SAGA OF A NEUROSURGEON SERIES, BOOK ONE

YOUNG
COYOTE

**GARVEN WILSONHULME'S WAY TO SUCCESS—
NO QUARTER ASKED AND NONE GIVEN**

CARL DOUGLASS

Neurosurgeon Turned Author Writes with Gripping Realism

Since 1978

PO Box 221974 Anchorage, Alaska 99522-1974
books@publicationconsultants.com—www.publicationconsultants.com

ISBN 978-1-59433-314-9
eBook ISBN 978-1-59433-315-6
Library of Congress Catalog Card Number: 2012942355

Manufactured in the United States of America.

Disclaimer

This is a story, a fiction, where all but a very few names have been changed to protect the people deserving of great respect and are, in all cases, cast in a deservedly positive light. They are minor characters in the book and its story. Other characters and the part they play in the *Saga* are loosely based on real people, including the author, whose names are changed; the places they work in the book are fictitious or different from where they were actually encountered by the present author. Some of the experiences described and the characters depicted are amalgamations of persons, places, and actions, and some diluted and altered autobiographical remembrances. There are healthy dollops of whimsy running throughout even the autobiographical hints.

The world of Garven Wilsonhulme is indeed fiction, but while not exactly real, it is faithful to an era of neurosurgical training and experience that is almost entirely a thing of the past. The independence and cowboy experience of being trained in a blood and guts trauma hospital in that era is not an exaggeration. There are some of those old men (and women) out there who will smile as they read and remember. If nothing else, the experiences of those semi-pioneers are the stuff of legend, humor, and pathos that invite endlessly fascinating yarns by all those consummate raconteurs.

The world of medicine and surgery is far more sophisticated and genteel now, far more of a closely controlled corporate money and legalistically driven environment. No longer can residents work 120 hours a week by federal and state law. It is all but unthinkable for a trainee to act with cavalier unsupervised independence in the closely monitored environment of the programs of the twenty-first century. A Garven Wilsonhulme would never make it into or through the training or the vicissitudes of neurosurgical practice in today's world without a very considerable amount of refinement and bowing to the ethical, moral, legal, and scientific standards of the present day. But then, neurosurgeons are eminently tough and adaptable. Maybe even Garven could make his way in the new paradigm as he did in the era of forty and fifty years ago when this *Saga* took place. The author would like to think he could.

Dedication

The series of books is dedicated to those giants upon whose shoulders I stood, including: Harvey Birsner, M.D., my partner and friend; Shelly Chou, M.D., PhD., my great mentor; Kemp Clark, M.D., The Chief; Stephen David Durrant, PhD., Professor of Biology/Evolution/Comparative Anatomy, a curmudgeon, humorist, inspiration, and friend; Lyle A. French, M.D., PhD.; the grand master at Minnesota; William Wallace Newby, PhD., Professor of Biology/Embryology, my greatest friend and help; Lito Porto, M.D., The Indian; J. Charles Rich, M.D., my worthy opponent in premed and the consummate neurosurgeon and contributor to the neurosurgical community; Theodore Roberts, M.D., my start; Duke Samson, M.D., the great builder of neurosurgery and foremost of brain vascular surgeons; Charles Sternbergh, M.D., the rock of integrity; Clark C. Watts, M.D. J.D., my friend and support during the lean years.

"Life's splendor forever lies in wait about each one of us in all its fullness, but veiled from view, deep down, invisible, far off. It is there, though, not hostile, not reluctant, not deaf. If you summon it by the right word, by its right name, it will come." Franz Kafka, *Diaries*

Acknowledgments

The author acknowledges with appreciation the direct contributions to the books of Harvey Birsner, M.D., Keith Hooker, M.D., Kim Oliver, M.D., Brent Pratley, M.D., Charles Stewart, M.D., and all of the general surgery and neurosurgery interns, residents, and professors in California, Utah, Minnesota, Texas, Virginia, and the men and women of the navy who served with me.

"Garven stood over his tormentor, who lay before him completely *hors d combat*. Garven wore a disappointed look on his face. He still had murder flashing from his eyes but nowhere to commit it. The two nearest witnesses were impressed, almost shocked. The rest of the football players loped up to the fight scene, chattering excitedly about what they had missed. As Tadd, the former best fighter in Cipher, Arizona, began to come to, nauseated and puling, the boys described and rehashed the spectacular fight to each other.

Garven left the field with the rest of the boys fully integrated.

"Welcome to Cipher," Lyle said respectfully.

The intrepid red hawk perched on the cross-tree of the telephone pole was oblivious to the boys, and intent on the jackrabbit she was eyeing. But the old coyote watching from behind a creosote bush was well aware of the boys and the cacophony they created. Garven caught the predator's cruel eye in a moment's glance, and it seemed that the creature gave him a quick wink."

CHAPTER
One

The town of Cipher, Arizona, is set twenty-seven miles back of the canyon rim that permits a striking view of the Painted Desert—far enough back that the inhabitants of the town miss the view and see only sand and red rock. The paucity of plant life makes for views little different from the mountains of Mars. God made the Painted Desert as beautiful in its own way as Lago Maggiore in Northern Italy or Mount Timpanogas in Utah are in theirs. Cipher—well-named—on the other hand, might as well be where the Creator rested on the seventh day and left behind some unfinished work.

The town was small and poor, drab, dusty, and plain—plain ugly. In 1940, the city consisted of seventy-eight habitations, most in need of paint, one all-purpose store, an elementary school, one vintage Mormon church, two competing up-to-date beer joints, a service station, a café, and a junk yard. Given the social milieu, the principal industry of the municipality was jury duty. Third Street was at the edge of town, and coyotes and desert hawks ruled the sands outside the town's meager streets.

Garven Aloysius Carmichael, age ten, sat on the top wooden rail of a broken fence watching a sandlot football game that raged with the intensity and—to him—the importance of Armageddon. Garven was a competitor with a ferocious will to win, and sitting on the fence rail while the drama of the game unfolded in front of him and without him was maddeningly frustrating. His problem was that he was the new kid in a town that required time to adjust and more time to assimilate. The establishment of the town's boys had no reason to open ranks and to let him join them. Garven was scrawny and short, had a high pitched pre-pubertal voice, and, worst of all, was the new teacher's son. With all of his social debits, Garven sat silently watching for the wedge of an opportunity to enter the fray.

Besides the dry field that served as the town's only park or playground, Cipher's main site of recreation was a small man-made reservoir created by the CCC boys in the mid-thirties called, pretentiously, Lake Arizona. Cipher had one road in and the same road out. The road was unpaved and dusty; at the height of summer, the dust was six inches deep on the average and in some ruts, nearly twelve. Alongside the battered sign announcing the name of the town and its population—one hundred (the sign was twenty-four years old), and elevation—3028 feet (a guess made by the CCC surveyors)—there was a sign hand painted by one of the CCC boys when he and his mates finished the dam that was considerably the worse for wear and now read, "…est Little Town by A Damsite". Closer to the junction of Arizona state highway 56 and the turnoff to Cipher was a well-kept series of signs maintained by a shaving cream company. THE BEARDED DEVIL…IS FORCED TO DWELL…IN THE ONLY PLACE…WHERE THEY DON'T SELL…BURMA SHAVE.

The road continued through town towards pallid rust-colored hills that, except for the green-taupe sage-brush and creosote bushes that were sparsely dotted on the rocky slopes, were as devoid of life as Saudi Arabia's Empty Quarter. The road led into the corner of a small and desolate Apache Indian reservation, wound around aimlessly to accommodate the remaining Native Americans, then gradually diminished to a trail that became the dust of the desert as if it just wore out. The desolate bleakness of the road was broken only by two signs set fourteen miles apart. The first advertised Stinker service stations. The sign featured a cute but faded skunk and read, SAGEBRUSH IS FREE, STUFF SOME IN YOUR TRUNK. The second, nearer the boundary of the reservation, was once a source of indignation for the Apaches who placed a very high premium on female modesty and chastity. APPROACHING NUDIST COLONY. KEEP EYES ON ROAD AT ALL TIMES. After forty years, the Apaches had come to ignore the signs and accepted them as part of the drab, unchanging landscape.

Of the one hundred forty-one men, women, and children living in Cipher—not counting the reservation Apaches—one hundred thirty-nine were Mormons, some active, some jack. The two exceptions, as of less than a week, were ten-year-old Garven Aloysius Carmichael and his mother, Rachel, who had moved into the floridly dusty and scorching town after Garven's father deserted them in Phoenix. The town could not induce any other teacher to come there, and Rachel found it expedient to relocate without leaving a forwarding address. The mayor and the Mormon bishop, the two officials of note in Cipher, and the only two persons other than Garven privy to her circumstances, felt they had made a fine deal. Rachel had smiled, agreed, and had tried not to appear as crestfallen as she felt when she saw the one-room adobe school house—her future. She hated the town, the dust, the daily encounters with coyotes (not all of them four legged), and the demeaning professional status to which she had been reduced.

Rachel's husband picked his son's names because of the note of refinement they held. He first heard the names in the Seguro Gulch Bar and Grill and took a fancy to them because they had been the moniker of the only Englishman he had ever met and disregarded the fact that the Englishman was as dissolute an alcoholic as he was himself. Garven's father was convinced that the auspicious names would stand the boy in good stead one day when he became an important businessman.

During most of his ten years, Garven had dedicated himself to the prevention of any other living soul knowing about the 'Aloysius'. 'Garven' was strange and therefore bad enough. He was a loner by nature, and his interactions with other people had inculcated in him a crafty wariness and cunning that matched the coyotes roaming on the outskirts of the new town he saw during his solitary walks. He and his mother moved into the trailer provided by the school district rent-free the day before the ten-year-old assumed his wistful perch on the fence rail to watch the boys at war. Garven's father had not been a superior provider when he was at his best; and when he deserted them, he took most of the furniture of any value; so, the move-in had taken only a few hours. It was July 12, 1940.

The boys, arbitrarily divided up into their Gog and Magog teams, raged up and down the gravel-covered scrabble ground of the playing field, churning up dust clouds with every tackle, run, or altercation. Had there ever been any vegetation growing in the field, it was long since trampled into the coarse parched dust and forgotten by the generations of boys who battled there. The field was located west of Carterville Road (Third Street West) and was owned by the city. It would be a gross exaggeration to say that the 'park' was, in any way, maintained by the Cipher City Corporation.

The game that so captivated Garven was being fought out under the canopy of a cloudless azure sky. The temperature on the ground was 120°, and the ground was bricky dry. The game itself was a combination of the intensity of a pirate crew scuttling a ship and putting the passengers to the cutlass and the desert version of Athapaskan Indian lacrosse. The contest started in the morning with no clear rules; it was more like the improvisation of a knife fight. Garven supposed that, if one of the players was unable to get up after a play, the others might consider calling a foul. Each day, the boundaries of play and the rules of engagement were painfully worked out in a fist fight after every contested play. The scene was an irresistible draw for Garven.

A narrow wedge of opportunity presented itself, and Garven ventured out onto the playing field. It was opportune because Jimmy Rodgers had developed a bloody nose, one of the few universally recognized indications for a brief time-out in the Cipher amateur football league. The opposite team was grousing about the delay, as if anyone in the entire county, especially a kid, had any kind of a deadline.

"Need anybody else to play?" Garven asked the milling boys.

"Nope," answered Lyle Durche, the self-appointed leader and spokesman, being the biggest kid in that general age group in town.

"Oh, c'mon, lemme play," Garven said, trying not to sound as if he were pleading.

"Who are you, anyway?" one of the other boys asked.

Garven was the first newcomer they had ever seen. The demographics of influx and efflux in Cipher were simple and stable.

"Garven," he answered simply.

"Jimmy's nose had stopped bleeding.

"Okay, let's play," ordered the big kid in charge.

"Hey, we need somebody. You got two more guys than we do."

"Jimmy's little brother don't count, and you know Edgar will have to go milk the cows before we finish," said the boy who had appointed himself in charge of fairness.

"Then let him play until Edgar has to go. What's it matter, anyhow? He's as scrawny as Jimmy; can't make that much difference."

"How old are you, Gary?"

"Garven."

The questioner had never met anyone named 'Garven' and made the next obvious observation, "That's a funny name. You come from the city?"

Garven reflected on how painful it would have been, how painful it always was, when other boys learned about his really funny name, Aloysius.

He said, "Me and my mom, we moved here from Phoenix."

"Jeez…Phoenix," one of the boys muttered in slight awe.

None of the boys had been to the capital city or more than two hundred miles from Cipher, for that matter. Garven gained an immediate measure of respect. Such were the vagaries of social acceptance at that level.

"We gonna fish or cut bait?" Lyle, the big kid, asked, perturbed at standing around in the baking sun.

"Let's play. C'mon, Gary; you're on our side."

Garven let it go.

The raucous and joyful mayhem started again immediately after the yelled debate over who last had the ball. By the persuasion of superior size, Lyle Durche's team naturally won that discussion since no one could really remember who had had possession when they stopped for Jimmy's nosebleed, anyway.

Garven was on the same side as Jimmy and his little brother. The three of them brought the team average weight substantially below that of Lyle's squad. The captain and only big player on their side was Hyrum Smith. Hyrum also called all the plays in view of his size-dictated authority. The concept of democracy had not filtered down to the boy level in Cipher as yet. Since none of the boys on either side could pass the football with the least accuracy, all tactics concerned the running game.

"Jimmy, you block Tadd so's I can run a sweep to the right. Gary, you and Jimmy's little brother wait back and block anybody who gets through. Clark and Steve, you run in front of me and block for me when I head out for the left side," Hyrum instructed.

"When do you want me to hike it?" asked John Tatum, the fat twelve-year-old who played center.

"Jist hike it when I do like this," Hyrum told him, making the well-recognized finger flipping sign with both sets of fingers. "I'll count a bunch of hut numbers, but fergit them. Jist watch me. Got that?"

"Okay."

Garven had his own thoughts about how to run the play, but thought that he had better not press his luck, since he was only the new boy. He held his peace.

"Hut one! Hut two! Hut three!" yelled Hyrum to set up his deception.

But before he could get the next 'hut' out or flip his fingers in the agreed upon signal for the hike of the ball, fat John fired it off from between his legs with the momentum of a torpedo. The thirteen-year-old signal caller and running back was not ready for it. The ball hit Hyrum square in the chest, and Lyle's team were across the line of scrimmage screaming like attacking Huns.

Jimmy Rodgers slowed down Tadd Stricklin as he came barreling across the thinly defended line. Garven had hunkered down unobtrusively and anticipated the onrushing boy. He curled into a ball and propelled himself directly into Tadd's knees, so the bigger opponent tripped and fell on his face in the dusty gravel. Garven's block gave Hyrum enough time to get control of the ball and to get started around the left side of the unmarked line of scrimmage. Lyle was lumbering with full menace towards Hyrum from right to left.

Garven sprang to his feet as soon as Tadd went down and cut across the field as fast as he could travel. He picked a point of contact between himself and the hard running Lyle. Lyle was oblivious to anyone but Hyrum carrying the ball. The honor of both boys' teams was at stake.

Garven was small enough to escape Lyle's peripheral vision, and the much larger player did not see Garven's head before the smaller boy crashed into his midsection in a spear block. Lyle took an ungainly fall to the left. Garven still churned up the dust with his feet, all the while keeping his head driving into Lyle's gut. They hit the ground together with a sudden exhalation by Lyle, who then lay on the ground gasping for breath. Garven wondered briefly if his own neck was broken. He could move everything and could not hear any funny sounds emanating from his neck; so he figured he was all right. Hyrum went on for the touchdown.

He came back and chucked Garven on the shoulder.

"Good block," he said, and he was unused to granting such lavish praise.

"Crap," gasped Lyle when he could get his breath.

"Losers walk," Hyrum said, gloating over his team's first touchdown of the day.

Lyle's team lined up on the opposite side of the field, glowering with unaccustomed disgruntlement at the eager team facing them. They were not magnanimous in their usual role as winners, and were not even close to accepting defeat with equanimity. Lyle muttered something about that new kid, and glowered darkly at Garven across the sun-bleached playing field.

"Whoever catches the kickoff, give the ball to me," Hyrum said with his usual authority.

Garven nodded affirmatively like the rest of his teammates, though he had no intention of giving up the ball if he got the kickoff. Tadd kicked the pigskin way over Hyrum's head on purpose far to the left where the weakest kids were assigned. The ball sailed accurately into Garven's waiting hands, although he had to run over the top of Jimmy's little brother to make it happen. He saw Hyrum put out his hands to take a lateral; so, he could run the ball instead of the smaller Garven.

This was his big break, and Garven had no intention of handing off the ball. All the glamor was in carrying the ball, and Garven was about to make the best of it.

He faked out Lyle who came in too fast. He dodged and paused, ran and darted his way through all of the would-be tacklers until he was running easily with only Tadd between him and a kickoff return touchdown. Tadd was faster than he looked and covered more ground than Garven would have anticipated. Garven could only get another ten yards before Tadd read his mind and met Garven in a stand-up tackle that jarred the smaller boy's joints loose. He fell to the ground with Tadd draped over him. Tadd checked around for the other boys who were beginning to limp his way. Assured that no one was close enough to witness, Tadd hauled off and slugged Garven on the cheekbone with his clenched fist.

"Wanna make somethin out of it?" whispered Tadd with fight in his eye.

Garven was still on the ground and, as a result of that, he did not get his head knocked about, just scraped up on the gravel. He had a florid bruise on his cheek in a matter of seconds. He was not drowsy, and he was not intimidated.

"I can wait," Garven answered in a steady voice.

He held Tadd's eyes in a direct stare. Tadd blinked first.

Garven's cheek smarted and started to discolor and to swell. He ignored it.

"You okay?" Hyrum and Steve asked as he got up.

"Yeah," Garven responded tersely, "I'm okay."

Hyrum punched Garven's shoulder.

Garven and his teammates huddled, and as usual, Hyrum called a running play with himself in the starring role.

"Could we try something else one time?" Garven spoke up.

He was greeted with expressions of consternation.

"I guess we might could," said Hyrum with a tinge of surprise in his voice. "Watcha got in mind?"

"A pass."

"Kin you pass?" Clark asked, his expression full of exaggerated disbelief.

"A little. But I thought Hyrum could do the best job if we could block for him long enough for him to get set."

"Yeah, good idea," said Hyrum, warming to the idea now.

"Then everybody but me and Jimmy's little brother block for Hyrum. Me and him will run straight down the sidelines on both sides. I'll go short, and he can go long."

"I can run purty fast," piped up Jimmy's little brother for the first time anyone had heard him talk on the football field. He was generally regarded as cannon fodder.

"Okay?"

"Okay," everyone said.

They were unconvinced; but it was worth a try since they never got anywhere on the ground, each of them thought privately.

Garven knew he was not big enough and secretly knew he was not able to pass well enough to do anything worthwhile in that department. He also knew that Hyrum would throw to the guy who ran short because he probably couldn't pass worth anything either. And Garven knew he could run the ball if he could get the chance. This was his best opportunity to get in with these guys, and he intended to capitalize on it. His main hope was that Hyrum could at least get the ball somewhere near him.

The team lined up in the usual single-wing formation facing the opposition. The town's footballers had abandoned the clumsy double-wing formation as soon as the new single-wing offense was introduced at the state finals the year before. Everyone took football seriously, and they kept up on the newest changes. Fat John had been firmly admonished after the lousy hike in their previous series of plays. He was determined not to screw up the delivery this time. He watched Hyrum's fingers for the sign, then centered the football right into the waiting hands. Fat John then extended his usefulness by falling in front of Tadd and Clint as the two of them crashed in after their usual target, Hyrum.

Hyrum set himself and looked frantically for a receiver. Steve, Clark, and Jimmy all got in some blocking, using a little more hands action than Lyle and his team thought fair. Hyrum looked at Jimmy's little brother who was streaking for the goal line, never looking back. Garven was in the clear, not far from the line of scrimmage with only Teddy Sorensen between him and the goal. Hyrum threw a short, wobbly, end over end pass for which Garven had to backtrack two steps, but it was roughly on target. Garven uncrossed his fingers and caught at the ball. The football bounced on his chest, juggled briefly in the air, and Garven caught it again.

By this time, Lyle, Tadd, and Teddy, on the opposing team, figured out what was going on and converged on the scrawny ten-year-old with the ball. It was now only a matter of a foot race to the goal line. Garven was not very fast and was steadily losing ground, but the distance to the goal was growing shorter. With eight yards to go, Garven was ahead of the three tacklers by four yards. At four yards to touchdown, Garven could hear and almost feel the hot breath on his neck. He saw the line scratched in the dust directly ahead of him less than a body length away. He visualized success and in his mind's eye, he could see himself crossing the goal line first. He could feel victory, acceptance, and even a little glory.

Garven felt two sets of hands grabbing at his legs. He eluded the first pair and heard an oomph as his tackler fell prone in the dirt behind him. The second set of fingers tripped up his dust-churning feet, and Garven tumbled headlong over the line, clutching the sweat-soaked football in a desperate clasp. Tadd Stricklin was still on his feet behind Garven and arrived a full second late, just in time to throw a vicious kick into the wiry little boy's exposed thigh. The other two tacklers saw the unnecessary bit of villainy and looked at each other in a questioning glance. Lyle was about to stick up for the fallen and abused newcomer, even though Garven was not on his side, when he saw the new boy spring to his feet like a wounded tiger. He decided to watch how the city boy handled himself.

Garven was in real pain and having trouble fighting back tears. Lyle and Teddy watched the struggle in fascination. Each boy knew they could witness the new kid's ruination. To cry after being hurt in Cipher, Arizona, was the worst thing you could ever do. Garven clenched his teeth in a concentrated effort that shut off the pesky tears. In a blur of movement, he whirled his thin body about so that he was in direct line with the taunting face of the much larger boy. Tadd had the reputation of being the best fighter in Cipher, pound for pound; but Garven could not be expected to know that. Even Lyle felt a small pang of sympathy for the new kid, Gary or whatever his name was.

Garven's expression was one of complete concentration on his objective. He kept his flashing hazel eyes locked onto the pupils of the larger opponent, drawing Tadd's attention irresistibly to the intense focal point. In the brief fraction of a second that Tadd looked at Garven's eyes, Garven threw a low kick at blinding speed and caught Tadd precisely on his left testicle. The pain was so sudden, surprising, and so terrible that Tadd had no time to react. His mind wanted him to crumple to the ground, but his body had not had time to comply. He had a completely stunned expression on his face as the first two sharp pointed fist blows bolted through his fogging vision and into his tender nose and exposed teeth. Before he could hit the ground and find relative safety, two more vicious jabs pounded his broken nose and cut his cheek. They were thrown with blinding speed. Tadd did not want to fall, or to cry, or to pass out; but he did all three in rapid succession.

Garven stood over his tormentor, who lay before him completely *hors d' combat*. Garven wore a disappointed look on his face. He still had murder flashing from his eyes and nowhere to commit it. The two nearest witnesses were impressed, almost shocked. The rest of the football players loped up to the fight scene chattering excitedly about what they had missed. As Tadd, the former best fighter in Cipher, Arizona, began to come to, nauseated and puling, the boys described and rehashed the spectacular fight to each other.

Garven left the field with the rest of the boys fully integrated.

"Welcome to Cipher," Lyle said respectfully.

The intrepid red hawk perched on the cross-tree of the telephone pole was oblivious to the boys intent on the jackrabbit she was eyeing. But the old coyote watching from behind a creosote bush was well aware of the boys and the cacophony they created. Garven caught the predator's cruel eye in a moment's glance, and it seemed that the creature gave him a quick wink.

The boys hollered and swore without prejudice from old boys to newcomer. He even taught them a song he learned in Phoenix:

> On top of old Smokey,
> Where nobody goes.
> There sat Betty Grable,
> Without any clothes.
> Along came Gene Autry,
> Clippety clop
> He jumped down beside her....

Within hours, the minutiae of the confrontation were known in exquisite detail by every boy and most of the girls in the town. Even without his repertoire of songs new to the protected enclave of Cipher, Garven Aloysius Carmichael was in.

CHAPTER
Two

There was precious little to occupy the minds and hands of the boys of Cipher in the 1940s. Most of the state and national interest was being poured into the war effort, and all of the able-bodied men were gone. The women left behind had to scrabble a living out of the dusty earth, which left them little time to be watchdogs or disciplinarians. The tradition for the youth was to run free and to engage in wonder. During wartime this tradition was carried to its extreme, and the wonder had more to do with mischief than any other experiential education.

Garven solidified his positive social standing as rapidly as he could. The trouble came because Lyle Durche loved Indians—the Hollywood variety, not the local reservation types—with their war paint and feathers, especially their feathers. He knew the location of a virtually unlimited source of feathers— McNaughton's turkey farm. Clarence McNaughton was an elderly holdout against the failure of the turkey ranches that had once dotted the countryside around Cipher. He still had a few dozen of the stupid birds. His turkeys were the old brown-gray color instead of the newly favored white variety, and the feathers looked every bit like eagle feathers to the boys.

Clarence was not much inclined to change. He had survived decades of problems with turkeys and had a balanced love-hate relationship with them. Once he lost almost every bird when a chance sudden rainstorm descended on Cipher. The turkeys all looked up curiously at the rain, opened their mouths for some inexplicable reason, and drowned. He hated them for being stupid.

But Clarence also loved them. For all their animal dumbness and despite the trouble they caused him, they were his sole source of livelihood. He protected them as he would his own children, better, in fact, as it turned out, according to his sons. He had become a virtual recluse, never daring to leave for fear men would rustle his whole flock, the women of the town would make off with a dinner or two, or the kids—the pesky rapscallious kids— would come and torment them.

To their credit, it was not Lyle, Garven, Tadd, or Teddy's desire to torment Clarence McNaughton's turkeys. All they wanted was a few tail feathers.

The four boys slipped out of the copse of quaking aspens at the edge of the cornfields that bordered the turkey enclosure. They crawled under the barbed wire fence and frog walked in among the domesticated birds. Their presence caused a minor stir among the flock, and when a tail feather was extracted from a tom's backside, the noisy bird gobbled loudly and trotted around for a while before settling back down. Lyle figured that Clarence would presume that the birds were just naturally restless, and would not trouble himself over the hyperactivity and increased vocalizations.

Garven was the first to recognize that Lyle had figured wrong. He saw the sheriff's car moving slowly down the dirt road between Packer's and McNaughton's corn fields.

"Cops!" he whispered loudly to Lyle. "Let's get out of here."

Lyle looked up and just then saw the old turkey rancher making his way towards the enclosure containing the boys and the birds in a most resolute way. He could tell the man was in earnest by the over and under twelve gauge he was carrying.

"Teddy! Tadd! Get your butts outta here! Cops! And Clarence has his shotgun!"

The three older boys had had some little experience with farmers' shot guns loaded with rock salt and bacon rind, and it took no convincing to get them all moving. The four youths made a beeline for the weak point they had made in the barbed wire fence.

Clarence yelled, "Stop, you little varmints! Stop or I'll shoot you. I swear I will. I'll teach you to molest my turkeys!"

Stopping, as an option, was never even entertained as a thought let alone as a subject for discussion. As soon as Clarence hollered, the boys took off as hard as they could go, all attempts at further concealment abandoned to the practical need to put distance between themselves and the dreaded rock salt and bacon rind. One shot blasted out with the noise of a field artillery piece, but with no indication that it had come any where near any of the fleeing boys.

Sheriff Rantel yelled from somewhere in the corn fields, "Stop! Stop in the name of the law!"

The sheriff used his favorite movie line as often as he could.

Garven was the first one under the fence, the first one into the corn patch, and the first one to reach the grove of quaking aspens. He dug in under a pile of deadfall and stayed there scarcely breathing. Lyle's enthusiasm was kindled to the maximum by a second shotgun blast that sent the small missiles close enough to his head to be heard clearly. He headed abruptly to the left as soon as he hit the cornfield; and when he reached the middle of the thick tall stalks, he lay down and did not move again that afternoon. Tadd and Teddy made it to the canal and jumped in just ahead of the sheriff and the deputy. The old banks of the partly full canal were undercut, leaving room to hide effectively for field rats, raccoons, a passel of water snakes, rowdy boys, and other varmints.

"Ketch them kids, sheriff, or I'll have your job!" Clarence stormed about shouting impotently.

"I will do the very best I can. But you know these town kids; they can hide better'n Indians. I don't know what is gonna become of this next generation. Used to be kids obeyed their parents; then at least when a policeman said 'no', they knew he meant it. But now they don't even give no respect to law enforcement. Just wonder where it's all gonna lead."

"Stop yer jabberin' and look. Election is comin' right up. Believe me, you are in a peck of trouble if you don't get those rotten kids!" Clarence ranted.

Sheriff Rantel let Clarence get out of earshot, not too far a distance since the old man was so hard of hearing, then said to his deputy, "Zeke, you scour this place. Look in every hidey hole you can remember from when you were a kid a botherin' Clarence's turkeys. We can't afford to have those brats put one over on us. We got a election comin' right up. We have to show everybody that we are effective guardians of the law."

Zeke, the deputy, looked hurt at the suggestion that he had had a criminal past; but since he was a doer, not a talker, he set out methodically to probe every niche and pile. The hunters walked and crawled and drove about in their vehicles. The hunted stayed silently in their places. Six hours passed and it was fully dark when the sheriff, his deputy, and the irate farmer had to concede defeat. Rantel vowed to come back first thing in the morning. Garven and his friends left their hidey holes as soon as the first light of false dawn provided enough visibility. All four boys got a well-deserved licking when they finally got home. No one ever told the cops. Families took care of their own.

******

KerJacky Shanklin and Lightning Ivens made their way to the curb of Main Street, the only paved road in Cipher. Heat mirages shimmered off the near melting asphalt. If you did not live in the city or had so little to do that you could take notice of town characters, you would be impressed at the glacial celerity with which the two old friends moved. Garven Carmichael and his friends watched the show with impolite and obvious good humor. KerJacky was slow because he was drunk, as always, and because the two carbon fragment fluid toxin had ruined his cerebellum and his balance. Lightning Ivens got his nickname years ago, owing to the peculiar festinating gait he developed from Parkinsonism that caused him to walk progressively faster until he almost fell forward, then to be frozen in position for minutes on end. KerJacky's face was dotted with abrasions and scars of varying sizes and ages from his frequent falls.

His regular explanation for being on the sidewalk was, "I joost was walkin' along, mindin' my own business, when kerstoopid sidewalk came up and hit me in kerface."

His strange speech mannerisms came from his Swedish background and from the *spiritus frumenti* along with the uncertainty of his gait.

Garven Carmichael and his two best friends, Lyle Durche and Tadd Stricklin, shielded their eyes from the brilliant noonday sun of July 4, 1943, just over two years after Garven's acceptance into the young male society of his new home-town. Life had been good since the fight on the football field. No one had even learned about his middle name, "Aloysius"; he had only had to have one more fight to establish his bonafides as a real scrapper; and the fight had only cost him the penalty of writing "I will not fight again. I will negotiate" three thousand times on the blackboard at school under his mother's rueful gaze. The three boys soon tired of giggling about and mimicking KerJacky and Lightning and scanned about for a spot of trouble to lighten the boredom of the hot summer afternoon until the Independence Day races started.

After he broke his arm on his first ride on a bucking horse, Garven had made friends with the only adult male he had ever respected, Dr. Peter Wilsonhulme, who made weekly clinic visits to tiny Cipher and to the relatively nearby hamlets of Navajo, Stevensville, and Partaway. Otherwise, Garven's entire waking day was spent in the company of boys with nothing more useful to do than to torment KerJacky and Lightning or the spooky old lady who lived across from the church. Right now, Garven and his companions could find little more to do on the sleepy Independence Day than to watch the two old men make their weary way down the precipice of the Main Street curb as they all waited for the annual parade.

For Garven, the second most important event of the year, after Christmas, took place after the Fourth of July parade. The yearly town races determined the pecking order for athletics as much for the younger boys as the basketball season did for the high schoolers. With his usual grim determination, Garven intended to win the 100 yard sprint and the high jump, the only two events anybody cared anything about. He planned to try the all-ages mile race this year. The boy's mindset would not permit him to visualize anything but victory. He only thought in terms of success, and every enterprise he undertook seriously was colored by the element of intense competition. He had secretly trained for the track and field contests by running hard and long every morning before dawn when it was cool enough that he would not burst a blood vessel or something from the heat. Some mornings, an old coyote ran along the crests of the low sandhills watching him. Garven had divined the definition of success for boys in Cipher and now had only to achieve it.

He won his heat in the 100 yard dash with the twelve and thirteen-year-olds with ease. While the second heat was set up and run, Garven took his place in line for the high jump. There were so few boys from any of the age groups in Cipher that were willing to compete in the high jump that no age or size distinction was made. Lyle Durche, by virtue of his superior size, was the odds-on favorite and had won the event for as long as any kid in town could remember. Lyle and Garven cleared the three-and-a-half foot bar fairly easily using the best scissors kick form. Garven then lined up in nervous anticipation for the final heat of the sprint.

The starting whistle sounded and nine boys sprinted in the blistering sun for the bragging rights for the year. Garven's shoes were heavy and awkward, and one of the brown laces broke at twenty-five yards, so he had to curl his toes to keep the shoe from falling right off. Erich Taylor, a skinny twelve-year-old, had regular racing shoes; and by virtue of that advantage, he came in first. Garven squeaked out a third place by sheer determination. He muttered invectives at himself, at the curse of poverty which denied him decent running shoes, and at Erich on general principles. His concentration was off on the high jump, which caused him to have to make three tries to clear four feet to let him stay in competition.

Dr. Wilsonhulme and Garven's mother watched the boy and took note of his intensity.

The doctor commented, "That boy is the most competitive kid I ever saw. I love his single-minded drive."

Rachel replied thoughtfully, "I fear it. What is that boy going to do when he is done with childhood in Cipher? There will never be enough for him here, and he will never have enough from me to be able to get out and make something of himself. What will come of all that competitive energy then, especially if he stays cooped up in this little burg."

"I don't think you will have to fear much for Garven, Rachel," the doctor said seriously. "He shows every indication of being able to get what he sets his heart and mind on."

"Maybe that's what I really fear the most, Dr. Wilsonhulme. Garven will not let anything get in his way. I don't think I like that side of him. How is he going to act when he hits a real obstacle?"

"Decisively, I presume," smiled the doctor.

Dr. Wilsonhulme was coming to know the Carmichael boy well enough to make such an observation. Garven found an excuse to visit his clinic every time Dr. Wilsonhulme came to Cipher to hold a clinic on approximately a fortnightly basis. The boy seemed to be taken away from the drab dullness of existence in the ugly little town for the short time he spent with the doctor, peppering him with questions. Dr. Wilsonhulme could see that he was opening horizons beyond the low vistas the town provided, and, like the boy's mother, had some concern that he might be raising Garven's expectations above what reality offered the son of a poor mother struggling to get by. Dr. Wilsonhulme occasionally remarked to Rachel Carmichael that her son showed promise. He was coming to believe that more firmly as time passed. The boy did not belong in this intellectually destitute village. The middle-aged doctor began to ruminate about what he might do to help the boy.

Garven had tightened his laces. The last heat of the 100-yard races included the win, place, and show competitors of all boys up to age fifteen from all heats. Garven felt like David against the several Philistines who had won the upper age heats, not that he was smaller or less powerful, but in the sense of winning against any Goliath who challenged him. He concentrated on his mind's eye view of himself crossing the finishing line first. The starting whistle sounded.

Garven's start was explosive; fast enough to drive his right heel into the bent knee of Darryl Knight, the fast fifteen-year-old starting next to him. Darryl faltered and restarted, losing precious momentum. Garven and Tadd Stricklin were neck and neck until the last fifteen yards with Tom Latherty running a close third. Tom gave a mighty and awkward effort to pull out in front of the two younger boys and succeeded only in making the last yards of the race a three-way tie. Tom's sawing elbows flailed, and his feet tore at the dusty track. He moved across Garven's left in a premature move to place himself at the advantage in front of the wiry runner beside him. Tom did not quite make the transition to front runner; his right foot neatly but accidentally crossed Garven's left. Garven stumbled and almost dived into the dust of the track.

His mother and the doctor took a short gasp as they watched. Garven growled under his breath and demanded an instantaneous surge from his straining body. It was not enough. He passed Tadd by an inch but could not overtake Tom Latherty and had to settle for second place. Garven Carmichael had no cerebral provision for second place. His look was murderous.

Tom panted up to Garven, extended his hand, and said breathlessly, "I'm sorry about bumping you. It was an accident."

Garven leveled a malevolent gaze at the fifteen-year-old and ignored the proffered hand.

"You tripped me. That was no accident. I won that race," he said gracelessly.

Tom took a step back in reaction to the emotional force coming from the thin boy facing him with his fists clenched. Garven had a reputation as a hot-head and a fighter. Tom did not want to have a stupid fight with a thirteen-year-old especially right there in public.

"Take it easy. It's just a race. I said I'm sorry. And look, it was an accident. Really."

"There's no such a thing as 'just a race'. There's only winning," Garven hissed.

Garven's mother and Dr. Wilsonhulme walked up to the two boys in time to catch the last two verbal interchanges. Rachel knew the violence behind the rigid stance and the piercing look in her son's eyes only too well.

She soothingly said, "Garven, stop this. The race is over. There was some contact between you and Tom, and you stumbled. I know how badly that feels. But you know that you accidentally kicked Darryl's leg at the start of the race; so, he couldn't catch up. He has won the race for the past three years. How do you think he feels?"

"What do I care?" Garven snapped in annoyance at his mother's interference.

Tom Latherty took advantage of Garven's shift of attention to back away from the confrontation.

"As long as you live, never use that tone with me again, young man. I am too good to you for that!" Rachel said and hoped she displayed an exaggerated calmness she did not feel.

Garven saw the hurt look on his mother's face and the displeasure on Dr. Wilsonhulme's. His anger began to cool and his thought processes began to reform.

"I'm...I apologize, Mom. I didn't mean it," he stammered. "I mean...I didn't mean to say anything mean to you."

Rachel tacitly accepted Garven's apology by a small nod of her head. The doctor caught Garven's attention, making the boy uncomfortable.

Garven said to him, "I would have won that stupid race if he hadn't tripped me. It just made me mad. It was his fault."

Dr. Wilsonhulme quietly leveled his full attention on the angry boy. The older man said, "That's an excuse, Garven. There's nothing to gain by blaming other people or things than ourselves. No one who hopes to get anywhere can afford to make excuses. The only thing that matters is what you do, what you are responsible for. You are too young to get into that terrible habit of blaming someone else for what happens to you. Do you understand what I'm telling you, son?"

"I guess so. I think I do," Garven replied reluctantly. He had a near worshipful respect for the doctor's pronouncements.

"I don't really care much whether you win a race like this or not, Garven, but I am interested enough in you to care that you accept responsibility for the results of your own actions."

"But I would have won if he hadn't tripped me."

"Maybe, but you didn't win. That's what matters here. 'Sorry' doesn't cut it. 'It's not my fault' doesn't either. Life is tough. You have to learn to overcome obstacles, all of them. Outside of this little village, no one cares what you have to do to succeed; you just have to do it. It isn't a matter of what other people do. You're just whining."

That cut. Garven did understand. The doctor had often before taken the time to talk to him in a teaching way, always giving Garven the sense that he could be somebody and could do something even though he was poor and lived in a town that was just another word for zero.

The boy's facial expression softened, and he said thoughtfully, "I guess you think that lesson is more important than the race, huh?"

"The lesson is an old one. Did you ever hear of Rudyard Kipling?"

Garven shook his head, embarrassed because he assumed the name was one he should know.

"That's all right. What matters is what the man said. He was a poet. He said:

"When the buckled girder,
Lets down the grinding span,
The blame for loss and murder

Is laid upon the man.
Not on the stuff, the man."

Garven thought he understood.

"The doctor's pretty wise, son," interrupted Rachel. "That's why he's a doctor."

"It's more that I'm old and have lots of white hair," said Dr. Wilsonhulme with the proper touch of self-deprecation. "Listen, I have to be getting back to Emmett. You going to come by the clinic and see me next Wednesday, Garven?"

"If it's okay," the boy solicited with familiar expectation.

"Sure. I will probably put you to work if you keep hanging around."

That sparked a gleam in Garven's eye and the beginning of a smile.

"Really, doctor. If he's a bother…" Rachel said feeling a tinge of self-consciousness for her son's overuse of the busy doctor's time.

"He is not a bother," said Dr. Wilsonhulme with emphatic feeling. "I am growing fond of this boy. He's bright and feisty, full of whiskey and vinegar. Maybe he ought to be a doctor. Maybe I'll be an influence."

"And maybe you'll just put ideas into his head—ideas he would have a hard time realizing, you know," Rachel said soberly. "You'll have him wanting nothing else but to be a doctor like his hero."

The older man blushed slightly and looked as though he enjoyed the compliment.

"That's how you get to be a doctor, you know. You have to want to be one more than anything. You have to imagine yourself to be a doctor. Most medical students could see themselves only as doctors, nothing else, even if they have no clear idea of what a doctor is or what one does. If that boy of yours is going to get someplace, he is going to have to channel his considerable drive into that kind of thinking."

"Mom, Lyle and Tadd want me to go to the rodeo this afternoon. It's almost time. Okay?" Garven asked, trying to absent himself from the uncomfortable discussion of himself in the third person that adults so often carried on.

"Go on, boy. Have a good time. Try not to get into any trouble for a change!" she ordered fondly.

"So long, Garven. See you on Wednesday," the doctor said as Garven began backpedalling.

"Yes, Sir. See you Wednesday. Bye, Mom."

"He has a lot to learn, that hot-headed boy of mine," Rachel told the doctor as they walked to his car.

"He's only thirteen. He is made of good stuff. He has real willpower and determination. I don't think anything is ever going to stand in that kid's way.

And I say, good for him!" declaimed the doctor as he climbed into the driver's seat of his vintage Buick.

Dr. Wilsonhulme thought about thirteen-year-old Garven Carmichael all the way back to his home in Emmett. He saw a coyote and her two pups cross the road in front of him and reflected on how well the creatures adapted and survived in their harsh environment. Maybe Garven had some of that kind of grit. Time would tell.

Rachel turned her thoughts to Garven and to the doctor. She wondered what would come of the lofty ideas the kindly old man was instilling in her impressionable son's head.

CHAPTER
Three

Abram Conrad had a rickety outdoor privy that was eighty years old if it was a day. It was unpainted, had never been painted, and probably had never had five minutes of maintenance expended on it in its entire existence. As a result, it leaned precariously towards the east as a ramshackle, bleached grey wood monument of times past; and, as most of the townspeople regarded the offensive structure, they were times best forgotten. The flimsy privy represented what city attorneys might characterize as an attractive nuisance tempting generations of boys to tip it over. It just begged to be toppled, but no one had ever succeeded in getting past old "Fieldmouse" Conrad's vigilance.

Mr. Conrad's worst day every year was Halloween, when the local mischief makers seemed to feel it a duty, a rite of passage, or a sacred quest to tip over his toilet. He did not care that other people in Cipher liked to keep the dirty thing right in their houses; he liked his right where it was. He never slept for the two nights before and the actual night of Halloween, which was too much for the hard working old farmer, particularly as he became a septuagenarian then an octogenarian. This made him very tired and, in direct proportion to his sleeplessness, cranky. He had successfully fended off attackers and besiegers for all of these years, and he was bound and determined that he would do it again in 1944.

He loaded his ancient double-barreled shotgun with rock salt, bacon rind, and hard red winter wheat and positioned himself in his rocker on the porch to wait for the nightmare of the season to replay itself. He would have used real bird shot. His choice of ammunition was not determined by any delicacy of spirit or by fear of the consequences of injuring one of the fully deserving kids, but rather because the old iron barrels would no longer tolerate even lead shot, let alone the newfangled steel shot.

Mr. Conrad thought it was pesky of God to make him so he could only sleep four hours a night, but that he fell asleep at the drop of a hat when he sat on his davenport or in his rocker during the day. He fell asleep this evening on guard; the sun had barely dipped over the horizon.

Garven had his binoculars trained through a knothole in the decaying old fence around the Conrad place. He scrutinized the old man's eyes as best he could.

"I think he's asleep. These old binocs aren't good enough to be sure, but I think so," he said to Lyle, Tadd, Chuck—a new kid who moved in two years ago and had gotten to be friends with the other three even though he was disgustingly fat and belched all the time—and Teddy.

Garven did not call attention to the fact that his vision was not all it should be. He had been forced to admit to the traveling school nurse who had challenged him the year before that he could not see the chalkboard in class. She had gotten his eyes tested and, horror of horrors, Garven had had to get a pair of glasses. He never, never wore the spectacles in public, and only very surreptitiously slipped them on in class when he had to see something on the board. Heaven help any boy who dared to hurl the standard epithet "four eyes" at him.

"Lemme see," demanded Lyle.

He was not about to go into that yard without some assurance. He thought Fieldmouse was asleep also.

"One of us has to go in and see if he's asleep or awake," announced Tadd.

He knew he was safe because none of the other boys would entrust a mission of such subtlety to him. He would never be able to pull off the necessary theatrical performance if the old man challenged him.

"Yeah, and it ain't gonna be me," said Chuck.

Lyle, Tadd, and Teddy shook their heads in vigorous agreement with their fat friend.

"This is like war," Chuck said. "Like President Roosevelt said, 'I hate war. Eleanor hates war. I hate Eleanor.'"

The boys all snickered at the tacit understanding that FDR had to hate the ugliest woman on the planet. For some reason they all turned and looked at Garven.

"What are you all lookin' at me for?" Garven asked, his voice heavy with suspicion and reluctance.

"Cause you are the only one who can talk his way out of trouble if the old dirt-dauber is awake or if he comes awake while you're in there."

They all knew that. Garven was the smartest, and that came in handy at times like this. He wasn't the biggest or the strongest, but he always managed to come out on top and was respected in the boy society of Cipher, Arizona even if he was not really liked that much by his peers, the four co-conspirators excepted.

"C'mon, Garv. You know you have to be the one. The rest of us get too tongue tied when we get caught. And besides, Lyle and Chuck here are like elephants in a dish shop—something like that," said Teddy, speaking up for the first time.

The other four boys set up a nattering coaxing barrage that Garven could not tolerate, and could not resist; so, he assented.

"Quit…stop the yapping. I'll do it," he finally relented with a mixture of unspoken response to the flattering entreaties and of an unadmitted eagerness for the challenge. "Somebody has to."

Garven slipped through one of the openings in the fence where a board had dropped off due to the scorching heat corroding the ancient nails. The fence looked like the dentition of a seven-year-old. He padded silently, Indian style, like John Wayne did in the movies, across the paddock adjacent to the house and up to the porch. The whole traverse took five minutes to go fifty yards. He found the old man snoring.

Garven flashed the high sign, and the other boys tiptoed into the yard. They were all reassured when they saw the old man deep in slumber. The gloaming was closing in fairly comfortingly also, but there was still too much light to feel any great measure of ease. However, it was now or never. They would not be able to guess when the old Fieldmouse might nod off again. If he woke up, they would be caught red-handed.

The four boys started to push on the privy side with the obtuse angle leaning away from them. It was surprisingly sturdy and resistant to their efforts. Chuck and Teddy went around and started to dig out the ground under the oblique side until there was a noticeable instability in the foundation. The digging was easy; the ground was soft, too soft. Chuck and Teddy were glad it was getting dark so they did not have to think about what they were digging in. The stench was almost overpowering; they could all but feel it on their skins.

"Pee U and a half," hissed Teddy as his digging efforts stirred up the dormant odors in the heretofore undisturbed percolating mud. "This'd gag a maggot."

"Okay," Chuck whispered harshly.

There was no response.

"Push it over," he said more loudly.

Garven and Lyle must be deaf, he thought.

"Push it and let's get out of here!" he said loudly enough that anybody four feet away could hear.

They pushed. The outhouse rocked but did not give. All four boys tried one more time but could not get the stupid thing to fall all the way over.

"It must have been made out of six-by-sixes," Lyle said admiringly. "They don't build them this way anymore."

Garven giggled. It seemed perfectly silly to be rhapsodizing about the fine qualities of a decrepit old outhouse they were trying to tip over, especially in the atmosphere of almost palpable noisomeness.

"Whew!" exclaimed Tadd. "I think I'm gonna puke!"

The boys pushed and rocked the structure. They hummed and quietly sang their favorite ditty that came into town with some of the men who were back from the war:

Hitler has one ball, that's all
Goebels has two, but they're small.
Himmler is sim'lar,
And Goering has no balls at all!

Some progress was made. The whole structure shifted sideways, and Chuck's foot slipped into very soft stuff up to his knee. He blanched in the dark just thinking about the malodorous mixture. His foot popped out of the soft mud and increased the ambient aroma momentarily, a feat that the boys would have considered near impossible given the intensity up to then. It was getting hard to hold their breaths long enough to keep out many of the feculant fumes. Still, the flimsy old building continued to resist.

"We shoulda brung a rope; and half of us could pull; and half of us could push." Tadd said.

"Good idea, but a little late," said Teddy.

The boys were sweating from their efforts. They were now totally absorbed, concentrating on solutions to the engineering problem before them. Garven gave some thought to elementary physics and came up with a strange piece of memory tucked away in the recesses of his mind, *Give me a lever long enough, and a fulcrum strong enough, and I can tip over the world,* he recalled suddenly from something the doctor had taught him. That might not have been exactly right.

"Archimedes' Principle!" he exclaimed right out loud then remembered to keep it quiet.

"Huh?" said Chuck.

"Who?" asked Lyle.

"What're you talkin' about, Garven? Sometimes I think you just like to use big words and show off," chimed in Tadd, getting irritable from the frustration of pushing on the stupid immovable privy.

"We need a pry-bar!" Garven said authoritatively.

"Right!" said Chuck capturing the vision.

They all felt around in the growing darkness for a suitable lever. Teddy found an old wagon tongue that was dry, but not rotten. It felt like it would hold up to their pushing. The boys jammed and pounded one end under the foundation support of the little building on its obtuse side. It made quite a bit of noise, but by now, the boys were so absorbed in their task that they were all but oblivious to their surroundings and to their former vigilance towards Mr. Conrad. They wanted to get their job done and over with as soon as possible to get out of the horrendous stink.

They heaved and pushed, lifted and rocked. They were making progress, but the stinking building would not quite go over. Lyle crouched down and put his muscular shoulder under the lower third of the lever. The boys gave a well-coordinated mighty heave, expelling their breaths in weight lifter grunts that seemed peculiarly loud in the otherwise quiet desert night.

The out house toppled over onto its side, exposing the throne to the night air. The rotting boards of the oblique side of the diminutive building shattered to pieces when they hit the ground, renting the silent night air. Lyle pitched face forward into four feet of odoriferous liquid muck with the consistency of warm tar. Garven and Chuck howled with laughter, putting the brakes on to avoid joining their large retching and sputtering friend.

Abram Conrad screamed in Teddy's ear from two feet away and banged him with the barrel of his shotgun in the blackness of the starry but moonless Halloween night. The boys had forgotten all about the little old farmer and his shotgun.

"You cursed, rotten, scummy delinquents!" yelled Fieldmouse.

Teddy all but jumped out of his skin. He shot off the ground more than two feet and had taken three running steps in the air before his feet ever got back to the ground, like a character in the funnies. There was a chaotic flurry of moving arms, legs, and bodies and spattering slime and offal as the boys ran into each other and the old farmer, trying to get out of there. Lyle came out of the muck with a great sucking noise. He was covered with a camouflaging inch-thick coat of fetid reeking putrefaction. Mr. Conrad could not see the large teenager in the darkness, but had little difficulty locating him with his olfactory apparatus.

He wheeled his shotgun around to where the worst of the smell was coming from and let fly both barrels. Lyle was surprisingly quick for a big, dumb looking fellow and had already started zigzagging his way out of the side pasture. He was nicked by a few hunks of salt and bacon rind, but, for practical purposes, was missed by both barrels. The old man had to fumble in the darkness to reload the double-barrelled shotgun. The barrel and stock cracked open with an ominous metallic noise and slammed shut with authority. By this time the boys were nearly at the fence.

"Bang!"

Off blasted one barrel. The pellets hit the fence well away from any of the boys, but nonetheless spurred an even greater effort on their part.

There was no way to be sure where one of the gap-tooth openings in the fence could be found in the inky blackness. Each boy found his own way across with inspiring alacrity. Teddy climbed over like a scalded monkey; Tadd vaulted the rickety structure landing with the upright boards square between his legs. He let out a high-pitched squeal and fell on his head on the other side, blissfully unconscious. Lyle felt hurriedly for an opening and finding none, took the simple expedient of running right through the intact structure. The dry and rotting boards gave way before the athletic young brute like so much paper mâche. Chuck tore off two boards and heaved his bulk through to the other side and was off into the night before Abram Conrad could fire off the second barrel load. For a fat kid, he could really run when he had to.

Garven fell over a tangle of old baling wire that littered the field. Mr. Conrad ran right past him, wheezing and cursing. Garven knew that he was stuck on the horns of a dilemma. He could lay there and hope the old man's eyes never saw him, or he could make a run for the fence and hope that Fieldmouse would not shoot any straighter than before. It occurred to him that the mean old sod-buster (as the movie ranchers called them) would out-wait him and would find him when it got light.

He bolted. There was a clicking rustle of rusty baling wire that still ensnared him, trailing behind Garven as he ran. Occasionally in the thirty yards or so, the wire would trip him up; and Garven would stagger; but he never quite fell. He clattered over a stack of rotten one-by-sixes, placed his hands on top of the fence uprights, and vaulted into the air to swing over the barrier.

"Bang!" the second ten-gauge barrel cut loose, shattering the remaining quiet of the night, and creating reverberating echoes against barn walls.

The pain was instantaneous and dreadful. Salt pebbles, stony hard bits of heavy dry pork rind, shotgun wadding, and a few dozen grains of flinty red winter wheat tore through his pants and into his flimsily covered buttocks and posterior thighs. The stinging was the worst thing Garven had ever felt. It was like a thousand bees were on him at once, bees that could keep on stinging continuously. He hit the ground on his chest on the far side of Conrad's property, and was momentarily dazed and out of breath. Something animal in him responded, and he got up and ran a few more yards into the blackness to where he was sure the nasty-tempered, old skin-flint could not see him and lay down. He rubbed his butt furiously trying to get rid of the bees. The more he rubbed, the more dirt he ground in, and the deeper he imbedded the debris from the hand-loaded ammunition; and the more he stung.

He wanted to scream, to cry out in a keening wail, to bawl, to curse like a miner; but all he could do was to keep very quiet and to curse and sob inwardly. The desperate wisdom of this course of action was reinforced when he heard the dangerous click of the shotgun mechanism somewhere too near him in the dark.

The searing pain would not let up (which is why the salt, bacon rind, etc. is so desirable in dealing with two legged varmints); so, Garven struggled to force himself out of the adjacent field and onto the badly broken city sidewalk. He began limping for Lyle's place knowing he could not go home. He was glad to see the last of Conrad's yard and his putrid outhouse.

"Stop right there, young fella!" came the squeaky old man voice from the shadows. "You take another step and I'll shoot you so full of holes you won't be able to hold a glass of water!"

Cripes and double cripes! thought Garven. *How did that feeble old man get clear out here?*

He failed to take into consideration the time he had spent mulling in the dust of the field.

"What is it? What do you want?" Garven asked innocently.

"Abram Conrad. This is my place. You just knocked over my terlet. On my propity. What have you got to say for yourself?"

"I don't even know what you're talking about, Mr...uh, what did you say your name was?"

"Conrad. Everybody in these parts knows me. Who are you? Speak up pronto. I've a good mind to blast you!"

He was sounding a little less certain now.

"I don't know anything about what went on here tonight, but I'm just on my way to the place I'm visiting. How come you're pointing that thing at me?"

Despite his conviction, Mr. Conrad was wavering. He felt foolish pointing his gun at the skinny kid before him. The kid sounded genuine like he was the real McCoy.

"What did you say your name was?"

"Jim Green."

It was the first thing that came to Garven's mind. It sounded pretty lame to him, but at least, he had not hesitated in his response. That was one good thing.

"Who are you staying with?"

"You mean, here in Cipher?"

"Of course, where else would we be talking about?" the old farmer asked impatiently.

The kid seemed too dumb to be able to come up with a good lie.

"Mabel and Alfred Sweat. They're my uncle and aunt. On my dad's side," Garven lied.

He was getting better at it. He could feel the old man vacillating.

"Them old man Ephriam's kin?"

"Yeah. He's my grandpa, or grandpa-in-law or something like that," Garven stammered with just the right degree of confusion that the village moron would be likely to display.

He was pretty satisfied with his performance. The hardest thing was to keep from squirming from the pain in his butt skin and to keep the whine out of his voice.

There was a thoughtful pause.

"Okay, I'm gonna let you go this time. I still don't rightly know about you, but I'll give you the benefit of the doubt this onct. I want you to come tell me if you run into any boys covered with rotten filth or full of buckshot, you hear, boy?"

"Oh, yes Sir!" Garven responded enthusiastically. "I'll surely do that! You can count on me!"

He thought he'd better let it alone; he was laying it on a bit thick.

Garven spent the next two and a half hours at Lyle's house having his three friends pick the debris out of his backside. The pain of the extractions was excruciating, and it was bloody work. His poor butt looked like a miniature minefield after a battle. The worst part was when Lyle poured a bottle of mercurochrome into the raw pits and fissures. Garven squealed like a butchered piglet, and he was beyond caring whether anybody heard him or not. He finished off the night with a whipping from his mother with a weeping willow switch. Fortunately, she had determined of late that her son was too old to be whipped on his bare buttocks. It did not seem right for the growing boy to be exposed to a grown woman, even his mother, that way. Garven thanked the god he did not believe in for small favors. She had not seen his freshly pitted butt.

******

Before V-J Day in 1945, Dr. Wilsonhulme reluctantly curtailed his practice, owing to chronic arteriosclerotic coronary disease. He tired too easily to make the trip to the small Arizona towns. He inched away from his active medical practice in as small of increments as he could get away with. His advancing age, his progressively poor health, his wife's well intentioned nagging, and the fact that he scarcely made expenses factored increasingly in his decision to begin his retirement. He had carefully saved a portion of every month's income for his and Vera's retirement during his long years of practice, and was sure that he had more than enough to keep them. In the two years following the near incident up at the Independence Day races in Cipher when thirteen-year-old Garven Carmichael, the teacher Rachel's son, had looked ready to kill over a foot race, the doctor had recognized a developing closeness with the boy.

Peter Wilsonhulme and his wife, Vera, had never been blessed with children, and they had begun to lavish an inordinate amount of attention on Garven. Vera had a deep and unfulfilled maternal instinct, now more appropriately grandmotherly; and when Peter began bringing the boy to their home in Emmett, she had become as taken with the wiry overactive kid as her husband, who made a habit of befriending strays.

Garven had surprised them all—his mother, and both Wilsonhulmes—by his avid, even voracious, appetite for books. Garven read everything he could find at the library, everything Dr. and Mrs. Wilsonhulme could buy for him in his age range, and everything Rachel brought home from school. The boy developed an unquenchable interest for medical matters, and before he turned fourteen, had an unshakable idée fixe that he was going to be a doctor.

Aside from his contact with Dr. Wilsonhulme in his admittedly humble clinic, Garven knew next to nothing about what a doctor is or does, but that did not dissuade him from developing a single-minded quest. Garven was as naive about what it took to be a doctor, especially the high cost of the education, as he was about the qualitative nature of a medical career. Nonetheless, he was set on emulating his hero, the quintessential country doctor, in the person of Dr. Peter Wilsonhulme, and he would not be turned aside.

Vera developed malignant hypertension, a condition that defied adequate control and which caused her already weakened heart to hammer away with unnecessary force, until Peter knew she could not last much longer. He wanted his wife's approval for a plan that had been germinating in his heart for several months and feared making such a fundamental decision without the benefit of Vera's down-to-earth wisdom. He feared that he would be without it soon.

"Vera, I have an idea I'd like to have you consider."

"Uh oh," she said. Whenever you get that formal, I know we have trouble, or it is going to cost us lots of money."

Peter smiled blandly at his wife's sagacity. "The latter, dear. It's no trouble. I was thinking of spending all of our money, though."

Vera cocked a comma shaped eyebrow at her husband. Satisfied that he was still in possession of his faculties, and fairly certain that he was serious, she waited for the other shoe to drop.

"I have been thinking for a long time about Garven Carmichael. You know how fond I am of him, and I know you have become his grandmother."

She smiled.

"He is about the only bright boy in all of these forsaken little desert cities up here and certainly the only one with any ambition to get out of his rut. I think he is really serious about pursuing a medical career, at least as serious as a fourteen-year-old can be. He can't get anywhere with the education he will get in Cipher, Arizona and its schools, which is not to say anything negative about his mother. Rachel is a fine teacher, but she has her limitations, and the school facilities are dismal."

He took a breath.

"So, what do you have in mind, grandpa?"

"I'd like us to support his education. A real education. We have enough money to last us as long as we live and then some. We could send him to one of the great eastern prep schools and never miss the money. What do you think?"

"I will have to think some on it, Peter. It sounds like a wonderful thing to do for a boy, something very satisfying for us and beneficial for him, but I do have a concern for his mother. Where does she fit in all of this? Wouldn't we, in effect, be stealing the boy away from her? You realize that she would be completely alone then. That boy is all she really has to show for a very tough life."

Peter nodded his understanding of that thorny consideration that had escaped his man's way of thinking, he had to admit.

The Wilsonhulmes thought hard about the doctor's suggestion that they offer to take over Garven Carmichael's education in the ensuing weeks before

Garven's fifteenth birthday party. Rachel Carmichael had politely but firmly insisted that his fifteenth birthday be spent with his friends in Cipher. She, as a matter of course, invited the Wilsonhulmes, but clearly desired control over her son's destiny and used the party as an assertion of her status. Rachel wondered if she was not being overly protective or defensive. She wondered about her own motives, but not overly long since she was busy, and the idea did not seem particularly consequential.

Garven's only problem in school was that he had completed the eighth grade material early, and Rachel was hard-pressed to provide him with enough to do. He was becoming more quarrelsome with his friends and less and less respectful at home. The problem among his schoolmates was always the same. Garven did well in school and almost no one else even cared about the school work. Inevitably, about once a week, one of the larger, and often older, boys would make an allusion to the fact that Garven was the teacher's boy, her pet. He reacted with a defensive snarl that alienated the other students, but thank heavens, he had not started a fight. The problem between Garven and his mother was that he perceived, correctly, that she made a very definite effort to take the other students' parts in squabbles and to be most parsimonious in ladling out praise. Garven was beginning to take umbrage at the lack of praise for his academic work even though it was better by a long ways than his nearest competitor, and at the demerits he was increasingly accruing for infractions of citizenship.

Indians (the local Jicarilla Apache tribe) were tolerated as needy inferiors or "Lamanites" by the town's majority. Garven generally regarded them with indifference, not joining in the red skin baiting racial slurs that were a source of such entertainment with his schoolmates, or feeling any inclination to associate with or to defend them either. He was unaware of having any formed opinion about them and was content to leave them alone in their second class citizenship status. That all changed two days before his birthday in a way that resulted in consequences all out of proportion to the superficial significance of the actual event.

Boys in Cipher, Arizona and in most small towns taunted each other with friendly insults, which are tolerated for the most part with a shoulder shrug and a rejoinder as long as certain off limits areas were respected. The two most significant of those areas concerned one's mother and one's sexual predilection. In the spring of 1945, there could be no quarter asked and none given from a peer who suggested any ugliness in the sexual comportment of one's mother or that there was the faintest, remotest, teeniest possibility that one might be the slightest bit effeminate. "Queer" was out of the question, and someone had to die if such a malevolent insult were even intimated.

Edward Sespootch was the largest boy in the school by virtue of his hard life on the Apache reservation, and the fact that he was eighteen years old and still in the seventh grade. Edward was not at all interested in school, hated the rest of the white students who looked down on his humble clothing and long straight black hair, and whispered so he could hear that about the only good Indian was a dead drunk Indian. Even among the members of the local tribe, Edward was treated shabbily because his father was a Ute, not an Apache, and his mother was considered tainted for having married an outsider to the tribe.

Chuck learned the hard way not to taunt Indians, at least not Edward Sespootch and provided an object lesson remembered by every white kid in the school. He told Teddy Sorensen, in Edward's hearing, the following story:

"Hey, Teddy, you hear about the time old Ed Sespootch asked his mamma if it was true that Injuns had bigger dongs that white boys?"

"Uh uh," answered Teddy, uncomfortable because he knew that Edward was listening.

"His mamma said, 'I don't know Eddy, dear. What makes you think so?'

"Edward said, 'Well, me and the boys went behind the school and took ours out and measured 'em. Mine was twict as long as anybody else's. Do you think that's because I'm an Apache?'

'No, dear. I think that's because you're eighteen years old and the rest of your friends are thirteen and fourteen.'"

Edward took exception to the joke and got himself expelled for two weeks for sweeping up the floor with both Chuck and Teddy even though Chuck said he had not meant anything by it, and Teddy protested that he was just an innocent bystander.

Edward Sespootch attended school because the law said he had to attend, and, for some fool reason, kept coming out to the reservation to fetch him when he sloughed school as he did with obstinate regularity despite the whippings from his father, the tears of his mother, and the obvious disapproval of his teacher—that white-eyed witch.

Edward was in a particularly foul mood on that memorable day, two days before the teacher's boy's birthday. He had received an especially brutal flogging from his drunken father and had been bad-mouthed by the deputy who brought him back to school for the umpty-umpth time. He was dirty and disheveled and dog tired.

Rachel Carmichael looked at the errant Indian boy with anger. She had had a hard day trying to get disinterested students to diagram compound-complex sentences without success, and the Indian boy's sneering obstinate expression was more than she could handle with equanimity. Her look was one of contempt, and her worst mistake was to sniff and frown at his unwashed aroma as she passed his seat. Edward had had enough of school and of Mrs. Carmichael, the white witch.

He said sotto voce, loud enough for everyone in the room to hear, "Don't like the way men smell, teacher? That's not what I heard."

"What did you say, young man?" Rachel whirled back to look the hostile boy in the eye.

"You heard me."

As he said it, his peripheral vision caught the movement of Garven Carmichael rising from his desk chair.

"Do you want to share something with the whole class, Edward?" Mrs. Carmichael asked tightly in the ageless challenge from the annoyed teacher to the student with the unruly mouth.

"If you want. Everybody in this town knows you can't keep your panties on," he snarled defiantly looking directly into her shocked and dismayed eyes.

Rachel was speechless.

Edward's keen eyes took in Garven's form as he catapulted from his chair.

Edward readied himself for the inevitable conflict but could not resist one final unforgivable breach of the common ethic and said, as he moved into a fighting crouch beside his desk, "And the other thing I said was that everyone around here knows that cute little boy of yours is a fairy!"

Garven cleared two rows of desks in a dive and melded his body with the far larger Indian boy's.

Edward Sespootch may have lacked both formal educational skills and the social graces, but you had to give him his due. Growing up on the reservation taught the survivors to fight. The kids there understood the only rule of fighting—there are no rules. Edward was completely ready for his much smaller attacker's contact although he had had only a fraction of a second to set himself. He bit Garven hard on the back of his shoulder drawing blood and an inadvertent yelp.

"Titty!" Edward laughed at the thrashing boy who held him in a bear hug.

It was less funny when Garven's hard shoe toes slammed into his shins three times before he could move in defense.

Edward twisted to loosen himself from the younger boy's intense clasp; so, he could punch the kid into submission. His fists were big enough to enclose one of Garven's hands. Garven was surprisingly strong for a white city boy, and for someone as small as he was. Edward could not shake his attacker and, instead, managed to topple straight over backwards as he twisted awkwardly. He caught the edge of the adjacent desk with his occiput, opening a small gash, and crumpled onto the screw plate holding the desk to the floor, opening another gash. That hurt, and he was now aware of a fogginess in his brain. He thought it would be nice to rest a bit.

Garven loosened his grappling hold on the big Indian and brought both fists up in a staccato attack on his opponent's face. Blood spurted from both of Edward's nostrils. He was breathing very hard from his exertions and sent a spray of blood over Garven's arms and face. Two girls—Sarah Carlisle and Monica Young—screamed in the background, and neither fighter noticed. Edward brought a ham-sized fist around from the floor and caught Garven squarely on his ear. The cartilage snapped and a blossom of pain bloomed in the injured ear. Edward enjoyed the hit and swung the second fist around to cauliflower the second ear. He had not counted on the wrought iron legs of the desk and smashed his fist full force not on the soft ear but on the unyielding metal bar. There was an audible crunch of bone and gristle. Edward groaned and ground his teeth. There was no time to tend his new wound. Garven's small fists flew in a blinding flurry, pulpifying the larger Apache boy's nose and cheeks. Edward roared his rage and fought his way to his feet while fending off the wiry white boy with his intact left hand, and keeping his mangled right hand protected behind him. The fifth metacarpal was fractured and the distal segment protruded through the torn skin. Blood flowed freely from a small digital artery that was severed by the jagged bone ends.

Edward was hurt but still a formidable opponent. He was as large as the biggest man in Cipher and had no concept of the Marquis of Queensbury or his quaint rules. He kicked, gouged, and flailed at Garven with his left fist. His arm was large and defined with muscles, as well carved as the knots on a hickory branch. Garven was kicked in the stomach, and the fight seemed to go out of the boy along with his air supply. He was exhausted and dizzy and fell lamely to the ground. Edward raised his size twelve shoe sole over Garven's vulnerable face and contracted every muscle in the limb to stomp out the vicious little white boy's life. He saw his opponent, his victim, through a blood-tinged pink haze of uncontrolled fury.

"Edward! Stop!" the sheriff's voice penetrated the haze from the entry way into the classroom. He had been summoned from his office across the street by a frightened child.

Edward scarcely connected the source with the sound, but the sheriff's voice was familiar after all the trips from the reservation back to school after his truancies. He hesitated just over a second, time enough for Garven to shake his grogginess and to move his head before it was squashed like a melon. Edward stamped his foot down where Garven's face had been a fraction of a second earlier. The edge of the hard-toed sole grazed Garven's heretofore intact ear, neatly slicing it in half. Both halves stayed on his head but pumped blood on the already bespattered floor. He rolled further to his side and rose to a half crouch. Edward's calloused fist was doubled on the end of his coiled spring-steel arm. The final blow was unleashed with Garven watching his devastation in the awful slow motion view provided by the adrenaline-charged brain.

But the blow never connected. The mighty arm never uncoiled and drove the gnarly fist with all the Indian boy's body weight and force behind it. All Garven saw was Edward crumpling over him like a rag doll that had had its stuffing suddenly and mysteriously removed. The Indian's inert carcass covered the diminutive white boy like a bear rug.

Edward never saw the blow from the sheriff's truncheon, and did not know what hit him. The last thing he could remember out of the haze of postconcussion amnesia once he woke up fully a day later was being punched in the face by the furious teacher's kid. The sheriff, for all his ungainly egg-shaped body and small low-browed head, could move short distances with remarkable celerity and was far stronger than his unathletic figure would suggest. He cold-cocked the big Indian just as the boy was about to finish off the scrappy white kid who was down on the floor, ready for the death blow.

Mrs. Carmichael was afraid the sheriff had killed the Sespootch boy, and how was she going to explain that to the school board and to the Apaches who would come to the school and silently wait for her to make them understand? She was ashamed at her disappointment when the monster began to stir and show signs of life.

The Cipher volunteer ambulance crew carted both boys to the town's medical facility where Peter Wilsonhulme, M.D. waited. It was his last day of practice in Cipher. When he saw the Sespootch boy, he presumed it was another drunken brawl at the reservation. However, when Mabel Kendricks, his nurse and right hand, cleaned the blood and gore from the other boys face, he realized that it was his mentally adopted son, Garven, and deduced that the school must have had a riot. Dr. Wilsonhulme worked with unaccustomed assiduousness to repair Garven's transected ear. He brought to recollection everything he had ever learned or practiced about plastic surgery and put in dozens of tiny sutures. The ear was perfect. Oh, it would be a little crooked and asymmetrical in comparison to the other one which was cauliflowered itself, but, barring an infection, the cut ear would look as good as any high-priced Phoenix cosmetic surgeon could make it. He surveyed the ruined nose.

"Garven, this is going to hurt...a lot. I'm sorry. I have to snap your nose bones back into place with this pliers-like thing then tape it into place."

"Can't you knock him out, Dr. Wilsonhulme?" asked Rachel Carmichael, looking at her battered son sympathetically.

She flashed a malevolent glance at the recumbent warrior on the next gurney.

"Sorry, Rachel. Can't be done. From time immemorial, pugilists have had to endure this little procedure without anesthesia. It'd be better if you stepped out into the waiting room during this. Just for a minute or two," the doctor requested.

"No, Sir. I'm staying. I want to feel every part of this. I want to have this in me when I make decisions about this boy's future; so, I won't forget or get soft in the head. I'm not a fainter, if that's what you're worried about," Rachel answered definitively.

"Okay, my dear, but don't say I didn't warn you. Ready, Garven?"

"I guess so," Garven muttered. His voice sounded thick and like he had a bad cold with a congested nose.

Dr. Wilsonhulme inserted a long beaked pair of nasal forceps into the tender, swollen, blood-encrusted nostrils and in less time than it takes to say it, made a violent short wrenching motion. There was a sickening crunch of small bone fragments. Suddenly the battered nose assumed something of its pristine form, although it was badly swollen. Garven passed out. Mabel swiftly applied a tape splint to the fragile bridge of Garven's nose and taped it in place. She fashioned a cup bandage to keep pressure off both of his burgeoning cauliflower ears, cleaned up the bite chunk missing from his shoulder, and bandaged it.

Perhaps out of a sense of egalitarianism, or simply to avoid the appearance of favoritism or racism, Dr. Wilsonhulme was solicitous to Edward's needs next. Overly solicitous to Rachel's way of thinking.

Savage brute, she thought as she looked at her son lying there, swathed in bandages.

Dr. Wilsonhulme and Mabel soaked Edward's battered hand in iodine/merthiolate solution. The pain from the two chemicals was terrible and was mirrored in the stoical boy's brown face although he did not make a sound. He fought to avoid the ignominy of crying in front of all these enemy white faces.

"I'm sorry it hurts so much, Edward," Dr. Wilsonhulme commiserated with the stolid Indian. "I'll hurry fast as I can. It'll just be a minute, but we have to kill off all the germs. Understand?"

"Um hum," mumbled the young Indian through clenched teeth.

"Its okay to cry, Edward," said Mabel with genuine sympathy. "We don't ever talk about what goes on in here."

Edward recognized the universal language of kindness. It made his efforts to control his tears all the harder. Nonetheless, he appreciated her expressed concern.

"I'm all right, Mrs. Nurse. Thanks for your help."

It was the most he had said all at once in days. He fell back to his silent endurance.

Dr. Wilsonhulme warned the Indian youth of a moment of impending severe pain, read the acquiescence in Edward's eyes, and pulled on the fifth knuckle and on the boys wrist at the same time. The bone twisted but did not reseat itself. Edward groaned involuntarily.

"Sorry, son. I have to do it again. You up to this?" the doctor queried with real concern.

The boy looked pale for all his congenital and sun-baked bronzing.

Edward simply nodded his head feebly up and down.

This time the pain was worse, but the bone edges snapped under the torn skin margins. Dr. Wilsonhulme gently straightened out the bent hand and covered the unsutured skin with a bulky cotton bandage. While Mabel held the unstable bone fragments in place, the doctor expertly applied a long arm cast.

"Son, your boxing days have got to be over for a while, understand?" Dr. Wilsonhulme ordered with a stern avuncular look.

"Yeah," Edward returned meekly.

"Okay, Edward, just a little more. I think your nose's busted too. So, we have to fix that. We better put a few stitches in the back of your head and over your spine. I'll do that, then Mabel will bandage you all up."

The doctor's voice was kind and warm despite the clinical message.

Edward nodded affirmatively again. Dr. Wilsonhulme worked swiftly, setting aside his fleeting humanistic concerns as he deftly inflicted pain and repair. Edward was as good as a scarred-up new and settled off to sleep when he was assured that there were no more pains to be had after he and Garven got their tetanus shots.

"I want to keep the boys here overnight to watch them. You can pick up Garven in the morning. Since it's Saturday, you don't have to teach and can come in anytime. I'll stay at the Hansen's until Vera comes up from Emmett for Garven's party on Sunday," Dr. Wilsonhulme said to Rachel who had finally taken his advice and avoided the grim spectacle of Edward's clinical tortures.

"Oh, good grief! That party! I guess it's all off now. I'll have to call the boys' parents tonight. Thanks for reminding me," Rachel said with frustration.

"Not necessarily, Rachel. Kids are tough. Both of these boys will look like war heroes, but they will probably be full of wim, wigor, and witality in two days. The kids don't care how they look these days. You ought to know that just by looking at the Halloween costumes they wear for regular clothes. What a generation!"

"You really think we should have a birthday party after all this? I will be lucky to have a job. I'll be lucky if the red skins don't come to town and scalp me!" Rachel exclaimed.

"You're tired and frazzled now; things will look better in the morning. I don't really see any good reason to put off the party. The school board is not going to do anything. They will hold their breath for fear that you'll quit and leave them mid-school year. Then, they'll have to find someone else to herd these banshees around. As for the Indians, they are used to violence. You won't hear a thing from them; you can rest assured that Edward Sespootch will be the last person on earth to open his mouth about the events of this day. He knows that he will just get another whipping if he does. Poor kid, doesn't have a chance".

"It's more than I can do to muster up some milk of human kindness for that one; so, don't waste your breath, doctor." Mrs. Carmichael replied to Dr. Wilsonhulme's unspoken request for tolerance and forbearance. "But I'll give the party some thought if you really believe Garven will be okay by then."

Garven and Edward woke up on their hard-backed gurneys at about the same time and for the same reasons: full bladders and aching heads and limbs. They looked at each other and inexplicably smiled. They both looked like they had been in a grenade attack, and to teenagers, their looks were the soul of hilarity. The two boys grinned, then chuckled, then started to laugh. They were soon moaning in pain at the movements exacted by the uncontrolled catharsis of laughter—gales and guffaws of laughter. They looked like a pair of battered loonies. Mabel checked in on them at bedtime when they were midway into their lunatic giggling, tittering, and recurrent howls of unbridled mirth, and concluded that they were just fine. Crazy, which is to say, normal teenagers, but otherwise just fine. She was a crotchety old biddy with a soft spot for bad boys. She looked at these two with affection.

Words are precious, and Edward Sespootch was generally a very thrifty guy. He was feeling especially garrulous at the moment.

He doubled his output of sentences for the week and said to his recent opponent, "Hey, Garven, you sure can hit. I never even seen the punch comin'. My head is still full a cobwebs."

Garven knew perfectly well where the final blow to Edward had come from, and it never crossed his mind to tell the Indian about the sheriff and his truncheon.

He simply said with all humility, "Ah, it was nuthin', just a lucky punch. You are one tough hombre."

Garven could not have selected a better phrase. Although largely unspoken, the friendship between the two former combatants was sealed, much to Rachel Carmichael's chagrin and better judgment. The two boys were inseparable after their recuperative night in the Cipher Hospital (using the term loosely). Edward even came to Garven's party—the first time he had ever been to a party where there was not a single drunk, and there were even girls present.

Edward was crestfallen as he entered Rachel and Garven's house exactly at the six o'clock announced starting hour.

He stood literally hat in hand at the threshold and stammered out a brief and carefully rehearsed, "I…I'm…I am truly sorry for the fighting. I promise to be better."

He looked so forlorn and genuinely contrite that Rachel could not help but smile and invite him in. She did indeed forgive the terror from the reservation, but vowed never to forget the lesson she had learned that day in her school room. When she saw how chummy her son and the wild Indian had become in that brief interlude of peace following the battle, she was not so much astonished at the transformation as she was dismayed at the implications for the future she envisioned for her son.

Rachel did not see the party as being nearly as genteel as did Edward Sespootch. She took exception to Lyle Durche's usurping the role of greeter of guests. She took considerable exception to his introductory greeting that the guests found so amusing:

"Ladies and gentlemen,
Beggars and tramps,
Bowlegged mosquitoes
And cross-eyed ants.

I come before you,
To stand behind you
To tell you of something
I know nothing 'bout.

This Thursday, which is
Good Friday,

There will be a Mother's Day
Meeting for fathers only.

The admission is free;
Pay at the door.
Pull up a chair
And sit on the floor."

The party was, by anyone's evaluation, a rousing success. Garven had a great time; he and Edward regaled the other boys and the enchanted girls with the gory details of their fight and medical adventures. At least, Garven regaled, and Edward nodded in agreement. Garven even kissed a girl for the first time. Her name was Sarah Carlisle, and she blushed scarlet when their lips touched. Even though she was a painfully converted Mormon through and through, he liked her. He had a good blush himself.

Rachel determined then and there to make a change, some kind of change to save her son's future. She had been upset, even frightened, during the fight, and had despaired for Garven's very survival. He was becoming like one of the coyotes she so despised. Her feelings upon seeing her son becoming bosom buddies with the wildest human being she had ever personally encountered was, to her, a harbinger of the future that prompted a vow for a change. The thought of change was as yet unformed, a shapeless gray mist wafting through her brain; but it was born of a deeply felt need; and she intended to bring the thought to a plan, and the plan to an action before it was too late. Garven was not going to be a wastrel like his father. She would be damned before she would see that bright boy languish into adulthood in this godforsaken desert with its coyotes, scorpions, and snakes; and they were among the nicest features of the place, she groused to herself.

The events, the birthday party, and Rachel's rapidly developing dissatisfaction and concerns were fortuitous. Serendipity and perfect timing impelled Peter and Vera Wilsonhulme to stay over in Cipher to attend the birthday celebration. He and Vera had a good time being the honorary grandparents. Garven treated the older couple as if they were fully blood family, and Edward was even civil. The party ended with the obligatory ice cream and chocolate cake scattered all over Rachel's scrupulously clean floor, and the anticipated relief as the din quieted with the last kid—Garven's—exit.

"Be back in an hour or so. Me and Edward are going to raise some trouble over at the church after their Sacrament Meeting lets out."

"It's 'Ed and I', Garven, I'll thank you to remember. And I think the two of you have raised enough trouble for a long time to come, don't you, young man?"

"Nobody calls him Ed, Mom. He's Edward. He likes his whole name," Garven rejoined in defense of his quiet-spoken friend. "We're just goin' to find some girls. Can't you take a little joke?"

"The word is 'going'…going, not goin'," his mother said stressing the word endings emphatically.

"Yes, Ma'am; yes, Teacher."

Garven smiled affectionately and a trifle painfully at his mother as he backed down the front porch steps and was gone with Edward, looking for all the world like the comic strip characters Mutt and Jeff in bandages as they went.

Rachel gritted her teeth as the two boys sang another of their raucous songs as they walked off down the street:

> "Woke up Sunday mornin'
> Gazed upon the wall.
> The bedbugs and the Cooties
> Were havin' a game of ball.
>
> The score was nine to nothin'
> The Cooties were in head.
> The bedbugs knocked a home run
> And knocked me out of bed.
>
> Went downstairs to breakfast,
> The bread was very stale.
> Coffee tasted like tobacco juice
> They serve in the county jail.
>
> Indian rubber beefsteak,
> Disconnected cheese
> A weenie took a flip-flop
> and lit in a bowl of peas."

Rachel rolled her eyes and shook her head in not so mock despair.

Dr. and Mrs. Wilsonhulme excused themselves and thanked Rachel for the invitation to the party. They hesitated a little, and Rachel collected her thoughts from the swirl going on inside her head.

She said quietly and earnestly, "Please stay for a bit. I would very much like to have someone to talk to. This has been quite a weekend."

"It has. I have been meaning to discuss some ideas Vera and I have been tossing around. Maybe this is as good a time as any," Peter said, glad to have an opening.

He and Vera had fairly firmly agreed on making their offer to Rachel to assist in Garven's education, but their innate courtesy and social shyness had not permitted an opportunity until now.

Rachel bade them to sit, made each a cup of coffee with copious amounts of cream, sugar, and some Mexican vanilla which she knew they liked, and presented her concerns for her son and his future, taking care to avoid complaining or self-pitying. After rambling somewhat about her situation and her observations about Garven's present social condition and her fears for his future, she concluded with the thought that had become firmly formulated for the first time.

"My son has to get out of here. He has to get out of this town, or he is going to be a wild cowboy or a feral child. Or an Indian at the rate he is going. I may be a racist or something, but I don't think so. There can't be anything wrong with a mother wanting to prevent her son from failing or, worse, getting into trouble. I am going to try to get someone, maybe some of the nice Mormon people in Phoenix to take him for the school year. He needs to go to a real school, to meet bright kids with a future. The Mormons do it for the Indians; there must be some way for them to help my boy."

She said it more pensively than emphatically. Vera gave Peter the high sign with her raised eyebrows and a small significant nod of her head. Dr. Wilsonhulme drew a breath, sensing that this was his best opportunity. By virtue of his medical training, Peter Wilsonhulme was not given to being overly subtle, or to the use of euphemisms by his very nature, or to talking around a subject. He plunged right into the conversational pool.

"Stop me if you consider anything I am about to say presumptive or out of line, please, Rachel. I assure you that both Vera and I will understand. But we have come to regard you and Garven almost as family. Darn it, we do think of that boy like a son, or perhaps, more aptly, as the grandson we have never had and can never have."

Rachel smiled shyly in acknowledgment of the expression of affection.

"We hope you have come to feel somewhat the same about us. We are getting older, ready for retirement, and would be more than grateful if you could see your way clear to let us help with Garven's education. We share both your concerns and your pride. He is a special boy just as you have indicated, and it is clear that he is going to need special help to get up and away from here permanently. We have a proposal in mind. We've actually given it some thought."

"Really?" was all Rachel could muster. Peter had her undivided attention. Her pulse rate had quickened.

"Indeed. I know a school where he could get the education you speak of. It is not a school; to my mind, it is *the* school; and I know for a fact that he could get accepted."

Here, Dr. Wilsonhulme overstated his facts somewhat, but his assumption was based on a reasonably sound premise.

"Let me take a moment to explain. You see, a dear old friend of mine, a classmate from my prep school and undergraduate days, is now the headmaster at the Burton-Cagle School in Malibu, California. Perhaps you are not so familiar with the competitive world of prep schools, but accept my expertise on this: Burton-Cagle is the standout among the best schools in the West. It is by all criteria the best high school west of the Mississippi, and can compete with Andover, Groton, or the Harvard schools for number one in the country. It is my alma mater."

The doctor paused, sipped his coffee for a moment, and collected his thoughts briefly while the two women watched him. The desert sunset glowed through the open windows with subtle and warming mauves, pinks, and lavenders.

He returned to his task.

"Another thing you might not know, but can imagine, is that fathers apply for places at the school when their sons are born. It is, to say the least, an exclusive school. Each class has no more than fifty students with twenty times that number on a waiting list. It is snobbish, conservative, and a pain in the… behind at times, but the education received and the social connections to be made are incomparable. Since Vera and I have had no children and harbor no religious pretensions, we have contributed a rather tidy sum to the school over the years at the request of my old friend. Although, I can't be certain, I do believe that my recommendation and sponsorship of a deserving boy would carry the day. I have yet to do so, which makes this first-time recommendation all the more compelling, I think."

"What does a place like that cost? I'm almost afraid to ask," Rachel inquired with timidity in her voice but with a feeling more like temerity.

"I guess we're talking upwards of seven, eight thousand dollars a year." Peter replied.

Rachel gasped and emitted a short nervous laugh.

"That's more than twice what I make in a whole year. It's impossible!"

"Rachel, dear," Vera interrupted. "Peter can't seem to get to it. Although we are by no means wealthy people, we do have the means to support Garven through the Burton-Cagle School. We can probably even get him a scholarship. They do have a few; and as of last year, I am on the selection committee. The opportunity is open right now; it's the opportunity of a lifetime. I know it is hard for your pride, hard to think of sending your son away to school."

"With all those Philistines!" Peter chimed in facetiously.

Vera shushed her husband.

"But I know that above all else, you are a mother and have the interests of your child close at heart. I like to think of myself as a kind of aunt to Garven. I really feel like his grandmother. Let me give to him, too. I would be grateful to be able to share in the life of a boy whom I love."

There was a long thoughtful pause. Peter and Vera watched the elements of pride, concern, hope, and gratitude pass over Rachel's expressive face. She was able to think clearly in that brief space of time freed from all other interests and concerns. When she spoke, it was clear that she felt she had crossed her Rubicon.

"I am overwhelmed. This seems too good to be true, too frightening for a country girl like me to take in all at once, but I accept. I love you for what you are willing to do for my boy. Maybe, together, we can keep him from growing up to be another coyote in Cipher, Arizona."

"Of course, we will have to have Garven's agreement in all of this. After all, it is his future we are presumptuous enough to be planning here," intoned Peter trying to be fair, as the usually incomprehensible new generation always seemed to demand.

"That will not be necessary. Families are not democracies. My son will obey my wishes; and for this purpose, he will be obligated to obey your dictates as well, Dr. and Mrs. Wilsonhulme. Children cannot be entrusted with such a vital decision," Rachel stated with finality and the determination of her self-sacrificing maternal instinct. "He will agree, and he will be forever grateful that he did."

"Now you're a woman after our own hearts. You will be pleased to see that sort of attitude maintained vigorously at Burton-Cagle," said the doctor.

CHAPTER
Four

"It would be much more defensible if he were your own son, Peter, you realize that," Carter P. Des Moines said again.

The headmaster of Burton-Cagle School was faced with a real quandary about this application for admission to the venerable institution. It was one more point of pressure among altogether too many already facing the beleaguered headmaster.

"But sadly, I have no son of my own, C.P. This boy is as close as any could be. I hate to put it this way, but if obliged, I would call in my marks for this lad. He's worth it, and well, I wish you didn't make me say it, but the school owes me. You and I go back a long ways; that should count for something; our friendship should not be something I have to presume upon. I don't want to be in the position of equalizing the ledger. It shouldn't be that way," Peter Wilsonhulme said persuasively, making an effort to keep any note of pleading out of his strained voice. This discussion had been working up to this point for ten minutes.

"Have you any idea how many boys are applying for the freshman class this year, Peter?"

"Two thousand seventy-eight for fifty places, to be precise. The average grade point average is 3.6; most have had two or more years of a modern foreign language; all except Garven have had the necessary exposure to beginning Latin; the average income of the fathers is in the six-figure bracket, and many are the richest, and some, the most famous people in America," Peter crisply recited the daunting admissions demographics his wife had supplied him the evening before.

"Exceptional grasp of the facts of the problem I face. One thing you neglected to stress: the fathers of these boys are the best, the brightest, the most successful, and the richest in the world, not just California or even the U.S. They are not used to hearing 'no'," Mr. Des Moines rejoined.

"And ten percent of your students are scholarship boys. Whatever you thought about the decision to admit those less privileged boys, it was something you had to do. Include Garven in that group, if you must. You have to tell more than two thousand fathers no anyway, what does one more no to one more father matter?"

"I don't know how much longer I can contend with this stress, Peter. You know that there is a lot of pressure to admit—Jews, of all people. That came from the administration in Washington—you, know, *Eleanor*—and the socialists running the Los Angeles government for the time being. Would you believe that I have even had a letter from Eleanor herself suggesting we were wasting brains by not admitting girls? *Girls!* The meddlesome first lady even hinted that the time would come when we would see swartzers in the student body. I wrote her a letter discussing the snowball-in-hell timetable, politely worded, of course."

"I know all that, and I truly sympathize; but we are not talking anything radical here. This kid fits most of the bill: he's a W.A.S.P., a heterosexual, not a Jewish or colored gene in his background. He lives in a little Mormon town, but he's not part of that cult. Think of him as interesting. He'll add some diversity to this plain vanilla campus, but not too much. Think of him as a challenge. I think he is smart enough to get his Latin and his other deficiencies up to snuff in less than a year. You know you want to be able to say you have a student from such a picturesque place as Cipher, Arizona!" Peter said with an affectionate smile sensing capitulation.

"It'll cost you, my friend. I will have to sell him to the board and that will be costly. You will have to squeeze another couple of hundred thou out of the alumni to grease the skids for Garven Carmichael of Cipher, Arizona."

The two aging men laughed with each other with the warmth of a lifetime of friendship and returned favors. They shook on it. Garven Carmichael was as good as admitted. Somewhere, a father would scream foul when he learned that the son he placed on the Burton-Cagle list on his Christening day, would have to settle for The Cate School, Groton or Andover or Culver Military Academy, maybe even Dunn School.

Peter Wilsonhulme was more than pleased with his success, but the element of the conversation that stayed with him for some reason was C.P.'s casual observation that Garven would fare better as his son. Something to think about.

******

Garven spent most of his time after school let out in the spring on the Apache reservation being a wild Indian with Edward Sespootch, the wildest Indian of all, as his guide. He learned several essential things for maturation, like the art of excessive beer drinking, dirty fighting, how to swear in Apache, and stealth. He took long walks in the desert alone, sometimes shadowed by his old friend, the coyote, which now had only one eye. His mother acknowledged the value of his learning about the wild things and places in the desert and bemoaned his lack of enthusiasm for the Latin studies she arranged for him in Emmett with the retired Catholic priest. Rachel worried that her son was not cultivating the kinds of young men he would need to know at Burton-Cagle, but Peter and Vera Wilsonhulme assured her that he would be an instant success at the school being the only boy with an Apache Indian for a best friend and the one-eyed coyote for whom he seemed to hold affection, and who spent his summer living like an aborigine. Rachel was not altogether convinced.

Garven maintained an air of nonchalance about the impending radical change in his life, but exuded a marginally suppressed air of excitement and of wonder about the faraway places with strange sounding names that lay in his future. He had won acceptance in Cipher by his toughness; boys were the same everywhere, he reasoned; and he could make himself accepted at this fancy boys' school the same way if he needed to.

He got a job on the reservation helping Edward break horses, and by the end of the summer, he could manage to stay on a horse long enough to tame the feisty creatures the majority of times. He learned to accept bruises and falls as nothing more than temporary setbacks in the process and got back in the saddle immediately after getting bucked off. He never gave a horse an even break—the first rule of cowboying; and he had yet to meet a horse he couldn't make bow to his will. He was satisfied with himself and his prospects. He was bronzed from the sun with a mass of freckles on his face and shoulders. He was lean, toughened to the saddle, full of expectations for the fall, and completely naive.

On his last night in Cipher, it seemed warranted to celebrate, but in the dusty little desert town, there was not much to do to celebrate. The local teenagers' standard joke was to ask each other, "You wanna do somethin' or just drag main?"

Main Street was the only paved street in the city. All of his closest friends came to be with him that night, sort of fascinated with the impending departure. No one they knew personally had ever left.

"Wanna do somethin' or just drag main?" Lyle asked.

It didn't get much of a laugh from the collection of fourteen-year-olds or Edward.

None of the boys had driver's licenses. Chuck McInerny, Tadd, Teddy, and Lyle were all too young, and Edward, who was nineteen, was an Indian. Lacking a license did not keep Lyle from having his own car, a thoroughly beat-up '38 Ford; and the boys all piled in and headed for the Avon Café for some ice cream or something.

They were raucous, making a serious effort to offend as many of the towns-people as they could as they drove slowly along the pavement. They sang at the top of their lungs:

"Yankee Doodle went to town,
A riding on his lady,
And every bump that
They did hit;
Out would bounce a baby

And:

My name is John Taylor;
My dink is a whaler.
My balls weigh forty-nine pounds
Each!

And:

Ta ra ra boom te ay!
Did you get yours today?
Well, I got mine today
From the girl across the way!"

The inspiration for what to do to give Garven a serious send off came from an entirely unexpected source and by serendipity. The county sheriff's and town marshal's cars were parked alongside each other, facing opposite directions; so, the officers on duty that night could converse with each other comfortably through their open driver's side windows. It was a very hot night, sweltering, and there was a consequent torpor about the town. The natives were restful, the two minions of the law had decided and had left their units (a word the sheriff had picked up at the state patrol school) and were enjoying a couple of chocolate malts in the Avon. They could see the street and do their jobs just as well from there as they could from their cruisers (the marshal's favorite term, one he had gotten from a Jimmy Cagney movie). They could not actually see their police cars, but the last thing anyone wanted to bother was a cop car. Besides, it was too hot to make trouble that August night.

Garven got the idea first. He always seemed to be the one who got the great ideas first. *It was the curse of being smart,* he thought, because he seemed to get into more than his share of trouble with those great ideas.

"Hey, where're the cops?" he asked with some real interest, the idea already germinating.

"Probably in the Avon," said Chuck, whose mind tended to run to food.

"More likely shackin' up with Rita Rottencrotch," Lyle said.

His mind tended to run more towards more physical activities than did Chuck's. His reference was to Rita Rogenweiler, the town punchboard.

"Let's find out for sure. I've got an idea," said Garven.

Five sets of ears perked up.

"Go into the Avon and see if they're there; and if they are, where are they sitting," Garven directed.

His presidency was usually accepted without question when he had an idea.

"I want to know if they can see their cars from where they're sitting right now."

"Hokay, boss," Chuck said with his rendition of a Mexican accent.

He walked to the café barely glancing at the "WAITRESS WANTED" sign and the old advertisement in the window: "T-BONE, 75¢ - WITH MEAT, $3.25."

"Lyle, you got some drag chains and about four axle blocks?"

"Not on me," Lyle replied facetiously turning the pockets of his Levi's inside out.

"Funny," Garven said. "In the trunk?"

"Chains, but no blocks."

"My dad has all kindsa blocks in his shop," offered Tadd.

"Let's whip over there and get a coupla sets," Lyle said and cut a kitty right in the middle of Main Street, but discretely out of sight of the Avon and the town cops.

He had no idea what Garven had in mind, but since Garven's ideas usually panned out, and since there was nothing else to do, he felt fairly galvanized into action.

Chuck was waiting for them in front of the Avon when they got back.

"Wherra you been?" he asked petulantly, thinking he had probably been made the butt of a joke as usual.

"Gettin' some stuff," Garven said. "Don't get all bent out of shape. So, what did you find out about those in our community authorized to protect and to serve?"

"You mean Deputy Peterson and Marshall Jones?" Chuck asked.

Garven nodded.

"They're sittin' in the back booth orderin' one thing after another. Mabel Sessions's the waitress tonight."

That explained everything. Mabel was pneumatically endowed and never seemed to be able to find a waitress blouse that buttoned clear up to the top.

"They'll be there for a while."

"Okay, here's what we do," Garven said and proceeded to lay out his most current and well-thought out plan in detail.

Garven was quick and thorough when it came to these kinds of plans. The boys all had fiendish grins when he completed his description of logistics.

The boys jacked up the rear axles of both cars and set them down on the wooden blocks, so the rear tires just cleared the ground. They then attached the drag chains around the front axles which left the chains lying diagonally between the two drivers' front wheels, a readily apparent and therefore untenable arrangement. Garven found the entrenching tool Lyle kept in his trunk and dug a small groove beside the chains, deep enough to bury their full size and lengths. The boys covered the chains and, in the dim light of the evening, there was almost nothing to show for the work. You had to bend down to see the axle blocks. Chuck kept watch.

"Okay, we're ready," Garven pronounced after a final inspection of the work.

It was neat and camouflaged.

"Now, what? Do we just wait all night until the two cops get tired of lookin' at Mabel's busts or have to take a leak or somethin'?" Teddy asked.

He was getting bored again now that the excitement of the clandestine work project was over.

"No," Garven explained patiently, wondering why it was necessary to describe the obvious. "We have to get them to move out like a turpentined cat as soon as they hit their cars without bothering to look too carefully at the ground."

"A diversion, right?" asked Tadd.

He was getting the picture.

"Any ideas?" asked Garven in the democratic spirit.

"Throw a brick through the Avon's front window."

"Drive by and scream."

"Call in a phony murder at the edge of town."

"Something like that," Garven encouraged.

The other boys waited for their leader to come up with a better plan instead of exercising their imaginations any further.

"Well, I thought we might drive by yelling and screaming just like Lyle said," Tadd smiled.

"Then in the field by Dickinson's place, we throw a stick of dynamite and roar out of town. Maybe drop another bomb by the county fence." Garven offered as an addition.

There were no counterproposals. It was a perfect plan; they all knew that. They all knew how to get at the dynamite and blasting cap stocks in the county sheds. Every kid in town knew that, and not a single adult in town knew that they knew.

"I'll get it," said Edward, speaking up for the first time all evening.

For Edward this was almost animation. He was really getting into the spirit of the project.

"I'll drive him out to the sheds," said Lyle since it was his car.

The rest of the boys nodded and moved away from the vicinity of the cop cars to prevent some nosy busybody from making an association later after it hit the fan.

Edward picked up three new sticks of dynamite, knowing the unreliability of old ones. He knew how to use the stuff and was not about to get himself blown up in the prank. Garven and the others knew that and felt an easiness over the arrangements. The project was seeming more and more like an idea that was meant to be.

Lyle parked at the head of Main Street, three blocks from the Avon Café. He revved the little car's engine.

"Ready, Edward?" asked Garven, twisting his neck to look at the big Indian in the back seat.

He was the perfect one to lean out the window and toss the dynamite because everyone knew that they all looked alike.

"Uh huh," Edward mumbled and nodded.

"All the noise you can get out as soon as we get by the Avon," he said to the rest of the boys as a last reminder. "Go!" he yelled at Lyle who jumped a little at the unexpected shout.

He wasn't deaf, you know.

Lyle let go the clutch and floorboarded the accelerator at the same time. The rear wheels churned up a choke of dust; the car spun and quivered in place for a few seconds, then roared onto the paved street like a gray land rocket in the dim light of the town's two street lights. It was going close to seventy when they came within hailing distance of the café where the town cops were peacefully taking in a well-deserved supper and the proffered view. The car's performance more than justified Lyle's prodigious work that year to make it faster than the cop cars—the goal of every kid mechanic in Cipher.

As they approached then passed the Avon, the six boys yelled, screamed, whistled, and hollered. Lyle skidded to a wavering, screeching high speed stop and waited for developments.

The deputy stuck his head out the café door, an official scowl on his face. The boys shouted some unacceptable insults, gave the astonished and disgruntled policeman the bird, and roared off down the street. They saw the two officers run from the café entrance, hitching up their belts, making a beeline for their cars.

Edward threw the first dynamite stick into the open field, and Lyle drove on without pausing. The explosion was deafening and altogether too close. Edward had made the fuse a mite short.

They passed the county sheds, and Edward blew the high chain-link fence including two uprights into smithereens. The fuse was better this time. Lyle made a hard left on the last street in town, turned, and doubled back into the town center via Fourth North, the street facing the open desert. He had turned off his lights and cruised along in a cloud of powdery dust and turned down Center, drove two blocks, and parked. They were a block north of the Avon. There had been no hint of police activity.

The boys walked nonchalantly and innocently into the now busy town center and joined the small crowd watching the two cops as they furiously raced to jack up their cars and to kick out the axle blocks upon which their cars had been spinning for the first few minutes of the excitement. When the tires were once again on terra firma, the two officers jumped into their cars, desperate to avenge the insult and to make an example of the j-ds who were undermining the cause of decency in their fair city.

The powerful police car engines turned over and roared in anticipation of the chase. Each vehicle leaped forward like a great cat after its prey. And each vehicle made a sudden totally crazy swerve and rammed its front end into the rear fender of the other. The cop cars bounced off each other and then to the consternation of the watching crowd made an absolutely psychotic, grinding circular motion as if the two side by side vehicles were chasing each other in a destructive exercise. The cars shut off immediately. They were now facing ninety degrees from their original positions. The county car was pointed at Livingston's garbage cans, and the city car was aimed directly across the street at the Avon Café. Smoke wafted from the hoods of the battered vehicles. Heavy drag chains were tangled around the front wheels and lay askew in the street.

Garven's friends worried that he was going to have a stroke; he laughed that hard. They hung on each other and laughed and retold the events of the day until late at night. When his friends finally left his and Rachel's house, they could hear the boys singing for the benefit of the neighborhood:

> "A little miss, went out to pi. . .
> ick some flowers.
> She stepped in grass, up to her a. . .
> nkles fair.
> She said, 'Oh, my word, I stepped
> on a tur. . .key feather.'"

Lyle had a deep scratchy voice that might one day be a baritone. He made up in volume what he lacked in rhythm, tone, or being in tune. He yelled out a solo:

> "Two Irishmen, two Irishmen, fightin' in a ditch,
> One called the other one a dirty son of a…
> Peter Murphy had a dog, a dirty dog was he,
> He gave it to a lady friend, to keep her company-y
>
> She fed it, she fed it. She taught it how to jump.
> Jumped up her petticoat and bit her on the…
> Country boy, country boy, sittin' on a rock,
> Along came a bumblebee and bit him on the…
>
> Cocktail, ginger ale, five cents a glass,
> If you don't like it, you can stick it in your…
> Ask me no questions, I'll tell you no lies,
> If you get hit with a bucket of…
> …Fertilizer— you better close your eyes!"

Garven laughed and watched them until the red lights of Lyle's car turned the corner. Rachel was relieved that her son was going to be removed from such influences, however much she knew she would miss him. She felt very much alone.

CHAPTER
Five

Garven knew little about the demands of the exclusive school in California, the networking of the exclusive boys, and had not contemplated the possibility of homesickness. Until August 15, 1945, the day the fifteen-year-old from Cipher entered the gates of the most exclusive college preparatory school in the western United States, Garven Carmichael had not been one hundred fifty miles from his home and mother. He had a great deal to learn about life, the realities of his peers' attitudes, and about his ability to cope on his own.

The entire United States, Burton-Cagle School included, was having a great party. It was V-J Day! The streets overflowed with revelers. There were boys cavorting around the school's campus grounds in festive hats, and their parents were only a trifle less silly. V-E Day on May 8 had been more subdued than this final day of the Second World War. There was a feeling of a heavy burden having been lifted and of new beginnings. It was an auspicious day for Garven Carmichael to embark on the great adventure of his life; his mother and the Wilsonhulmes told him more than once.

Peter Wilsonhulme had driven Garven and his mother from Cipher to Los Angeles a week before the first day of the autumn semester; so, he could be properly outfitted and could see a few of the sights that were part of the familiar scene to the new student's contemporaries. Vera Wilsonhulme was too ill to accompany the trio; her hypertension had damaged her heart; and she was not up to the rigors of a non-airconditioned trip across the broiling Mojave Desert, or to the excitement of the crowds and the opening day ceremonies. Peter knew his wife's time was limited and accepted the fact with resignation. He had done all he could for her personally and professionally.

He kept his feelings to himself, aware of the burden his medical knowledge caused him.

After a quick passby of the school campus to orient Garven and Rachel, they drove down the coast highway to Los Angeles for some shopping. The doctor parked in the spacious parking lot of Bullocks on Wilshire Boulevard and led the wide-eyed boy and his mother into the department store that was larger than the town in which the fifteen year-old-lived. They marched directly to the boys department; shopping was not a pastime for the busy physician, just a necessity. He knew exactly the outfits Garven would need. There was no reason to shop about or to have extended discussions on the choices.

"This is Garven Carmichael. He is entering Burton-Cagle this year and will need a wardrobe, miss," the doctor said to the overworked saleslady causing Garven to blush with embarrassment.

She did not have to know his whole life's history in order for him to get a couple of new outfits. The saleslady did not have the faintest notion of what or where Burton-Cagle was. She was elaborately polite presuming that it would be to her benefit to be impressed. Garven silently begged the doctor to skip any more personal revelations with this stranger.

"He will need three blue blazers and a dark green one, four—no—five pairs of trousers. He will need a seersucker, two khaki, a light gray fine wool, and a summery light blue pair. You can get us three dark school ties to match the blazers; seven sea island cotton white, buttondown collar dress shirts; and a dozen pairs of assorted blue and gray socks."

"Yes, Sir," the saleslady replied, brightening up at the thought of the commission this sale would bring.

It had been a very slow morning thus far. She set about with dispatch to fetch the requested items, having judged his size without troubling the lady or the gentleman with questions. No one would expect the boy to know his own measurements or sizes, of course.

Garven was set for the school year in less than an hour and was growing anxious to see the ocean, the palm trees, and the movie stars. He was restless, not bored; every building, street, tree, and odd character was new to him; and he was fascinated. He had never seen a Negro before, and the city seemed full of them. He heard people speaking Spanish and Chinese and wondered briefly how they could make sense out of such gibberish. He saw thousands of cars, more than he could have imagined existed. He smelled exotic foods, felt the cooling salty sea breezes as they approached the beach, reveled in the gentle warmth of the oceanfront sun, and was thrilled to walk on the pale sands of the beach and to see the near-naked forms of gorgeous girls—hundreds of them. All his appetites were whetted; all his senses alerted; and he experienced feelings that had not surfaced nearly as strongly before. He tried not to gawk at the girls with his mother right there. He wished Lyle Durche and Edward Sespootch could be there so the three of them could have a snicker over all the flesh they were seeing.

"What do you say about us getting some Chinese, eh, Rachel? Okay, Garven?" asked Dr. Wilsonhulme, feeling vicariously exhilarated by Garven's youthful exuberance, by the ocean and its breezes, and by his old man's appreciation of the abundant femininity.

"I'm not sure, doctor," Rachel said shyly.

Her reticence betrayed her inexperience. "Isn't that awfully strange food; mightned we get a stomach upset, you know, the unusual things those people eat?"

"Nonsense. Where's your sense of adventure? You game, Garven?"

"I guess so," the boy said, grinning but not quite knowing what he was getting himself into, and besides, the prospects of leaving the wonders of the beach disappointed him.

Dr. Wilsonhulme checked his watch and saw that it was only shortly after noon. "Still plenty of time," he said briskly. "Well then, I know a great treat for you. We can drive to Chinatown and get dim sum."

He turned on his heels and started up the beach as if the three of them had completed a thorough discussion of the subject of lunch and had jointly made a decision. It was his nature or that of his medical training to make decisions and to present them *fait accompli*, presumed Rachel, and she smiled at his kindly and officious presumptiveness.

The meal was the most unusual experience of Garven's life to date, and probably of Rachel's. The restaurant was compact, smoky, and full of chattering Chinese families. Their good humor was infectious; the place was cacophonous with laughter and rattling bowls and clattering kitchen carts. Diminutive Chinese girls fairly ran along pushing their carts full of a dizzying array of small pots of the most peculiar foods. At least, Garven presumed they were foods by the haunting smells that wafted in on him from all sides. People haggled briefly over the price of each small bowl, then, satisfied that proper form had been followed, ate with relish.

Garven watched incredulously as the Orientals picked up selections from their bowls with thin sticks and ate what appeared to be chickens' feet, duck skin, seaweed, mounds of unrecognizable brown, pink, and yellow substances, steaming but otherwise uncooked balls of dough, crabs the size of big scorpions, pieces of shredded meat dripping clear sauces, and what was obviously some sort of sea creature with a dozen or so legs. Garven thought he recognized the tentacle of an octopus going into one hungry mouth. That was too much, he decided, and wondered what would look like that. There was no steak or potatoes or bread, nothing he could recognize reliably.

Despite himself, Garven was hungry. The doctor was ravenous with anticipation, and Rachel was overly quiet and apprehensive.

"May I help with the selections?" asked the doctor politely, shielding the amusement on his face from Rachel as he watched her reaction to the dim sum dishes.

"Oh, please do, Dr. Wilsonhulme," Rachel said. "I really wouldn't know what to choose. Besides, I don't think I am very hungry. Don't get me too much," she said, and under her breath, "And I think I am going to be allergic to a lot of this stuff."

"Okay with me," Garven chimed in unasked.

A series of small carts passed their table, and Dr. Wilsonhulme made his selections by pointing. The delicate and giggling girls spoke no more than the rarest word of English and then directly to the point.

"Shimp," one girl explained when Peter indicated a pinkish delicacy hiding in a translucent rice flour wrapper.

"Pok," explained another at the implied question about a cylindrical amorphous consistency, heterogeneous green-flecked lump.

"Fly lice" was a recognizable dish, Garven thought, although the description was suspect.

"Fistchy" was the last thing Garven thought he understood although the stuff in the perfectly formed gray spherule looked nothing like fish.

Garven shook his head when Dr. Wilsonhulme selected bowls of what he said were, "100-year-old eggs".

The serving girl said, "Edge."

The boy was less queasy when he found that the eggs were not all shriveled up or, worse, turned into a gray-green liquid with fuzz on top after sitting around for a century.

Peter collected enough "edge", "shimp", "pok", "fly lice", "fistchy", and black mushrooms that were the size and shape of a dog's ear for everyone; selected some pork buns, tofu squares, squid, and a dish of lychees and a dish of custard for each; and set about to demonstrate the use of chopsticks to his enthralled audience of two. There were no real eating utensils, and Garven surmised that he would not be able to fill his growling stomach if he didn't use the unfamiliar implements; so, he gave his most rapt attention. Rachel felt as if she had come to a new planet.

Garven was clumsy with the chopsticks but with a trial and error method that included stabbing, one stick in each hand, scooping, and surreptitious use of bare hands, managed to enjoy a great meal. He loved the strange stuff, especially the "shimp", which he had never before encountered. Like a typical fifteen-year-old boy with a hollow leg, he kept the charming Chinese waitresses running to their table. Rachel tried not to grimace, tried to use the frustrating chopsticks, and tried to find something she could recognize if not enjoy, but was not very successful. The doctor deftly picked up morsels of food and conveyed them to his mouth with obvious gusto. His was a cultivated palate despite his country doctor status. He knew how to enjoy himself, and Garven was determined to live like this man.

Cipher, Arizona was the epitome of boredom, the boy concluded.

I'll have more of this, he thought, having great fun.

The new parents and entering freshmen students gathered, as directed by the printed agenda, in the auditorium of the Leslie Theater, donated by the family of the late oilman. After the memorized and proper Protestant invocation, two senior students outlined the great joys of studenthood at Burton-Cagle and assured the boys and their parents with radiant smiles and youthful enthusiasm of the marvelous education and great times that lay ahead. An efficient spinsterish secretary, primly donned up in her best Whistler's Mother dress, handed out copies of the dorm assignments, physical education opportunities and requirements, and a bold printed heavy paper list of the rules and regulations for the student while at Burton-Cagle. The parents were pleased with the strict and efficient beginning, secure in the knowledge that they were doing the best thing for the tender boys they were about to leave behind. The boys were cowed.

After the necessary preliminaries were completed, Headmaster Des Moines rose majestically and walked, or glided, regally to his position at the podium. His patrician, aquiline face stood out in stark contrast to the black academic gown he wore. He bore an expression of patient leadership and august formality, a true American eagle with just the right degree of softening by a gentle smile. His voice was clarion clear, reedy, and well-modulated with a manly baritone pitch. The voice carried to the farthest corner of the auditorium without a microphone and without being raised in any unseeming strain. There was not a sound in the acutely attentive audience. Mr. Des

Moines spoke *ex cathedra*, and the parents and boys gave full sway to the gentleman and scholar.

"We are all mindful of the realities of the foreign war that has just been concluded by the gallant men and women of our military in far flung places around the globe. Our institution is amply represented among the brave sons of this land who defended the cause of democracy and our Christian way of life, and all too many of the families of our former students have made the supreme sacrifice in that cause. The reason they fought, and gave everything, is apparent if you will but pause and look about you. These young men in these hallowed halls are more than the hope of the future—they are the future. They are the seeds of our future generations, institutions, and, indeed, of our entire God-fearing society. The war has come to the only conclusion it could have had; the forces of right, truth, and democracy at long last have achieved supremacy. We will continue to prepare our lads to be leaders in America's effort, but I will do all in my power to ensure that these future leaders find a safe haven here, an oasis protected from a world gone mad where the elements of a gentlemanly education are preserved. We will dwell on that education. There will be time enough for service."

The headmaster paused to sip from a crystal glass of water.

"I will now speak to you boys, directly. Your parents may take a well-deserved short rest."

There was a polite ripple of laughter.

"Gentlemen, and from this day forward, you are gentlemen. I will briefly outline what is expected of you before inviting the attention of your parents back with us again to tell all of you what you can expect to gain with hard work and sacrifice through your years in this school. Fine men, even legends among men, have started their careers here; be mindful of the history of these walls and of the pride men take in their having graduated from the finest school in the world. You will note that there are no dissidents, no deviants, no social misfits here. We frankly haven't time to wreak the magnitude of changes that type requires. We at Burton-Cagle haven't time to waste on troublemakers, wastrels, slothful students, or on boys whose behavior betrays our trust. We will not tolerate lying, cheating, stealing, the use of alcohol or tobacco, taking our Lord's name in vain or other vulgar expressions. Gentlemen do not behave in that fashion and do not use such language. We will have none other than gentlemen here. Read the honor code with utmost care; you will be held to it in the most minute detail by your peers, your fellow students. One of the reasons your parents have selected this school is because of our continuing policy of corporal punishment in a modern age of softness and permissiveness."

Garven pricked up his ears at the word "punishment" and briefly and idly wondered what "corporal" meant.

"You will accord the administration of this school and every faculty member full respect: each is a 'sir' or a 'ma'am' every time he or she is addressed. This is not a democracy any more than your individual homes are. Just as your father is the leader of your homes, to be obeyed without question, we expect the same prompt obedience to the directives of the teachers, coaches, and administrators placed in positions of authority over you.

"You will leave this institution as scholars, leaders, men of Christian principles, and men of distinction. *Noblesse oblige.* Never forget that."

Knowing parents glanced at each other and at their boys with looks of satisfied pride. Their efforts were justified.

"The academic work here is exacting; the time for frivolity vanishingly rare. You will find the work difficult, trying, and tiring. The faculty is here to help, but you are responsible. Work will be done neatly, on time, and accurately. We expect you to succeed and will extend every effort to see that you do. Not all of you will live up to our expectations and those of your parents who sacrifice to keep you here. Sad as it is to report, not all of you will make it all the way."

The headmaster paused for effect. The boys fidgeted and looked down. They were properly daunted.

Mr. Des Moines concluded with an invitation to the parents to return their interests to his presentation and enumerated the accomplishments of the school and its students and faculty. He listed just a few of the prestigious Ivy League and other major universities now being attended by graduates of the class of 1944. He delicately mentioned the ever burdensome need for funding for the school's projects. He concluded with an invitation to the parents to come back soon and frequently and to enjoy the athletic events, the social ambiance, the superlative library, the grounds and playing fields, and the company of their stalwart sons.

"But," he requested, "do not correspond with your sons by letter, telephone, or in person before the Thanksgiving break. The boys will adjust faster and more completely if they make the manly separation now and if the apron strings do not stretch from home henceforward.

"No one ever died of homesickness, you know, mothers. Let these boys adjust. Let them toughen up and become men. We have been at this business of the education of boys and the making of men for sixty-two years, ever since the founders, Messieurs Burton and Cagle, were headmaster and administrator. I think we know best. We'll see you at the reception tonight then again at the Autumn Sports Olympiad before the Thanksgiving recess. Thank you for your support."

Garven, his mother, and their benefactor found his room in First Dorm, the most austere and uninviting of the living quarters, set aside for freshmen and their upperclassmen hall monitors exclusively. The exclusion from the sophomores, juniors, and seniors was a holdover from the old days of hazing that, rumor had it, got out of hand with some injuries to the heirs of a Los Angeles fortune or two. The consequent rule changes and tighter scrutiny resulted in the removal of all first year underclassmen to the protection of their own dorm and to the relief of the beleaguered faculty, and to the demise of the hazing rites no more than a year later. To have a freshman dorm seemed a good idea at its inception. The unforeseen ability to control the young boys in a single enclosure proved to be so convenient for the faculty that the change was institutionalized.

Garven met his three roommates already firmly ensconced in their corners, leaving Garven the right angle near the exit, which was considered to be the noisiest and least convenient of the otherwise identical facilities in the room. Each boy had one closet with no door. In the closet was a single rod to accommodate clothes hangers and a narrow shoe rack. There was no lining on the walls, and no shelving. The bed was a simple box securely bolted to the floor and covered with a thin, clean mattress. Pillows and bedding were to be supplied by the individual boy to his taste, the parents had been informed by the welcoming packets mailed out over a month earlier.

The decor was simple enough—there was none. The redwood planking on the floors, walls, bed boxes, and closets was unadorned, once long ago stained maroon, now weather and boy beaten to a sturdy but scarred patina. The planking was all approximated side to side with finely made tongue-in-grove joints that served to keep out the marine winds and rains that blew in from the Pacific with regularity during the late fall and early winter months. There were rules against defacing any school property including rooms, but nothing contradicted the use of nails in the walls or on the doors. There were hundreds of small holes all over the planking attesting to the multiplicity of tastes and placement of decorations or reminders by the boys of the past. The only rule, evidently, was that every nail and every decoration or personal object had to be removed before the room was certified as satisfactory at the end of each year. *The effect,* thought Dr. Wilsonhulme, *was as if some Lilliputian army had machine-gunned the walls in a bygone battle.* Rachel thought it disreputable and was concerned for her child's wellbeing; and Garven, like most of the other boys, viewed the room as just his sort of place. He could hardly wait until his mother left so he could put his personal stamp of disarray on his area.

"Hello boys," Dr. Wilsonhulme greeted the three roommates in a brief sweep of his head around the room as he spoke.

"Hello, Sir," they chorused a little off sync.

"I am Dr. Peter Wilsonhulme, and this is Garven Carmichael, your new roommate. This is Mrs. Carmichael, Garven's mother as you may have deduced."

The boys nodded and shook hands with the three newcomers. They gave their full names. They were perfect gentlemen. Garven wondered how long that would last.

"It's about time you got settled in here with your new friends, Garven. Dr. Wilsonhulme and I must really be going now. You need a little time to yourself before supper and lights out," Mrs. Carmichael said with a slight quaver in her voice.

She knew she must not cry although she was not so sure she could prevent it. She had to think of Garven.

"Let me give you a good-bye kiss, son," his mother said and hugged him firmly and planted a big buss on his cheek before he could protest.

"Ah, Mom," the mortified boy blushed. "Jeez."

Peter shook Garven's hand firmly and held the boy's smaller hand with both of his own in a brief and manly gesture of affection. An unruly little tear drop formed in Garven's eye, and he gritted his teeth fiercely until it dried up and he was sure that there were no others. Peter and Rachel exited the door with only a brief backward glance. For the first day in his short life, fifteen-year-old Garven Carmichael was alone. That is, he would not be with his mother. Despite his external placidity bordering on bravado, there was an internal infernal feeling as if he had a ball stuck in the passages of his chest.

"Hey, Garner," the most mature of the roommates said.

"Garven. My name is Garven."

"Hey, okay. Sorry. Glad you're here. That bed okay with you?" he asked and gestured toward the door and Garven's things.

"I don't see why not."

"I'm Stephen Randall VII," the gregarious boy offered, repeating his previous announcement.

"Pierpont D. Graham. D. for Daniel. My close friends…and roomies, I guess, call me P. Pot," said the chubby, soft looking boy from the corner opposite Garven's bed.

Garven smiled openly at the introduction and simply said in his best western drawl, "Howdy."

He was glad they were repeating their names. He had been too nervous to remember the names when the boys introduced themselves to his mother and Dr. Wilsonhulme. He admitted to himself that he was bad at names.

"I'm David Applegate; my dad's the Applegate of Jessen, Applegate, Sawyer, and Withers," the last remaining roommate chimed in making the incorrect assumption that everyone would instantly appreciate the association with the famous firm of attorneys.

He was two-thirds correct. Garven was noncommittal and avoided betraying his ignorance.

"Hi, David. I'm Garven; I guess you heard that four times already."

"I have a hammer. Need some nails?" P. Pot asked. "I have some big ones so's your stuff won't fall down."

"Thanks. I never thought of that, I'll admit."

Garven was glad to have something to do with his hands. He didn't fancy himself much of a conversationalist at best, and there did not seem like a lot more to say. He found a few unpockmarked places in the planking of the wall and hammered in three or four nails at intervals. He hung his sweaters and athletic gear on two of them and his grungy pants on the last one. As he neatly unpacked his new clothing from Bullocks and placed each pair of trousers and each coat carefully on a hanger in the closet, Stephen started to ask him the standard questions.

"What does the 'A' stand for?" he asked

"Pardon?"

"The 'A', your middle initial. What is it for?"

That rotten "Aloysius" again.

"Nothing, no name, just an 'A'," Garven lied.

"What's your dad do, Garven? I got it right that time, didn't I?" Stephen asked slightly apologetically emphasizing the name for practice so he would be sure to remember it.

"Garven. That's right."

"So, what's he do? What is your dad's profession?"

Garven paused for an awkward second before replying. He was from a town where everyone knew everyone else's business, and he had never had to discuss his father before. He debated momentarily about telling Stephen and the other two boys the truth but thought better of it.

"He's a doctor, a…an internist. In my home town in Arizona," he lied fluidly.

The lies were coming easier now that he was becoming more comfortable. These guys had no way of checking his background—and he could not very well say he had been deserted by his father—the four plus jerk. You could not tell the cream of society that your father's the town ne'er-do-well, and a deserter to boot.

"Who's that guy who brought you here, Garven?" asked David to make his entrance into the conversation.

"Oh, that's my dad's partner."

This one he had anticipated and was prepared.

"What does your dad do, Stephen? Hey, is it Steve or Stephen?" asked Garven to turn the attention away from himself for a little while.

"I go by the whole Step-hen. Dad's in the import-export business. We do a lot of business in South America. He works for the United Fruit Company," the self-assured boy answered.

"What'd you say your father does, David?"

Garven began to make the rounds on this subject.

"He's an attorney, works for the state department right now until he gets released from the war. He's in DC most of the time."

David interpreted the unspoken question correctly and spared Garven any embarrassment by answering, "Washington. Washington, DC."

"Oh, sure," Garven quickly said. "How 'bout your dad, P. Pot?" he asked the chubby boy.

"He's in manufacturing. His company makes copper and steel plating; used to be for bus parts, now for some sort of munitions. Sort of hush-hush."

"Where're you guys from?" Stephen asked everyone.

"Pacific Palisades," answered David.

"Just around the corner," observed Stephen.

"Um hum."

"Houston," said P. Pot taking his turn.

"I'm from Providence, Rhode Island, Providence." volunteered Stephen when Garven failed to respond. "How about you, Garven? You said Arizona, right? Do you come from Phoenix?"

"Just outside," said Garven. He was aware that he had created a mildly fictitious life for public consumption and would have to be careful to remember the elements of it in future conversations to be sure he was consistent.

"Pretty hot country," said Stephen. "We like to stay at the Camelback Inn in a little place outside Phoenix, called Scotsdale. You live near there, Garven?"

"No, that's on the other side of Phoenix," Garven answered to avoid the complication of having to defend a knowledge about a place he had never heard of.

"Lets go eat. I'm starved. I'm always starved," said P. Pot.

It was after nine o'clock when Garven was finally able to get away from the hectic interplay of meeting new boys and teachers and of sharing backgrounds. The food was good that evening, better than he was used to having for regular meals at home. He saw quite a few parents sharing this last supper with their sons. They were impressed with everything about the school, including the great food their sons were going to have. Worried mothers had one of their fears assuaged; their sons were not going to lack nourishment.

Garven had never been overly mindful of class distinctions before. He recognized that he was in the company of the rich and the privileged and felt somewhat intimidated by the power that represented. He felt the weakness of his own background as never before. Garven was determined to be one of these people, no matter what the cost or compromise.

Alone in the darkness of the upper playing field shortly before official lights out, Garven had time to contemplate his situation. He was aware of an aching loneliness that had been sublimated to the necessity to keep up appearances earlier in the day. He was aware for the first time in his life that he was poor. He had not thought about it before; his status was not so different than most of his friends back in Cipher, better than some like the Sespootches. Here, he was a distinct minority, a scholarship boy, as he had learned. The stratification of social class level was clearly demarcated in Garven's mind, and he knew that it was in the rich boys' minds as well even though the veneer of courtesy had forbidden an overt acknowledgment of the relative status. Garven gnashed his teeth at the impotence of his position. He silently swore an oath that he would get up and out of his level; he would be their equal, no matter what. The pangs of acute homesickness and the sense of frustration at his differences with the other students were too much there in the quiet darkness. Garven started to cry. He was angry with himself for doing so and knew that none of the other boys would be such a sissy, but he could not help it, and gave in to the emotions completely and sobbed out his pain.

The crying was brief, almost violent, and strangely restorative. It was nearly time to be in his room for official bed check at lights out. Garven regained full control of his emotions, vowed never to cry again, ran water from the hose bib at the edge of the field over his eyes until he was sure the redness would be gone, and trudged determinedly back across the turf to his dormitory.

The three roommates were in bed when Garven returned. He quickly threw on his pajamas, brushed his teeth, and slipped between the sheets just in time. The hall monitor walked into their room unannounced, looked at each boy in his bed, and, satisfied, left without comment. Each boy was lost in his own thoughts, and sensed the need for mental and emotional privacy in the other boys that night. Garven fell asleep determined to prevail. Some time in the night, he heard the muffled sounds of crying from P. Pot's corner. Garven was satisfied that he was not the only sissy.

The early weeks of school were intentionally made so busy that the freshmen boys had no time to dwell on their loneliness. Garven learned something of the deal Dr. Wilsonhulme had made to permit him to enter the school. Part of the staggering tuition was paid by the general scholarship fund for the less advantaged boys. In return these boys were expected to work ten hours per week. Garven's assignment was the most conspicuous possible. He served in the supper line, and was deeply embarrassed each time he had the duty, three days a week. The scholarship duties, the school work, and the athletic obligation exhausted the small boy from Cipher; and he was grateful for bed each night. The policy worked; he had no time for homesickness and seldom thought of home. He was a neglectful letter writer.

The supper line duties were made bearable by the presence of another scholarship boy, Hank Greenlee, from a place called Soldier Summit, Utah. Hank was unfailingly cheerful and had an incredible repertoire of off-beat songs. On their first night passing out trays together, Garven recognized the tune of *My Bonnie Lies Over the Ocean*. It took him a minute to catch the words:

> "May bunny lice soda devotion;
> May bunny lifesaver de sea!
> Mack Bonifice rover commotion,
> Oh, brickbat Mahoney for me!
> Chorus:
> Brickbat, oh, brickbat,
> Oh, brickbat Mahoney for me, for me
> Brickbat, oh, brickbat,
> Oh, brickbat Mahoney for me."

Garven laughed and tried to pick up on the nonsense lyrics with little success because Hank went on from one ditty to the next:

"My Bonnie has tuberculosis,
My Bonnie has only one lung.
She coughs up a bloody solution,
And rolls it around on her tongue.

Oh, come up, come up,
Come up my dinner to me, to me
Come up, come up,
Oh come up my dinner to me."

And to the tune of *Old Black Joe*.

"I'm comin'; I'm comin'
For my head is bendin' low
I hear the angels' voices callin'
HASTEN JASON, BRING THE BASIN.
OOPS, SLOP, BRING THE MOP!"

And right into "Hi, Ho Kafusulum, the Harlot of Jerusalem" and "The Fightin' Sixth Marines" —sung very sotto voce because of the lurid quality of the lyrics.

Garven laughed until he was too weak to work as swiftly as required, drawing frowns from the real kitchen staff and from the faculty. It was a fight to regain his composure, and it was therapeutic.

The scholarship duties put him in the company of the other less advantaged boys at the school from all classes, freshman to senior. Garven made a strong effort to avoid being typecast as one of those boys and was successful in alienating most of them, including Hank Greenlee. Since he was, in fact, one of them, and every boy in the school knew his status just as he knew each of theirs, Garven would have been a thoroughgoing loner, a coyote prowling the edges, had it not been for his roommates.

The educational requirements that applied to all of his classmates, and from which he had received a temporary waiver owing to his background, came as a shocking surprise to the boy from the one-room desert school. Rachel had done her best to drill the essentials of English into the thick heads of her students, but the task of satisfying the needs of boys and girls from kindergarten to grade twelve with her own limited background proved to be inadequate for Garven's needs in competition with the well-schooled boys entering Burton-Cagle. He had been exposed to poetry but only of the patriotic genre accepted in Cipher. He had learned mathematics only to the level of long division and multiplication to where he had become facile with carry overs. Garven could not manipulate fractions, and he did not know about algebra or trigonometry. At Burton-Cagle, Garven was going to have to measure up and soon, he was told.

CHAPTER
Six

The first item on Garven's rude awakening list was Latin. On the first day of classes, the boy from Cipher was given his first lesson about what it was going to take to be an educated gentleman. When he turned up his nose at the prospects of learning the archaic language, the Latin teacher made a diversion from his prepared text to give Garven a glimmer of recognition that the educationally elite all had been taken through the exercise of learning Latin, if only to be able to share the memories of the pain of conjugating the verbs of the long lost language. Garven had never so much as heard a Latin word to his knowledge, and could not think of a possible practical reason to spend his time learning the esoterica otherwise.

"My name is Cecil Lemuels, Dr. Cecil Lemuels," the wizened old gnome informed the freshmen in their first class on their first day of actual school work. "I am the chairman of the language department. Your regular teacher, Mrs. Hankins, will take over the class tomorrow. Today, she has an excused absence—she is ill. I welcome the opportunity to share with you my enthusiasm for Latin.

"The study of Latin is the most important task you will encounter at Burton-Cagle. Knowledge of the language of the Caesars, of the Stoics, and the Philosophers is essential to the life of an academic and a gentleman. You cannot rub shoulders with the truly educated without it. Latin is called a dead language, but it is not. While it is not spoken as such anywhere, except as what is now called Romanic in a small segment of Switzerland, it nonetheless lives on as a vital part of many languages. It forms the basis of English, French, Spanish, and Portuguese."

Garven made the mistake of rolling his eyes upward in theatrical disbelief and boredom as Dr. Lemuels was beginning to eulogize the ancient language. The bored young man had the misfortune to catch the glance of the humorless old teacher mid gesture.

"Well, young man, would you like to share your insights with the rest of the class?" Dr. Lemuels asked quietly and sternly in response to perceived student disinterest that the old teacher had practiced in classes for decades.

It was hardly the first time that he had encountered overt lack of enthusiasm for his important discipline.

"No? I thought as much. What is your name, young man?"

Dr. Lemuels fumbled through the papers on his desk trying to find the class seating roster.

"Garven Carmichael, Sir," Garven said meekly and apologetically ruing the impulse that had caused him to attract unwanted attention.

Dr. Lemuels cupped his hand behind his ear in the universal speak-up gesture and said, "Please speak up. No need to be bashful. I'm sure the class would like to share your thoughts."

They tittered.

"Garven Carmichael," spoke up Garven a trifle brusquely due to his mounting discomfiture.

"Ah, yes, Mr. Carmichael. And pray tell me what your career plans are. What profession are you going to pursue?"

"I am going to be a doctor, Sir," Garven replied, calming down now that he was on less tenuous ground.

"Any idea how a knowledge of Latin could be of benefit to medicine, to medical education especially, Mr. Carmichael?"

"Not really," said Garven, uncomfortable again.

He was pretty sure that the teacher was about to enlighten him whether he liked it or not.

"Latin is the *language* of medicine, young man. At least it forms the primary foundation for anatomy and pathology and for most scientific measurements. Let me give you a few examples if I may. The stem, 'cent' comes from Latin, 'centum' which means hundred. In the metric system, the scientific system of measurements based on tens, hundreds, and thousands, the cent is a major form in fractions; so, we have centimeter, centiliter, etcetera. Even the word 'etcetera', now that I think of it, is Latin; it means 'and the rest'. Are you beginning to get my drift?" the teacher asked, warming to his subject.

"I guess so, Sir," Garven replied trying to become as inconspicuous as possible.

"Then there are 'deci' and 'milli' for tens and thousands, and so forth. This makes an easy system to work with, don't you know? Can you imagine how far along our scientific efforts would be if we were stuck with the old English language of weights and measures, the stone, furlong, fortnight system? Can you imagine doing the arithmetic where the units for weight were fourteen pounds, the unit of length was an eighth of a mile, and the time unit was fourteen days! The English still use that system, you know. The barbarians!" Dr. Lemuels said with mock severity and indignation.

The class, except for Garven laughed in great appreciation of the drollery of their teacher.

To Garven's relief there was even a polite bit of laughter from the taciturn old man. The teacher acknowledged the class's appreciation of his amusing style of delivery with a self-deprecating little smile and nod of his balding gray head.

"You must know Latin to know anatomy. I can make the same assertion next year when you begin your adventures in the Greek language. '*Abdomin*' is Latin for belly; '*articul*' for joint; '*cauda*' for tail as in the caudal sac; '*costa*' for rib; and so on and so forth. Like it or not, you will learn Latin, all right; or you will not learn medicine!"

Garven had been forgotten in the passion for his subject to his relief.

Dr. Lemuels returned to the mundane requirements of teaching the rudiments and ordered, "Open your texts to the introduction, if you please. We will cover the entirety of this material today. Before Wednesday when we gather next, I expect you to have not only read but to have committed to mind the general schema of verb declensions contained in the first twelve pages."

In the following hour, from nine to ten, Garven encountered a modern foreign language for the first time. Two years of German or French was required for every student in addition to four years of Spanish. The latter was deemed universally necessary because of the need to deal with the lower class immigrants flooding into California and the other border states. It would be of practical benefit to every upper-class American to know something of the language of the servant and migrant worker class, Garven was informed. The pursuit of French, so emphasized in the eastern prep schools, was becoming passé in the minds of the Burton-Cagle curriculum directors.

The modern world had seen an ascendancy of power for the English speaking people and a decrease in the influence of the French even in the arts and diplomacy that had followed the seats of power to America. German, of course, was still a language to be reckoned with even in the wake of the world war.

"It is still the language of science," Dr. Wilsonhulme had told Garven and had insisted that the boy become proficient in German in order to avail himself of a medical education.

Garven knew better than to repeat his mistake of the previous hour; that of underestimating the importance the teacher attached to his subject. If German was to be considered the most important subject to study at Burton-Cagle, who was Garven to argue?

The German teacher was a severe, stolid German matron, a no nonsense authoritarian. Her hair was pulled back in a bun, so tightly bobby-pinned in place that it smoothed the wrinkles on her forehead. Her once fine blond hair was now uniformly gray. Her features were coldly Aryan despite the rotundity from too much dumpf noodle and schnitzel.

David, his roommate, sat next to Garven in German and whispered to Garven very quietly before the bell sounded to begin that, "I hope we don't have to make the *Hitlergruss!* My *sieg heil* is rusty, it might not sound all that sincere."

Garven controlled the urge to turn the corners of his mouth up, not relishing another opportunity to entertain the class.

"Ich heisse, Frau Mueller," the precise German lady began, enunciating each syllable and word in the foreign language. *"Unser buch fuer dieser classe wert Erzael Mir Was sein. Wir wollen neur Hoch Deustch in unser class sprechen und scriben,"* she continued with her careful pronunciation and accenting.

Garven was pleased with himself that he could get something of the drift of what the woman was saying in the unfamiliar tongue. He was dismayed to look about and see several of his classmates assiduously taking notes. Quite obviously, he would have his work cut out for him if he was ever going to compete on an equal footing with his educationally privileged new competitors. Garven first felt threatened by their superiority, then challenged. He would somehow get it, Latin and German and all.

He copied the assignment from the blackboard: Vocabulary (from *The First German Book with Exercises* by Betz and Price: *aus, auser, bei, mit, noch, seit, von, zu, hinter; Accusatif—bis, durch, für, gegen, ohne, um, weider; Genative—anstatt, vährend, wegen, ausserhalk, langs, dieseit; Dativ - unser, euer, ihr. Ihr* was about the only thing he thought he might understand from the class that day. It would take him a while to be sure of modified vowels, diphthongs, umlauts, and the arrangement of the vowels into the vowel triangle. The other thing he understood was that he was faced with a major project of catch-up to be on an equal footing with several of the boys who responded, albeit haltingly, in schoolboy German, to the teacher's questions posed in the new language.

Everything was new to Garven and, therefore, confusing. Even the floors and the desks and the rooms. It was all somewhat overwhelming to the lad from Cipher who had never before been in a gathering of as many as 100 people in one place, had never heard a foreign language except Apache, and had never seen the ocean or even a green hillside. The newest concept of all, to date, was the third class of the day—freshman mathematics. It was like a language unto itself, some secret interplanetary code of the gods, indecipherable by mere mortals. Garven was again dismayed to see his classmates taking notes on the obscure communications from Dr. Heinrich Oldendorf, head of the mathematics department.

"Frections," Dr. Oldendorf said in his heavily German accented voice that was hard to listen to over and above comprehending the mathematical jargon he sprinkled into every sentence. "Frections are not zu eacy zu understandt, boyss. I vill help you but you must verk very hart to learn dem. Ve vill learn to add dem, subtract dem, und to multiply und divide dem before dis year ist ofer. Many off you schon, uh, already, know dees dings zo dis vill be a gute review fuer you. Da rest vill haf der verk cut out feur dem, don't you agree?"

Garven thought the teacher was probably the master of understatement and, shortly into the semester, came to know just how accurate that judgment was. Even on that first morning, the mathematical concepts fairly raced across the blackboard.

Dr. Oldendorf rapidly scrawled four equations:

$$3/4 + 1/2 =$$
$$3/4 - 1/2 =$$
$$3/4 \ / \ 1/2 =$$
$$3/4 \times 1/2 =$$

Garven stared blankly, confused and unable to proceed. A veritable forest of young arms shot up in Garven's peripheral vision.

"Jess Matheson," the math teacher said and pointed at a nerdish boy with thick round glasses on the second row.

Garven thought he was about to develop an instant dislike for the boy whom he had never met. He surreptitiously compared his own thin glasses to those of the nerd's.

"Five-fourths, one-fourth, one and one-half, three-eighths," the nerd responded briskly and matter-of-factly in his squeaky voice.

Garven knew he hated Jess.

"Fine, my boy, ve vill haf to find someding more challenging for you, I see. It can be arranged. In fect, pleeze, see me after da class."

Garven averted his glance hoping against hope that he could avoid being called upon to display his ignorance. This was going to be a very tough year, he could see.

"Luther, Luther Foreman, come vorfard und write on the board fur me," the teacher directed.

He listed off numbers verbally to be written numerically: "Eighty-five; seven hundred fifty-six thousand two hundred seventy-three; one billion; one hundred million; one thousand one".

The next boy on the row was summoned to, "Add orally by fives until you reach sixty; add 445, 823, and 574. Keep your columns straight, young man."

Garven was starving when lunch break came. It was the only period when he felt fully oriented all day.

Lunch was a choice of noodle soup and bread or bean soup and bread with a piece of cantaloupe. Dessert was bread pudding. The boys were encouraged to return for second helpings of bread and bread pudding. There were no parents present for this carbohydrate fare, Garven observed.

Russell Knight, whom he met in math class and liked because he had not understood a thing either, commented on the bread pudding, "Careful with that stuff, Garven. I heard from one of the scholarship boys that they lace it with saltpeter."

Garven looked blank.

"So you don't get it up, can't get it up. Can't have a bunch of gentlemen flubbing their dubs at old Burton-Cagle, can we now? Nosiree!" Russell informed his friend.

Garven laughed, "Covered in the rules, no doubt."

Civics was the one o'clock to two o'clock slumber hour class. The sun shone warmly through the west facing windows, and there was a splendid view of the sloping lawns fringed with jacaranda trees set in irregularly shaped flower beds that were resplendent with petunias, marigolds, lupine, wild geraniums, hibiscus, and empatiens set in the careful disarray of an English garden. The stucco walls of the southwest style buildings were covered with vivid reds and purples of bougainvillea. In the far distance was the sparkling Pacific, dotted with sails. On the walkway beside the windows were waxy scarlet antherium with their protuberant yellow stamens standing at half mast.

On the evening previously, Stephen had told Garven, who had never seen such a flower, that they were also called "The little boy plant. Use your imagination," he had said with a knowing smirk.

The view from the classroom window was warm and very restful.

Garven fought sleep and developed a headache doing so. He would have to work out some way of keeping awake in Civics class if he were ever to pass. Thank goodness he had a textbook, and it was in English for a change. He decided not to worry overmuch about Civics, especially since the dullest teacher in the school, probably in the universe, had been given the task of conveying the dullest material imaginable. It was going to be like reading the phone book.

Freshman English, the next class, was to be a mixture of the didactic— the word left for morons like Garven to look up the meaning—and the creative with an introduction to poems and short stories, largely British the first semester, and concentrating on American authors in the second semester, according to the teacher. Prose writing would begin in earnest in the third semester, she announced as soon as the class settled down.

"This is your homeroom even though it is not your first class of the day. I am your homeroom teacher and, therefore, your school counselor. My name is Gertrude Aftenborough…Mrs. I am a naturalized American citizen, originally from Bristol, England. I have been assigned the task of teaching you to read, write, and to speak the King's English. I will accept nothing less in here; leave your slang expressions, your mod talk at the door. I will feel free to offer a correction when needed wherever I encounter you should I hear you doing injury to the native tongue. This is the most important class you will take at Burton-Cagle; the most important subject at the school. Your speech will immediately alert your listener as to your education, your social status, and to your intelligence. Your writing will determine your livelihood in good part. I am a stickler for details. Consider yourselves forewarned."

Garven was pleased to know that he was in yet another single-most-important class at Burton-Cagle. There was a certain fetching charm to the dowdy and impeccable pronunciation and to the care for the details of her communication that appealed to Garven. He was glad for the moment, at least, that Mrs. Aftenborough was to be his counselor and homeroom teacher. Despite her accent, which he found pleasant, he could understand her perfectly. He could have had another battle-ax like Frau Mueller. He would never understand a word that German warrior-woman said, he was sure; and it was a fearsome prospect to consider trying to talk to the scary Aryan. Mrs. Aftenborough had a softer, more human approach although she was a firm no-nonsense teacher. Garven warmed to her.

"Consider these sentences," Mrs. Aftenborough was saying as she chalked the words on the board behind her desk: "WITH WHO DID THE PRINCESS CONFIDE HER INNERMOST FEELINGS?"

She turned to the class briefly, then resumed chalking. "I LAY DOWN AT THE CLOSE OF A WEARY DAY."

The final sentence read, "THE GENTLEMAN SPOKE COURTEOUS TO THE DIG-NIFIED LADY."

Mrs. Aftenborough faced the class, glanced at her wristwatch noting the lateness of the hour, and said, "Your assignment is to correct any errors in these sentences; highlight the error, tell why it is an error, and to cite the rule from your textbook that covers the preferred usage."

The sentences looked okay to Garven. Probably some trick. He would have to dig into the first chapter of his book before tomorrow to get a clue about what Mrs. Aftenborough had in mind. The first chapter in its entirety was assigned. Garven reckoned that he would be able to cover the work assigned thus far today in about thirteen or fourteen hours of hard study if he did not take time to sleep or eat or work in the serving line. He had originally concerned himself about keeping up with his peers; now, he wondered if he would survive. He had not even been to Spanish class yet. Cripes.

Garven and his classmates were dragging as they entered the last class of the first day. He guessed that there really was a valid purpose to learning "spinach" as P. Pot called it, but the vision of him ordering his Spanish-speaking servants around in their native language seemed remote at best, however far in the future that vision might be expected to occur.

Garven woke up, took notice, and fell in love the moment the instructor of Spanish walked—more like floated—into the classroom. She was not just beautiful. She was striking. Her heavy, jet black hair wreathed her olive complexioned fine features in curls and lay comfortably on her graceful shoulders. She was petite, standing about five-three, Garven figured in a careful appraisal. Her arms and lower legs were bare, showing her flawless, soft, light pecan brown skin. Garven was embarrassed by his ogling of her Mediterranean proportioned, curvaceous body. He looked secretly around at his fellow students and saw their unabashed appreciative curiosity.

"Look at those bazoonkas! Jeez! I would give a leg for a minute alone with that señorita," whispered Stephen to Garven when the vision looked the other way.

Garven had to chuckle but a frown of jealously kept returning. "Shhhh," he hissed.

The last thing in the world he wanted was to get off on the wrong foot with his true love. If she called on him right now, he would probably pee his pants anyway.

"I yam Margarita Innocenta Perez-dePomposo," the lovely young woman informed the enthralled class. "I yam your Spinish teacher for thees yeer. I yam new here and want your help, hokay?"

"Hokay! Jubetcha!" chorused the silent mental telepathy of every boy in the class simultaneously. *"Ju can count on me!"*

"Spinish is a beautiful language, not hard for ju to learn, I theenk," Miss Perez-dePomposo continued. "I want eet to be lots of fun, hokay?"

"Ohhh, Hokay!" the telepathic chorus chimed in thought as one.

"Today, we weel learn to speak a leettle, how to say 'hi!' and 'good-bye!' How to ask someone who they are, that kind of theeng."

The room full of alert boys hung on every word, anxious to excel in Spanish. They did not have to be told that this was the most important class at Burton-Cagle; they came to a consensus on that opinion by an automatic telepathic vote.

"Me llamo Señorita Perez-dePomposo," she said with flash of her pearly, even teeth.

Her lips were pink with a perfect Cupid's bow.

Garven was fascinated by her mouth.

"Como te llamas, amigo?" she asked Donovan Bell-Geddes, the shyest boy in the class and in the whole school.

Donovan blushed and stammered. He had not understood a word and could not have responded if she had spoken to him in the clearest prose English. He stared at a fascinating spot on his perfectly shined two toned shoes.

"What ees joor name? *Como te llamas?"* the lovely young woman cooed encouragingly placing her delicate fingers on his pudgy shoulder.

"I...I...I, I am Donovan, Donovan Bell des...I mean Bell-Geddes," he stuttered in consternation.

That cool touch on the shoulder was more than a pent-up fifteen-year-old could be expected to handle.

"Me llamo Donovan. Try eet, geeve a try for me," the vision standing over him said encouragingly.

Now he knew. Donovan was no dummy, just painfully shy.

He summoned up courage from that well-spring hidden deep in all of us and rasped out, "May yamo Donovan," and deflated into his chair.

The teacher did not condescend to him with overworked praise; she just blessed him with the radiance of her smile and walked on to Garven.

Cripes, my turn to pee my pants, he thought. *Just don't let me say something completely dumb,* he begged the God with whom he had not lately been on frequent communication terms. *Please.*

"Hola, hombre!" she greeted him with gusto.

"'*Hombre*', that had to be good," Garven said to himself without knowing exactly what the Spanish word meant.

"Hola," he ventured in self-protective monkey-see, monkey-do fashion and smiled a tentative and innocent smile.

"Ah, amigo, that ees good. Good for you!" she praised.

His day was made. He felt her presence withdraw, and it was cooler around his seat. He was actually sweaty.

"Jeez."

Señorita Perez-dePomposo wafted lightly around the room leaving a praise here, a feathery touch there, and, everywhere, the scent of gardenias. She charmed the boys into saying their first tentative words in Spanish and corrected their accents until they wanted to sound like her. They jotted down the homework assignment with unnatural relish. Garven had twenty-two serious competitors for the object of his *amor verdadero.*

The spell was broken by the clamor of the closing bell. The excitement of the first day of tryouts for the sports teams caused a regrettable lapse in the delicacy of Garven and the rest of the class's feelings. The heady adrenaline of competition overcame the weaker chemistry of pheromones and even the recent brief testosterone storm. The courtliness of the young men in the señorita's classroom was a transitory illusion that gave way to the rush of enthusiasm that cleared the seats, the classroom, the hallways, the stairs, and their minds of anything frivolous such as learning or love or comity and left them able to focus on the really important issues of the day—the sweat and bruising of the playing fields where their real mark at Burton-Cagle would be left when all the other considerations had dimmed out of memory.

Every boy at Burton-Cagle was obliged to participate in at least one interschool sport each semester. The perfectly lame or dorkish could at least be a team manager, but not even the worst geek could get out of the manly obligation to participate in athletics. Football, American-style football, anyway, had been terminated at the school several years ago with a tacit and, finally, an explicit understanding with the other prep schools in Southern California. There was unanimous agreement that the sport was too dangerous, too time consuming, and too expensive to continue. Cate School in Carpinteria, Dunn School in San Luis Obispo, Thatcher in Thatcher, and all the rest had deleted the sport within a season or two of each other. The Thatcher School still maintained its preeminence in matters equestrian including competitions. But, otherwise, the loosely associated schools offered the same choices to their boys. Fortunately, no girls' sports were necessary to complicate matters.

Garven was offered his choice of going out for the soccer team, for lacrosse, for baseball, or for tennis that semester. He had seen the tennis players; they looked like pros. Garven had never so much as had a tennis racket in his hand. That choice was easy. He had not been much of a baseball player, too small, too weak a wing to throw far enough, he had to admit to himself. He did not know anything about lacrosse, and decided that he had enough new stuff to contend with for one day to take on a weird new sport. Soccer it was.

He did not flatter himself that he would be any great shakes at that game because he knew next to nothing about it. But, at least, it looked simple enough. He was fast and sure on his feet; he could do it, he decided. As in his football career at the sand lot in Cipher, he would make his bones at Burton-Cagle on the soccer field.

CHAPTER
Seven

Vera Wilsonhulme passed away before Garven completed the first semester of his freshman year; and her husband, Peter, was devastated. He had not previously plumbed the depths of his feelings for his wife, upon whom he had depended for so many years. He turned to Rachel Carmichael for solace, as if to the daughter he never had, and found that she was unable to give of herself in the degree he needed. When she had been deserted by her husband, her ability to generate such emotion, such compassion, had been extinguished. She tried, and he accepted her scant overtures as all she could give; but there was left an empty space in the center of the aging physician. Peter Wilsonhulme increasingly turned his attentions to the boy away at school. He began to think of him as his own.

Garven wrote a consoling letter. He realized the significance of Vera's death in more than selfish terms, which was unusual for him. At first when he received the telegram edged in black, he felt threatened, anxious that his benefactor would lose his enthusiasm for keeping him in the inordinately expensive preparatory school. He recognized the unworthiness of those thoughts, especially since his status quo was otherwise maintained, and carefully crafted a thoughtful reply. He wrote in his best hand:

Dear Dr. Wilsonhulme,

I wish to convey my sincerest condolences on your bereavement. I hope you know that Mrs. Wilsonhulme and you have been wonderful to me and that I feel like your grandson, really your son. Mrs. Wilsonhulme was every bit like a mother to me, and I will miss her terribly. I hope you can find a way to be happy. I just know she has gone to heaven with the other angels.

Love,
Garven Carmichael

Garven had some help from the school English department staff, and was especially taken with the big word, "bereavement" contributed by his teacher. She assured him that the good doctor would be pleased.

******

Garven had taken quite naturally to the game of soccer which he had heretofore considered foreign and alien and had found it a beneficial outlet for his pent-up fighting spirit. He delivered his punches to the unfeeling ball instead of at the boys who challenged and at times wronged him. He demonstrated a talent beyond his size or even his running ability, which was no better than average. He developed a wiliness, an evasiveness in handling the soccer ball that made it seem to obey his mind not just his foot and leg. He was fast becoming the star of the freshman team, and had gained an in with his teammates and, indeed, with all his classmates that he could not have purchased. He was bursting with enthusiasm when Dr. Wilsonhulme arrived in Pacific Palisades for the annual pre-Thanksgiving Sports Olympiad.

Peter Wilsonhulme set aside his overbearing personal sense of despondency in order not to detract from Garven's infectious ebullience. Although the boy had properly offered his regrets at Mrs. Wilsonhulme's passing as soon as they saw each other in the Los Angeles Union Station, it was evident that he was so keen on the upcoming sports events that he could not maintain any focus on the doctor's misery, nor would Peter let himself spoil the boy's excitement. He wrote it off to the natural egocentricity of youth. They did not mention Vera Wilsonhulme's death again.

Peter found himself forgetting the depth of his sadness for minutes at a time as he watched the boy play his position of striker on the freshman team. He was so good that Peter recognized that he outclassed the other young boys. He needed to be on the junior varsity team, a rarity for a freshman, as Peter remembered. When Garven dribbled around an opponent or broke free of his pursuers, he looked in the direction of Dr. Wilsonhulme who cheered unreservedly. His pride in the boy was boundless, and Garven basked in it.

The game was with Cate School, which was the Burton-Cagle School's archrival, even more than Thatcher. The yearly soccer rivalry highlighted the undercurrent of competition on all other levels—for faculty, for bright and wealthy students, for endowment foundation funding, and for national reputation. Burton-Cagle had the reputation that rated a slightly superior national standing characterized by more prominent mentions in the Petersen and Dunberg Handbook on College Preparatory Schools in the United States, and the resultant modestly higher endowment fund, greater percentage of doctorates on the faculty, and more solid building program. What Burton-Cagle had never had, however, was a better soccer team.

That fact had been passed off publicly as being inconsequential.

"We like our boys to have fit bodies, but our real emphasis is on their minds and spirits. We will not have their attentions diverted by football. We will not have that crude sport in our institution. Lacrosse and soccer are fine manly games that teach sportsmanship and endurance. Winning is incidental to the real benefits," Headmaster Des Moines stated often and sincerely, and bit his lower lip every time he said it.

In truth, the headmaster would have made a Faustian trade to have his school's teams have a winning season, at least to whip Cate and Thatcher solidly in both lacrosse and soccer, if they beat no one else. He would love to see the smug and condescending smile on Harold Goeffry's face disappear just this one day. The headmaster of the Cate School was always the perfect gentleman, which served to rub the perennial defeats all the deeper into Des Moines's wounds. The Carmichael boy had scored two goals to tie the game at the half, and the heady scent of victory, the very possibility of victory, was in the air. Des Moines could not stand the internal tension generated by the anticipation. He broke a long-standing personal rule of noninterference and visited the coach and team during the rest period.

"Doing rather well today, Mr. Penrod," Des Moines said benignly to the English teacher who was also the long-standing coach.

"Thank you, Sir. We're trying our best. Who knows?" he queried conspiratorially. "This might be the year."

"Indeed. Although we wouldn't want to overemphasize that aspect of the game, it would be a rewarding experience to garner a laurel in sports to match our kudos in academics and for our service on national committees."

"I'd certainly settle. It would be enough for me not to have to hear Tom Battlefries condescend to me with his usual, 'Harumph! Fine game, old man. Better luck next year!'" the coach said in a near perfect mimicry of his aging British-born opponent.

Des Moines smiled in appreciation of the performance and the sentiment.

"Mind if I have a talk with young Carmichael?" asked the headmaster.

"Certainly not. Garven, would you come over here for a moment?"

Garven trotted to where the two men stood talking. Coach Penrod moved away to engage the other ten starters in an animated discussion of field plays while Mr. Des Moines spoke to Garven.

"My boy, you are doing a fine job today, as usual. I wouldn't want it to go to your head, but a couple of more goals by you and a win today would result in considerable favor coming your way. What would you think of a promotion to the junior varsity squad that I coach?"

"Boy, that would be something. Could you really do that?" Garven asked incredulously.

"It is one of the few serious perquisites of being the boss around here. Do me proud today, Garven, and I am sure you will reap a commensurate reward. I don't care what you have to do, just put that ball into the goal net a couple of times. Let's, at least, see the freshman team come up a winner. It's about time!"

Garven was no dummy. This was the knock of opportunity. Having Mr. Des Moines on his side could not hurt, and he would give his right arm to be on the junior varsity. He re-entered the game with a fervent dedication that was immediately evident to his teammates and to the students and families cheering on the sidelines. They had never seen such hustle.

Peter Wilsonhulme cheered Garven's efforts until he momentarily forgot his recent bereavement. To no avail, however, Garven could not put the ball in the goal. He came close on two occasions, kicking wide once, and high the second time.

As he streaked down the sideline after a loose ball near the middle of the second half, he heard the passing note of discouragement in the voice of his headmaster as the man shouted, "A goal, lad, a goal. We're counting on you!"

Garven heard the emphasis on "you" or, at least, he presumed he did. He had to get a goal. He *needed* a goal—no, two goals. The center halfback (striker) from Cate snatched up the ball from Garven, who was going all out for it, and took control. The stringy boy streaked off in the opposite direction with no one to stop him. It was a personal thing to Garven. The defensive fullbacks were complete duds and Burton-Cagle's goalie was a reject, so far as Garven was concerned. Garven saw his chance dashing away. He pushed with all he had and ran a two player foot race for the Burton-Cagle goal. He was fairly fast, but Cate's striker was a bit faster.

Garven could see that he was slowly and inexorably losing ground, and would be out of range behind his determined opponent by the time the Cate boy was in range for one of his exasperatingly accurate goal shots. Garven had to do something now. He could never hope to get along side the striker, let alone in front of him. The faster player was already inside the fullbacks, having simply run past the two pre-pubertal fat boys. About the only thing Garven could do was to tackle the center halfback—a cardable foul—or try to make a baseball slide to deflect the ball before the inevitable kick into the goal. The goalie stood like a petrified thing, desolately awaiting the inevitable.

Garven had to succeed. He sacrificed everything and dived feet first for the ball at the last possible moment. Maybe he aimed a little high, in retrospect, but who could notice in the heat of the contest? His cleated foot caught Cate's half-back just above the lateral malleolus of his ankle and swept outward the needed three or four inches to contact the ball. The ball ricocheted out of the end zone and harmlessly away from the goal. There was a simultaneous snap audible to the sidelines, and the Cate player's ankle bone divided in a spiral fracture that separated both malleolar protuberances from their underpinnings. A bad break.

An ungentlemanly pandemonium erupted. Burton-Cagle supporters cheered wildly.

Cate's players and parents shouted, "Foul! Intentional tripping! Vicious!"

They shook their fists and looked as if they were about to storm the playing field. Cate's coach, Battlefries, usually stern and parsimonious with words on the playing field, was furious and read his practiced version of the riot act twice to Garven's coach. He was barely understandable. One recurring statement was clear, however:

"That's worth a red card, at least. I'd say that boy needs to be out of the game today and for good, if I had my way. He *tried* to hurt our boy. A good caning is in order, Penrod!"

Penrod did not like to have anyone shouting in his face. It was unseeming, even under the present circumstances. Besides, he did not see events quite the same way. Both he and Mr. Des Moines agreed that it was an unfortunate accident, part of the game. It was preposterous to think that a Burton-Cagle boy would ever intentionally harm an opponent.

"Try and keep your perspective, old man," Penrod said when the blustery speech by Battlefries subsided.

The injured player was borne off the field by the stretcher bearers, crying unashamedly with the pain. The referees and linesmen had a hasty conference. None of them had actually seen anything amiss, except that the action could have been construed as a dangerous play worthy, perhaps, of a yellow card, but certainly not a red card. The nearest linesman argued that the attack had been on the ball, striking the injured player was accidental, and the call should be no more than out of bounds. The head referee knew he would have real trouble on his hands, maybe even a formal reprimand from the council, if he failed to, at least, call a foul. He compromised with the call of dangerous play requiring a free kick on the goal but did not assess Garven any warning card.

The Cate assemblage was angry but in the interest of sportsmanship, gave no more vent to their feelings than isolated grumbles.

"Play ball," shouted the referee.

The boy chosen to kick against the goalie was inexperienced and had never kicked a one-on-one before. The atmosphere was full of emotionally charged tension. He concentrated as best he could in the milieu of swirling animosities and sub-rosa conflicts. He clutched at the last second and missed the goal by a wide margin to the roar of the Burton-Cagle crowd and to the moans of the Cate team and entourage. The injury to their striker and the subsequent humiliation of a missed free kick took the dash out of the usually frenetically energetic Cate team. They played defensively, tentatively, for the remaining fifteen minutes of the game.

On the other hand, Garven was blooded and played like a boy possessed. With no decent striker to oppose his team offensively, and the defenders feeling intimidated, Garven drove in three goals unassisted. He ignored his teammates and handled the ball by himself from mid-field each time. It was his day, his triumph. He did what was necessary. He got the goals.

Garven also got the rewards—he was elevated to the junior varsity team as their starting striker for next week's game; the headmaster positively shed a glow on the tired boy when he could get to him; and his benefactor, Dr. Wilsonhulme, hugged him with the pride and affection only accorded to a firstborn son who has brought honor, laud, and glory to a proud family. Garven did not notice the occasional sullen glance from his teammates. He ignored the inconsequential malevolent glares of the Cate boys and their parents.

Garven continued to shine on the playing fields through the rest of the soccer season, even playing center half for the varsity team when they lost their starter to a stupid surfing accident the week before a crucial game.

It was well that he stood out on the soccer team because he was barely mediocre in his studies. He studied until he was ready to drop every night, but he had started educationally behind the more advantaged boys, and was in a race to catch up as well as to cope with the ongoing demanding Burton-Cagle curriculum.

The grind of school wore on Garven. His elementary Latin textbook was *Latin Made Simple and Fun*. After three and a half months of struggling with the ancient tongue, Garven found it neither "simple" nor "fun". He had a difficult time being convinced that it was important to know a language only dead guys spoke. His education was progressing; at least, he did not voice his criticism.

"My young friends," fairly bubbled the old lady teacher. "Latin is more than a dead tongue, even more than a classical language. It is the foundation of our own language and of all the Romance languages, the industrialized nations' languages. It is a pillar and a connector of our culture and civilization to our history, our relationship to the past. Every scholar worthy of the title, and all truly educated men, are well-rooted in Latin. Each of you should look on your opportunity to learn the mother of all tongues '*ab ovo usque ad mala*'" (from beginning to end; lit. "from the egg, to the apples", referring to the appetizer and the dessert common to ancient Roman meals).

Garven could hardly wait for each class, he told himself. Mrs. Hankins carried on in paroxysms of enthusiasm for half an hour every class period, it seemed to him. Garven was willing to agree with her—to anything—couldn't they just call it a day? He asked himself every time Mrs. Hankins waxed eloquent on everything from Caesar to the senate to the medieval church. Despite himself, Garven became interested in the history. His interest got lost when she started to outline the language and left off with the only thing he found interesting.

"The parts of speech we still use came from the Latin. It is easier to learn Latin than it is English because it is more regular. It has no articles, and we must supply the a's, the's, and the an's to translate. We get nouns, pronouns, adverbs, adjectives, verbs, prepositions, conjunctions, and interjections from this language that was only one of several spoken in the Italian peninsula 200 years before the birth of our Savior. It became the most powerful language, developed different dialects that became the major languages of today, and carried on as the classical written language of the medieval churchmen. Latin is easy, too, because the word order, by and large, doesn't matter. All of the following sentences mean the same thing—'The man bites the dog.'

Homo canem mordet.   *Canem homo mordet.*   *Mordet canem homo.*

Mord homo canem.   *Canem mordet homo.*   *Homo mordet canem.*

"And all of these sentences mean the opposite—'The dog bites the man.'"

Hominem canis mordet.   *Canis hominem mordet.*   *Mordet canis hominem.*

Mordet homo canem.   *Canis mordet hominem.*   *Hominem mordet canis.*

Garven wondered if he would be forgiven for thinking they all sounded alike. Besides, he was uncomfortable with the recurring references to "homos". He had to admit that some of the assignments were more fun than the rest of his other classes:

"Memorize the signs of the zodiac from the Latin. *Aries,* the ram; *Taurus,* the bull; *Gemini,* the twins; *Cancer,* the crab; *Leo,* the lion; *Virgo,* the maiden; *Libra,* the scales; *Scorpio,* the scorpion; *Sagittarius,* the archer; *Capricornus,* the goat; *Aquarius,* the water bearer; *Pisces,* the fishes; and the names of the planets: *Iuppiter* (Jupiter), king of the gods; *Saturnus,* god of sowing; *Mercurius,* the messenger god; *Venus,* the goddess of love; *Mars,* the god of war; *Neptunus,*the god of the sea; and *Plut*o, god of the lower world."

German was his main nemesis.

"Count to ten, young man," the overbearing instructor, Frau Mueller, demanded of Garven.

He was standing in front of the class, feeling conspicuous.

"One, two, three, four, five, six, seven, eight, nine, ten," the flustered boy rushed.

"No! *Nein, nein, nein!*" the impatient German spinster fairly shouted. "In German," she said and added an afterthought, "*Auf Deustch, bitte.*"

Garven felt overwhelmingly stupid. He knew the German. He even knew that she wanted him to count to ten in German right then in front of the class, but he had gotten flustered. He felt humiliated.

Finally, he stammered out, *"Eins, zwei, drei, vier, funf, sex, seiben, acht, neun, zehn."*

His pronunciation was appalling. The timid fifteen-year-old freshman could tell that much just by the glowering teacher's expression before she removed all doubt.

"Zimply derrible. Your bronunciation ist derrible."

Garven did not fare much better on the *wortschatz*—vocabulary—or on translating the *gespräch*—conversation. When he looked up the vocabulary, he either misread the German-English dictionary, wrote down a definition one line above or below the one he should have written, or he did not pay attention to the spelling and hurried to get through, ending up with the wrong word again. He could not make sense out of the "conversation" because the verbs had been conjugated, and he could not find the changed spelling in the dictionary upon which he depended. It was a nightmare.

Deiter: *Guten Morgen, Franz. Haben Sie gut geschlafen, mein freund?*

Franz: *Ya, danke, Ich habe sehr gut geschlafen! Ich schlafe immer ganz gut.*
Deiter: *Wer weckt Sie denn?*
Franz: *Mein Vater. Wie spät is es, bitte?*
Deiter: *Halb elf.*
Franz: *Was machen Sie da?*
Deiter: *Ich lerne ein Gespräch auswendig.*

Garven's translation, full of erasures and crossouts, became:

Deiter: Good morning, Franz. Had you good [not in dictionary].
Franz: Yes, thanks. I /-/ -/ -/ very good [not in dictionary] I sleep always quite good.
Deiter: Who [not in dictionary] you [used in questions for the expression of
   lively interest or of impatience; to express meaning by the tone of the voice.]
Franz: My father. What time is it?
Deiter: Half eleven.
Franz: What to make you there?

Frau Mueller's response to Garven's early work was chilly.

"I vill get you a tutor, young man," she told him in one of his several mandatory after class meetings with the stern German instructress. "But either you perform on diss midterm exam, or I vill be opliged to place you on the Jeopardy List."

The headmaster's Jeopardy List was the last of a crescendoing series of warning steps. A frank "F" in a class required a faculty discussion about the propriety of continuing the student at Burton-Cagle, and a formal meeting with the boy's parents. Evidence of further inability to cope with the academic requirements led to automatic dismissal before term end. Placement on the Jeopardy List was an announcement that a failing grade was pending, and serious changes would be necessary. It was part of the innovative due process introduced to assuage the ruffled feelings of the well-to-do parents when confronted with their errant son's performance record. It was the justice of the Burton-Cagle system.

Garven was truly frightened. He was not in particular favor with his classmates owing to his lack of being a team player on or off the fields as they perceived it and were disinclined to be of any generous help. His teacher intimidated him, and, anyway, was not free to give him any more of her valuable time. The tutor, paid at Dr. Wilsonhulme's expense, was a young man living in Santa Barbara, a former student at Burton-Cagle, who needed extra money for his university tuition. The much-touted tutor, though capable and willing, could not keep many of his appointments with Garven. He always had a good excuse, but the excuses did the boy no good. Garven was beginning to understand the difficult foreign language, but he was sure he was getting it too little and too late for the looming midterm; and he needed every bit of help he could get.

The German midterm examination was to cover a four-page list of vocabulary words, present and past tense conjugation of irregular verbs, and translation into English of a German folktale. Garven memorized the list of words and their meanings and could remember most of the endings for the verbs by now, but he was woefully inadequate when it came to putting the information together to translate. He would never be able to get through the passage in the two hours allotted. He sweated blood in fearful anticipation.

With a week to go, it occurred to Garven to cheat, to write the vocabulary words on his white shirt cuffs, to secrete the textbook inside his pants, to bring a mirror to the test so he could peek at Jud Sanders's paper. Jud was the star German student and sat immediately behind Garven. The mirror trick did not work for several reasons when Garven tried it out. The writing was too small, appeared backward on the mirror, and the effort to see the paper behind him required too many conspicuous contortions. Garven was beginning to panic. By the late afternoon of the day before the fateful test, he was frantic with anxiety, failure of all his aspirations looming largely before his mind's eye.

Presuming that he would be unable to decipher the German passage and to get enough of it into English to pass, Garven decided to forsake all his pride and to go to Frau Mueller's office to plead with her for clemency, for a postponement—for anything. She always stayed late; so, he went to her office immediately after spring baseball practice. The good Frau was not in her office, it appeared, when Garven knocked. She had to be. He hadn't quartered his pride this much to miss his chance to talk to the unsympathetic Aryan woman. Somehow, he had to be able to communicate to her how much this test, how much staying in school and getting to be a doctor meant to him. She had to be made to understand. All rules of courtesy aside, he turned the knob when she failed to respond to his third and most insistent knock.

Frau Mueller, really, was not in her office. Garven had convinced himself so thoroughly that she was just avoiding him, that he was genuinely surprised not to find the teacher in her usual place. It had never occurred to Garven than the woman might have a social life, other commitments, other needs for her time, than to be where he needed her to be. Fifteen-year-olds do not have a complement of neurons that enable them to take into consideration, with any completeness, the needs of other people; and Garven was in no frame of mind to call on any of his brain cells to deal with anything but his own needs at that moment. His panic was complete. He was not even going to be able to mount an emotional appeal. In his excitement, he floundered around for a way out, he looked at the tidy room in desperation, taking it to be the source of his impending humiliation.

It was not that he meant to make the discovery, but he was looking about the room with his coyote's eyes. He would never have come to a teacher's office on a clandestine search. For one thing, he was not that brave; and for another, he was not capable of thinking clearly enough to be able to pull off a secret raid. It would never have occurred to him that the teacher would not have been in her room, that the door would have been unlocked, and, of course, that the complete set of examination questions, even with the German text to be translated, would be sitting out in plain sight in the middle of her otherwise empty desktop. Garven would not have seen the papers if not for their contrast against the grain of the dark rosewood desk. He was too frantic for it to have been a planned thing. It was a fluke, really a series of fortuitous serendipitous flukes. Garven considered it nothing short of providential.

CHAPTER
Eight

In the final analysis of what went through his mind on that occasion, Garven gave the whole matter almost no thought. He did not, for example, anguish for even a second about the school's honor code or about the question of common Judeo-Christian right and wrong. He scarcely had foresight enough to look out the windows and outside the office door to make sure that the old battle-ax was not going to pop in on him at any minute. Instead, he was galvanized into a flurry of action. He was no longer dazed by panic as he had been before he found the unguarded papers. His mind was clear, organized, and calculating.

First, he mentally memorized the exact position of the papers on the desk. Then, he extracted his spiral-bound notebook and sat at Frau Mueller's desk and began to write as fast as he could and still have any legibility. He invented a sort of shorthand as he worked and was able to get the main stems of the words down very rapidly. He could compare them to his own list later. His pen flew along copying "*sich anschliessen, das Auge, augenblichlich….*" The text for translation was a simple one from *Kinder und Hausmärchen*, Jacob and Wilhelm Grimms' *Fairy Tales*, one of several that was abstracted in his textbook.

"Once upon a time…" Garven began to copy. Then, he recognized that it was not necessary to copy the passage, just to remember which story the teacher had chosen. His task on the test was to translate from English to German; he wrote down the grammar section of the test as rapidly as his fingers could move and his eyes could delineate the print in the dimming twilight and his brain could assimilate the foreign words. Given the infinitive; *drehen, falten, gehen,* he was to supply the present, past, and imperfect and reflexive verbs. Given the nominative noun, he was to supply the definite article correct as to gender; *Arm, Bank, Buch, Hand, Feder, Zimmer,* and so on.

After what seemed like a half a day of frantic writing, but that was no more than twenty minutes by the clock, Garven finished and woke up from his absolute absorption in his copying task to realize within himself a nearly palpable sense of impending discovery. It struck him as if his chest had been squeezed by an unseen hand when the surge of adrenaline coursed through his veins at the realization of his compromising position at that moment. He silently padded to the windows and to the door again, looked out and satisfied himself that he was in no imminent danger of being discovered. He had broken into a sweat but felt cold and shaky. He stuffed the papers of salvation under his baseball shirt and left the room after taking excruciating pains to ensure that Frau Mueller's papers were back in the exact position on her desk where she had left them, and was sure that they did not look disturbed from his riffling through them.

He missed the evening meal and was too excited to attend vespers that night. He was sure his deeds would be as evident on his face as Hester's famous letter. No one noted his absence, and his roommates were oblivious to his emotional state, wrapped up as they were in their own concerns. Garven was up almost the entire night doggedly memorizing the results of his great windfall. He knew he had manna from heaven, and he could not afford to waste time on such a puny need as sleep when salvation from the Jeopardy List was at hand. By morning he was still so keyed up that he was not at all sleepy. He forced himself to eat although he had no appetite. He would not talk to anyone for fear that he would jiggle loose one of the precious nuggets of knowledge he had crammed onto the surface of his brain through the arduous night. His fingers were cold and trembling, his pupils dilated, and his skin dry and shiny when he took his place in Frau Mueller's classroom for the midterm exam.

Garven was full of unquenchable nervous energy as the test papers were distributed to the students. He was still unsure that the test he had seen would appear before his eyes this morning, and almost cried out when it did. He made himself be the very picture of control. He had a problem of not going too fast, of getting done so early that he would cast suspicion on himself.

It never occurred to him to make a few discrete mistakes. He had memorized the material so thoroughly that it was unthinkable to make a mistake; it never crossed his mind. Garven was not deeply or broadly intelligent, but he did have a remarkable ability to memorize and to hold in his mind the memorized material. He need not have worried about someone jarring him and disturbing the memory centers; so, he would lose some of the retained German. The material was there to stay, almost as if it were on a page printed before him as he concentrated. If he had wanted to, he would have been able to dredge the same pictures up a year or ten years from that day. He could not have confidence in that element of his cognitive function as he sat and wrote with a disciplined effort that day in Frau Mueller's German class.

Teenagers ordinarily avoided direct physical activity as a matter of deep principle, and baseball players are particularly skeptical of running and wind sprinting. Not so with Garven Carmichael that afternoon. He ran from his room to the diamond, ran circles around his teammates, and at batting practice ran around the bases when he hit the ball even when he did not have to. He did not deflate until eight o'clock that night; then he was so exhausted that he could not talk to his roommates for the second night in a row. He was asleep by eight-thirty and slept the sleep of the just until he was awakened by the early morning ablutions of his three roomies.

Garven's midterm grades represented his best performance for any grading period since he had come to the prestigious California prep school. If he could keep this up, he would finish out the year with a raft of Bs, a few gentlemanly Cs and maybe even an A or two. He did not know what would happen in German with a much improved midterm grade that would better his average—maybe enough that he could even be eligible for a B. Wouldn't that frost Frau Battle-ax? It was a little disconcerting that he had not gotten the test scores back from German, but no one in the class had either; so, he was not overly concerned. After two weeks, he was more concerned.

Garven had a reason for concern. His and another scholarship student's tests were at that very time lying in front of the headmaster, Frau Mueller, and the chairman of the department of languages, Cecil Lemuels.

"I find it hard to believe that anyone would be dumb enough to cheat and produce a perfect paper. A perfect paper! That is just not in the boy's own self-interest. I would be more suspicious if there were a few obvious errors, wouldn't you, Dr. Lemuels?

"But that is exactly what we found on the Daniels boy's test. He was virtually failing, and on this test had only two or three errors. In fact, he erased over the correct answers almost as if he wanted to call attention to his mistakes, to lead us away from the fact that he cheated. In his case we have proof positive of his calumny. His roommate brought in the boy's cheat-sheets. The writing on these little cards is so tiny I can't even read them. Oh, for the vision of youth without all its follies."

"We have no such incriminating evidence on the Carmichael boy, Dr. Samuels, Frau Mueller."

"He did it. Proof or no proof!" Frau Mueller declared flatly.

"I trust that both boys will break down when confronted by the student disciplinary council, but we are in a bind if Carmichael sticks to his guns and denies cheating. He would have almost had to have had a copy of the test in advance to do this well. I know how jealously you guard your materials, Frau Mueller; so, I have my doubts as to how he could have carried off a cheat without some detection. The prefects searched his room, you know, and there was not a single suggestion of a crib sheet. On the contrary, the wastebasket was full of the work notes of the boy that looked like he had been most diligent. His roommates have sworn that Carmichael studied frantically all night. I hardly think all four of them are in collusion," Des Moines explained to the two language teachers.

"I know this boy. He did not haf his German in mind vell enough to pass the test let alone to write a perfect test. Really, Headmaster, this cannot be ignored."

"Nothing is going to be ignored. In fact, I will have the pair of them in my office today, and I trust that both of them will make a clean breast of it before this day is done," Des Moines said confidently.

Dr. Samuels looked rather sad.

He said, "I hate to see this—promising boys ruined by a mistake."

"A mistake?! Spare me the euphemisms. This is a crime!" snapped Frau Mueller.

She was not a forgiving sort and was not in a mood to be persuaded or mollified.

"Let me handle it until the disciplinary council meeting. I do so prefer to have the students feel that they have made the decision. It is a good maturing experience for them all. I will have the incontrovertible evidence before them this evening. Actually, I hope both boys will have the decency to resign. It will be easier to break the news to their parents that way, I can tell you from past experience," the headmaster intoned.

"Better you than me, Dr. Des Moines," said the language department chairman sympathetically. "I would not have your job."

"I vould relish the opportunity! Especially that Carmichael boy. He has no pisness being here in the first place—zuch a pumpkin from Aridzona!" The militant German matron scowled her indignation. "I joost don't like that one!"

He was in the middle of his civics class in mid-afternoon when the prefect brought the terse note to him, interrupting the class momentarily and bringing full unwonted attention of the class on Garven.

The note said simply, "PLEASE PRESENT YOURSELF IN MY OFFICE AT THREE-THIRTY SHARP THIS DAY." It was signed with full formality, C.P. Des Moines, Headmaster.

Garven was as ignorant as anyone as to why such a summons should be given to him. It never occurred to him that he was about to meet the most serious accusation of his life to date. He was unprepared for the brusque confrontation from his headmaster, devoid of any preliminary pleasantries.

"I have the sad duty to inform you that you have been accused of cheating on your German midterm examination. The evidence is inescapable. I am sure you know the consequences. Or would you have me read the honor code to you?"

"No."

"What do you mean, no?" snapped the older man abruptly sensing a challenge.

He would broach no insubordination from this puppy.

Garven was calm and polite. It was not the first time he had been in a tight situation, even one suddenly thrust on him.

"I mean you do not have to read the honor code to me." He paused to collect himself, then continued, "I haven't the slightest idea what you are talking about otherwise."

Des Moines looked intently at the young face before him, into the steady eyes. He detected no guile. He was growing uncomfortable.

"Come now, my boy, you will feel better after a clean breast of it. Dash it! Give me your confession, and you will not have to face a single one of your fellow students with your disgrace."

Garven made no move to comply or to beg mercy or to explain.

"Now listen to me! I will have no dilly-dallying on this matter. Your guardian will be informed, and he is the only one who needs to know. Out with it! I am a busy man!"

His voice was rising in pitch and stridency despite his concerted effort to maintain a calm judicial manner.

"No," said Garven. It was an instantaneous feral response.

He felt desolate inside, but his face was a mask of innocence, unreadable.

The headmaster looked sternly at the boy. His fists were involuntarily clenched, and his jaw was tight. Ignoring the signs and entreaties, Garven knew he had to save himself and instinctively recognized that his only salvation was an unshakable denial. Confession might be good for the soul as the ministers had so often reiterated at chapel, but his soul was not his major concern at the moment; he had to save his hide.

He asked in as calm a voice as he could muster, "Just what is it that I am supposed to have done, Sir?"

"Don't you be coy. The evidence is right here before me," Des Moines indicated a folder of test papers. "You were all but failing Frau Mueller's class, then, by some miracle, you came up with a perfect score on her midterm examination. What have you to say for yourself, young man? Do I look like I was born yesterday?"

"No, Sir," Garven answered mechanically.

"No, Sir, what?" the headmaster queried testily.

"No, Sir, you do not look like you were born yesterday."

"Oh, for goodness sake, Carmichael, get off it. Let's have a confession and get on to the work of the day. This is nonsense."

"It's not nonsense to me. I think it is entirely serious. I have nothing to confess."

"Did you or did you not take crib notes to Frau Mueller's test?"

"I did not," Garven's voice was quavering a little, but he retained his resolute calm.

He knew it was his only hope.

"Did you or did you not copy answers from your fellow students during the test?"

"I did not."

His face was as uncommunicative as a soda cracker.

Des Moines pondered a moment analyzing, nearly voicing, then rejecting his idea. Finally he asked the question about what he considered to be the least likely scenario for cheating.

"You didn't have a copy of the test in advance, did you, Garven?"

The question came out more softly, almost apologetically.

Garven looked surprised at the question as if it was so far from his reality that he had to analyze its meaning.

He answered again, "No, Sir, I did not."

The headmaster wavered, began to doubt the certainty of his previous convictions. His voice noticeably mellowed.

"Then how do you explain your perfect showing on this test. It strains my credulity, I must say."

"For one thing, this is the first time I knew I had even passed the test. I worried myself sick over this thing. She was going to put me on the Jeopardy List, you know. I have to admit that I had been goofing off some and was spending too much time on baseball. I spent too much time on soccer before, and German suffered."

"I can well understand that," the headmaster said, his brow knitting in concern, the light of understanding coming on.

Perhaps it was just what he wanted to hear.

"Anyway, Frau Mueller took me into her office and scared the pants off me. I lit out of there and studied German like no one ever did before. I hate the subject, but I stuck to it. The night before the test, I was up all night studying. You can ask my roommates; you want their names?" Garven said rushing his sentences.

"That won't be necessary, Garven. I have already done that."

If the fact that he had been under investigation bothered him, Garven kept it out of his freckled face.

"Didn't they tell you what I just said?" the boy asked with a face entirely free of duplicity.

"Indeed," Des Moines had to admit. He waited until the silence between the boy and himself became awkward then, making up his mind, said, "I can see that I am not going to get my confession; this is not going to be easy. I do have to admit that I now have to entertain an element of doubt as to your guilt. Either you are as innocent as you say, or you are the best liar I have encountered in my years at this school. Maybe you don't have a conscience and are a psychopath, as the psychologists describe. God help you and the rest of us if the latter is the case. We'll see what your peers have to say. Think it over, my boy. Confession is still and truly good for the soul."

He could see that Garven had thought it over practically before he had finished his soliloquy.

"Be in the chapel at eight o'clock sharp. The accusations and faculty opinions will be in the hands of the Student Judicial Council beforehand. You can make your defense to them then."

Headmaster Des Moines looked down at the mound of papers on his desk as a gesture of dismissal, indicating that they had nothing further to discuss. Garven left, and the headmaster buzzed his secretary and asked her to send in the Daniels boy.

Garven arrived at the Hogan Memorial Chapel a little after seven—early enough to be sure he would be on time, and not so early as to appear overly eager or vulnerable. The chapel, like almost every building on the sprawling campus built after 1910, was a memorial and named after the wealthy donor. It was Danish Modern in style, having been designed by a firm of famous Scandinavian architects who had no idea of the terrain, flora, or climate of Pacific Palisades, California, and who created a spindly, open, unsuitable, and unattractive edifice that the elderly lady benefactor admired deeply. As near as anyone could discern, the principal reason for choosing the architectural firm was that they were famous, more accurately in vogue, in 1934 when the building was donated, and donations were otherwise very thin in that decade.

Twelve boys, three from each class at Burton-Cagle, filed in and quietly took their seats in the choir section behind the pulpit. Headmaster Des Moines and Mr. Tucker, the chemistry teacher and advisor to the Student Judiciary Council, assumed their places in seats on either side of the slender pulpit. Garven waited for Michael Daniels, but he was not in the room at eight o'clock sharp when Patrick Harrington Kent, student-body president and chairman of the council, brought the meeting to formal order.

"We will have a recitation of the charges against the student defendant," he said and looked in the direction of Donald Perry, the council secretary.

No one seemed to be looking at Garven. He fixed his eyes straight forward on the pulpit, presenting a pose he imagined Dreyfus had adopted in his mockery of a trial. Garven was ramrod straight in his chair. Despite the difference in their relative guiltiness, Garven felt like Dreyfus.

"Cause number one: Violation of the Burton-Cagle Honor Code by cheating in class.

"Cause number two: Perjury. Lying to the Headmaster."

Student body president, Kent, still standing, now turned his attention to Garven who felt very small in the large, quiet church room.

"How do you plead, Mr. Carmichael? Guilty or not guilty to either or both charges of violation of the Burton-Cagle Honor Code?"

There was a pause.

"Please stand, Mr. Carmichael," Patrick requested, as an afterthought.

Garven stood and said clearly but very quietly, "Not guilty."

Mr. Tucker turned to the headmaster and whispered, "What'd he say?"

Mr. Des Moines broke the quiet and ordered, "Speak up, please, Mr. Carmichael. The acoustics are not good enough for a whisper to be heard."

"Not guilty! I am not guilty of cheating or of lying," Garven spoke up loudly and clearly.

His voice was strong enough to remove any tremors.

The secretary read a harshly worded indictment from Frau Mueller and a bland communication from Headmaster Des Moines, summarizing the conversation he had had with Garven earlier in the day. Des Moines was free of judgmental statements, except that his concluding statement was to the effect that he considered Garven to have been lying.

Patrick asked Garven, "Do you have any defense witnesses?"

"No."

"Do you want anyone to help in your defense?"

"No.

Do you have anything to say for yourself?"

"I certainly do. I will be very brief. I did not cheat or lie. There is not the slightest proof that I did, just that German teacher's opinion. She doesn't like me, and that is about all there is to it. I am a scholarship boy, not good enough for her, not important enough to be here. I'm not in the same class as you, rich boys."

There was more sneer in his tone than he had intended when he rehearsed his defense in his room that afternoon.

"I studied hard. I did great on the test. She can't stand it. Now, she won't be able to get me out the regular way by failing me; so, here I am…this is the only other way to get me out. I see that a little something was left out when Don read those letters about me. Mr. Des Moines told me that the prefects sneaked and searched my room and talked behind my back with my roomies. Where's the report on that stuff? Do you have that kind of information, or would that help my defense?" he accused.

"There is no need to be uncivil, Garven," admonished the headmaster, barely controlling his irritation. "I can tell you what the prefects learned. There was nothing found in Garven's, I mean, Mr. Carmichael's effects that would incriminate him. His roommates verified that Garven was in his room studying all evening, in fact, all night, before the German midterm."

"Anything more, Garven?" asked Patrick.

No more than fifteen minutes had elapsed in the hearing; it was embarrassingly brief.

"No."

Patrick looked at the two teachers, then at Garven, then at the other members of the Student Judiciary Council.

"Okay," he finally said. "I guess that's it. You may return to your room. We will meet in council, and I will let you know the results tonight, myself."

Garven left without comment and without looking back. He was drained, emotionally exhausted from the effort to maintain his composure, from the internal struggle that willed him to break down and confess, to plead for clemency that he had consciously resisted, knowing his only hope lay in an implacable denial. He was not troubled by guilt nor by any great concern about what the teachers or boys would think of him. They had the ingrained distrust and dislike of him that always existed between the haves and the have-nots. He could deal with that another day. His problem that evening had been to survive the awful moment. Garven made a silent and intense vow that, one day, he would be rich enough to be impervious to such mean-spirited attacks.

In the subdued light of the chapel, the students were quiet, unsure how to proceed. Patrick had conducted or had been involved in any number of honor code violations, most of them regarding minor offenses. Most of the boys had been terribly cowed and had humiliated themselves by groveling and sniveling. Not Garven Carmichael. All of the boys and the two advisors recognized the hardness, the unbending nature of the small boy who had stared them down. They were inclined to accept Garven's demeanor, his challenging tone, as evidence of his innocence.

"It looks to me that it is just Frau Mueller's word against Garven's," observed Harold Stiplton, the senior from Denver. "A case of he-said, she-said."

"Me, too," echoed four other council members, the younger boys.

"What proof of either cheating or lying have we got?" asked Petter Benson III, turning to look at the headmaster.

"This is your show now, boys; but you can ask whether you think the evidence would hold up in a court of law. I have nothing more than a gut feeling that Mr. Carmichael was lying to me and then to you in the hearing. I honestly don't know whether or not I can trust my guts."

"The evidence is hearsay; it is not even hearsay, it's just speculation. We have nothing more than Frau Mueller's belief. Even she as much as admitted that she has no evidence, let alone, proof. I say it's not enough," stated Carlton Fisker, the other senior on the council.

"Are you ready to vote? Any more discussion?" asked Patrick.

The boys and their advisors all shook their heads. Patrick glanced at Don Perry, the secretary, and nodded his head.

"This is an open vote. Raise your right hand to the square to signify, okay?" Don requested.

"All those who vote guilty on cause one, cheating?"

There was no movement.

"All those who vote not guilty on cause one?"

Twelve arms came promptly to the square.

"Those who vote guilty on cause two, lying?" he inquired.

There were no affirmative votes.

"Not guilty?"

Again all twelve boys signified by squaring their right arms.

"There is a unanimous 'not guilty' on both causes before this council, Mr. Chairman, Headmaster, Mr. Tucker." Don sat down.

"I will let him know right away," announced Patrick and stood to indicate that the meeting was adjourned.

"Wait a couple of hours, please, Mr. Kent. I need to contact Carmichael's parents and have a chat with them before he gets the results of your deliberations, if you would indulge me," Mr. Des Moines requested.

"Sure, no problem," replied Patrick.

Several of the committee boys asked either why Michael Daniels had not been there, had not even been mentioned.

Patrick shrugged his shoulders indicating his lack of information, "All I know is—headmaster's prerogative."

"Say no more," commented the junior class cynic, Axel Holmquist.

The headmaster found Peter Wilsonhulme's home telephone number in Arizona and contemplated the disagreeable task of making his second unpleasant call of the day. Such was the *mantellum* of leadership.

The first unpleasant call had been to Rapaport Daniels, father of Michael, directly in his corporate headquarters in Chicago, knowing that the tycoon would be at his work at that time of day. He passed through three secretaries, each more protective than the preceding, before hearing the bluff voice of the chairman of Daniels and Carne Consolidated Food Company, the world's largest food and beverage holding company.

"It must be important for you to call me at this time of day, C.P. Something wrong with my boy? He sick?" came the rapid fire, insistent tone of the man who was used to crisp and to-the-point replies from his underlings.

"Nothing like that, Rapaport. I hope I haven't caught you at a bad time, but I fear this is something that can't wait. The boy is not sick, but there is a serious problem with Michael."

"Tell me," the tone was insistent but more subdued.

"I'll come right to the point. I think that is best," Des Moines drew a deep breath and considered the princely captain of industry on the other end of the line. "Michael has been caught in a flagrant violation of the school's honor code. Specifically, he cheated, used crib notes in his German exam. You realize the significance of that, do you not, Rapaport?"

It was a statement, not really a question. Mr. Daniels was a member of Burton-Cagle's board of directors.

Mr. Des Moines waited for Rapaport Daniels to collect his thoughts. He knew the food conglomerate chairman to be a man who never wasted words or time. He had a manner of speaking directly, and only after due consideration that caused his audience to give full attention.

"I would hope the two of us could find a way around this. No doubt Michael should be punished; when he gets back to Chicago, I'll have his head on a pike. But as I understand it, this is his first offense, and perhaps there can be found a way to correct him without the full penalty, without expulsion."

"You do realize that the actions of the Student Judiciary Council have to be automatic. We established a zero tolerance rule for cheating, lying, fornicating, and on-campus drinking three decades ago. They will have no choice. We can't make an exception for Michael; it would undermine the entire honor system. I just thought you should fully appreciate what Michael is up against," interrupted Des Moines.

There was another short pause.

"Then he will simply have to be kept out of that judicial council hearing."

"And how can I do that?"

"Exercise your prerogative as the CEO! You are in charge; you can't always let the inmates run the asylum. These boys are still children. A lot of that is left-wing nonsense anyway."

"That, that is most irregular...most, uh...difficult."

"Perhaps I can be of help. I do not want my family name held up for humiliation. I would rather see the name on a new library; in fact, I can envision the finest library building and book collection west of the Mississippi. It would be a great honor to commemorate the contributions of the founder of Daniels-Carne, my late lamented father, Seth Daniels, in such a worthy edifice. Wouldn't you agree, C.P.?"

Momentarily, there was no answer. Des Moines' success was beyond his farthest hopes.

"C.P.? What would you think of such a project?"

"Rapaport, do you know what you are suggesting? We're talking seventeen or eighteen million dollars for the kind of project you have outlined," Headmaster Des Moines replied with eyes tightly closed and fingers tightly crossed.

"Consider it done. I will rely on your leadership and discretion, C.P. Would I be too far afield if I asked whether there is already a set of plans for a new library?"

"Well, as a matter of coincidence, there is."

You old pirate, concluded Mr. Daniels to himself. "Good-bye, then, C.P.," and replaced his receiver.

Late that evening, Dr. Peter Wilsonhulme picked up the telephone in his home in Emmett, Arizona on the second ring. He recognized the voice of his old friend, C.P. Des Moines, immediately after the customary hellos.

"Anything wrong with Garven? Is he sick? Has he been hurt?"

"Nothing like that," reassured Mr. Des Moines. "There is a problem, though; and I'd like to discuss it with you."

He went on the describe the events and accusations of the last two days and finished with the description of Garven's somewhat suspect exoneration.

"Well, that's terrible, C.P.! Thank heaven the boy was proved innocent! I am sure you never doubted him."

"To be perfectly frank, if it hadn't been for me minimizing the evidence and the charges, I don't know where we would be right now. Peter, your Garven got by this time, but I really fear for him. He needs a firm hand; he needs some direction, the kind of guidance that only a father can give. I wonder if you have enough formal authority and control to be able to deal with this headstrong youngster. Just today, I saw the effective influence of a father come to the aid of an errant son. As I understand it, my friend, you are not even Garven's formal guardian. When push comes to shove, when he really needs your full capacities, are you going to have the paternal rights necessary?"

"You really think that is necessary? It raises a pretty delicate issue, you know. The boy is Rachel Carmichael's, that nice school teacher from the little town in Arizona. Maybe you remember her. I'll have to tread lightly."

"Nonetheless, you'd better start to tread. I don't think that being a benefactor alone is going to be enough. By the way, I am deeply sorry about the passing of your good wife. Now that you are alone, you might even think of adopting the boy formally. Think his mother would approve? It needn't diminish her parental role, you understand. Adoption could only help in my view."

"I can't think of anything that would mean more to me. You really think I should broach the subject, do you?"

"Get control of that boy as soon and as firmly as you can. I'll confide in you as one of my oldest friends, Peter. Garven won't survive another such accusation. He needs a serious change in status to compete in the situation here and with the privileged caste of boys we have. He needs you."

In less than a fortnight the cheating incident was no longer a subject of discussion, the Burton-Cagle planning and development office was in possession of a firm start directive for a new library; Frau Mueller received surprise approval of her application for a year's sabbatical to study advanced German literature at the Goethe Anthroposophical Institute in Bern, Switzerland; and Peter Wilsonhulme was sure he would be successful in his quest to adopt Garven Carmichael after the first emotionally charged discussions with Garven's mother.

CHAPTER
Nine

Rachel Carmichael had been over the issue twice before with Peter Wilsonhulme, and had worn down enough to insist that Garven be present at the next, and hopefully, final discussion on the subject of adoption. The matter was at a critical juncture with Garven back in Cipher for the summer. She was over the general reluctance to be involved in something decidedly strange and unheard of. Adoption of a fifteen-year-old who has a living mother? The doctor's attorney had cleared the air about that by pointing out the commonplace legal occurrence of guardianship changes. This instance was little different than if she and the doctor had married, and now he was adopting her son. She had asked about the propriety of having more than one legal guardian and was assured that it was not only legal but proper. Her real problem was emotional; would her son feel that he was being abandoned? Would she, herself, be abandoned in the process, for that matter?

"I haven't had the courage to talk to my son about this adoption business. I just don't know how to say it. It would seem so odd from his point of view," Rachel commented to Dr. Wilsonhulme before her son came back from the desert where he had been riding with the reservation boys.

He had been home for the summer vacation for two days. He now seemed so much more grown up.

"I think I have hinted at the possibility, but I haven't really said anything about it, at least not formally, either," Peter said.

"I am pretty nervous about this. I mean, I haven't made up my own mind; how can I expect a fifteen-year-old to deal with such an important change in a single meeting? That's asking too much, seems to me."

"Do you want me to bring it up?" Peter offered.

"No, I guess it's my responsibility. I have decided to go with whatever he wants to do. After all, it is his name, his life; and I recognize that it is to his practical benefit. You can never tell how teenagers think, though. It's up to the boy. I'll tell him." She was rambling, and felt more nervous than ever.

Garven came through the kitchen screen door after making a dust cloud by brushing off his clothes and boots on the stoop. He was weather-beaten and tired but looked happy and relaxed.

"Hi, Mom! Hi, Dr. Wilsonhulme!" he called out when he saw the pair.

He knew something was up because he had been required to come home early for a meeting. His mother had told him that the doctor wanted to talk to him and her about something important. His mother looked concerned, and Dr. Wilsonhulme appeared serious. He hoped it wasn't something to do with that cheating business. Couldn't they leave him be even during summer vacation? He had a passing thought that maybe his mom was sick.

"Come in, Garven. We're having a glass of lemonade." She extended a glass to her son.

"Thanks."

He drained the tall glass in a two-swallow teenage chug-a-lug.

Rachel was nervous, and it showed. Nonetheless, she knew she had to get it out; so, she spoke directly, afraid she would chicken out if she hesitated.

"Garven, with Dr. Wilsonhulme supporting you at the Burton-Cagle School, they, I mean the school people, feel there needs to be a clarification of his status. Your status with him, I guess I really mean."

"Huh?" asked the bewildered teenager.

At least they were not getting into the German test stuff. That was a relief.

"Look, what I'm trying to say is that you really don't fit into the scholarship-boy status, and your family is not the support for your schooling. You are somewhere in between because of Dr. and Mrs. Wilsonhulme's—rest her soul—generosity. He, I mean the doctor, would like to make it simpler, I hope better, for you. He would like to make an offer to you. A wonderful one, son."

Garven automatically looked at Peter Wilsonhulme who returned his gaze and then looked to Rachel for the next move. She nodded her head in Peter's direction; so, he assumed the prerogative to speak.

"Garven, my boy, you know how much my late dear wife cared for you, how much I do. We have felt like you were the son we never had. We know you have a wonderful mother, and have never wanted to interfere with you and her. With this school business, we thought we could have a closer relationship, a formal one that preserved what you and your mother have always enjoyed. When my dear wife died, I decided to act. I don't want to feel alone, son. I would like to adopt you, to have you be my son in legal fact. What would you think about such a thing, Garven?"

"Wow!" Garven exclaimed having no time to digest the import of Dr. Wilsonhulme's proposal. "I don't know what to think. That would sort of mean that I was someone else. Jeez. What do you think, Mom?"

"I've thought a lot about it, son. I am going to leave it up to you, to your decision. I am sad to have to say it, but the doctor has been more of a father to you than your dad, wherever he is. He deserted us and left us in tough shape. Dr. and Mrs. Wilsonhulme made most of the good things you enjoy possible. It is something to think seriously about. You don't have to answer just yet."

"In fact, Garven, we have to make every attempt to find your biological father and get him to relinquish his legal rights. I don't suppose that will be too hard when he has to face up to the law about desertion and his child and spousal support responsibilities. That will come to a handsome piece of change. He will probably want to be clear of it, and here is his golden chance," commented the doctor.

"What happens to me and Mom if you become my dad?" questioned Garven with an extra furrow in his forehead.

"Nothing will change. Nothing will ever need to change. I am your mother, and I will always be. I guess this is just a chance to get a father instead of an absentee dad for a welcome change," Rachel said.

"Well, give it some thought, Garven. You don't have to make up your mind right this minute. This is a big decision; you will want to take your time. I guess we should have an understanding before you go back to Burton-Cagle this fall; that's about the only kind of deadline there is," offered Peter.

Garven was quiet for a time. He absently held his glass of lemonade on his lap with both hands.

Finally, he returned from wherever he had been in his thoughts and asked, "Would I have to change my name?"

"I suppose not if you didn't want to, Garven," said the doctor.

"If I did, could I make the choice?" the boy asked.

"Of course, dear. It is entirely up to you. You could keep your exact same name, or have an entirely new one; whatever you wanted," his mother told him.

Garven returned to that place in his thoughts again. This time he returned with a calm, relieved look on his face.

"I've had enough time to think about it. I would love to be your son, Dr. Wilsonhulme. I can't even remember my real dad—my other dad. You're my real dad when you get right down to it. Let's do it. Let's do it as quick as we can, okay?"

"Okay, if that's what you want," laughed Peter.

Garven's mother smiled at his impetuosity, but knew her son well enough to recognize that this was a genuine and final decision on his part.

"Just one more thing, and I've thought a long time about this. When we do the adoption business, I want to change my name. I want to get rid of that 'Aloysius' once and for all!" exclaimed Garven. "I'll be proud to be a Wilsonhulme."

******

Socially, the sophomore year at Burton-Cagle was easier. The quaking freshman uncertainties were gone; Garven knew a lot more guys and had a pretty good idea of the pecking order at the school. He knew where he fit, or at least, he knew where he had fit before. There would likely be some nuances of change for Garven Carmichael Wilsonhulme. He was getting used to the name change, and definitely liked to drop a sentence or two that included a casual reference to "my dad, the doctor." It had been less than a month since the adoption was final, and Garven was still like the newly engaged girl who suddenly becomes left handed and has to write her upcoming new name a few hundred times.

"Hey, Carmichael," David Applegate called out to him when Garven was halfway up the front walk into the administration building.

"Hey, David," Garven called back. He was always a bit annoyed by being called by his last name.

And "Carmichael" was not even his last name anymore.

David caught up to him and, together, they walked into the office to sign up for room choices. The freshman dorm was set up to have four students to a room, the sophomore dorm to have three to a room, the junior dorm had only two bunks per room, and the kingly seniors and the few junior prefects had the luxury of single rooms.

David said, "Everybody's back. I guess we will have to make a choice since only three of us can be together. Think we ought to draw straws or something?"

"I don't think that'll be too big of a problem, actually, David. Stephen as much as told me his dad didn't want him to room with the same guys again, said something about him 'branching out'. Stephen felt icky about it, but I know it had something to do with that cheating business, when I was falsely accused, you know. I guess his dad was worried that he would be some of the dirt on him if Stephen had to be known as my roommate," Garven said with a tinge of sarcasm.

"Well, crap, all the more for us. Let's get P. Pot's name down with ours, then we can mess around for a while. Did you spend the summer with the wild Apaches again?"

Garven told David all about his summer, and the momentous change in his family tree. He emphasized his name change several times, then told David he wanted to forget that the change had occurred and just to go on normally. His last name was Wilsonhulme, not Carmichael. He wanted David to get that straight. He had to repeat the whole thing when P. Pot came up to their room.

Second year Latin was less deadly dull than first year. He did not have to spend all of his time with mind numbing memorization of long-forgotten vocabulary or in repetitive verb declensions. The Latin teacher started out with some simple translations and made an effort to pick selections that appealed to the martial spirit of the boys.

Postquam Cyclops haec facerat, Graeci fortes mortem exspectabant, sed Ulixes Polyphemum interficere in animo habebat. Ob magnitudinem vire non erat ullum iter facile ex periculo eorum, sed consilium parabant et suos animos bonos tenebant... Uterque Cyclopem timebat.... Polyphemus unum oculum solum habuit. Magna cum audacia Ulixis et socii sui in oculo eius finem arboris posuerunt.... Cyclops eos videre non potuit... Ulixes clamavit: "Nullus homo sum," sed Graeci in navi erant et laeti erant quod a Polyphemo furerant et ad Graeciam navigabant.

[After the Cyclops had done these things, the brave Greeks waited for death, but Ulysses had in mind to kill Polyphemus. Because of the great size of the man, there was not any easy way out of their danger, but they prepared a plan and kept their good spirits... Each feared the Cyclops... Polyphemus had only one eye. With great boldness, Ulysses and his companions put the end of the tree in his eye... The Cyclops was not able to see them... Ulysses shouted, "I am no man," but the Greeks were on the ship and were happy because they had escaped from Polyphemus and were sailing to Greece.]

And familiar or stirring quotations:

Sed non culpa mea est   But the blame is not mine. (Ovid)

Ditat Deus	God enriches. (State Motto of Arizona)
vi et armis	By force of arms
senatus populusqueRomanus	The Senate and the Roman People (SPQR)
carpe diem	Seize the day!
per capita	By head – per person or individual
post mortem	After death
habeas corpus	Thou shalt have the body
Virtus praemium est optimum	Virtue is the best reward. (Plautus)
Possunt quia possevidenturcum	They can because they think they can. (Virgil)
cum grano salis	With a grain of salt
sine qua non	Lit: Without which not – [something indispensable]

In second year chemistry, the students at Burton-Cagle started into laboratory studies to supplement their classroom work. The school was proud to be one of the first prep schools in the country to include the expensive equipment in their science courses. Mr. Des Moines had pointedly stated that fact in the opening day speech that autumn.

"In fact," he had said. "Burton-Cagle is the only, the *only* school west of the Mississippi to have a complete laboratory program available. This is due to the very generous grant from the Devlin Foundation. The Devlins have had five generations of boys here, you know."

Patrick Kilcannon became Garven's lab partner and as good a friend as P. Pot and David. Pat was a very bright young man, quick to catch on to the sciences. He helped Garven when he floundered with the chemical equations, and he seduced the country boy into a never-ending series of mischiefs. Garven had wanted to maintain the lowest of profiles when he returned that semester and to keep out of trouble. The German cheating accusation had been enough limelight to last him for the rest of his natural life. Pat was a flagrant extrovert, a born leader of gullible and impressionable boys, and the class prankster.

The first escapade concocted by the restless mind of the Irish trickster that fall was the manufacture of a chemical generator, specifically to make H2S—a small engineering feat. The physiology class was located immediately next door to the chemistry lab. The lab storeroom had once been a short hallway with a door that connected the two classrooms. The chem lab had usurped the old hall, and the assortment of high school chemicals and glassware were now stacked in smoky and dusty disarray on the hastily constructed shelves. To prevent the catastrophe of the door to the hallway being opened from the physiology side and causing an avalanche of expensive glassware and toxic chemicals, the door was nailed closed and the doorknobs on both sides of the hall removed.

Patrick had been fumbling around among the chemicals and beakers when he discovered that the missing doorknob had left a finger-sized hole connecting the two rooms. To his serendipitous surprise, he also determined that standard size latex tubing fit into that hole perfectly. Now, it only remained to discover what to do with the knowledge he had gained.

The laboratory instructor, innocently pursuing his duties to enliven the young minds with the mysteries of the world of chemistry, provided the answer to Patrick's quandary. Mr. Sessions followed the lab book carefully and demonstrated to the inquiring minds of his raptly attentive students, experiments that demonstrated the properties of the available principal chemicals and compounds from the table of elements.

On the fourteenth day of October, Mr. Sessions showed the class the properties of the handsome yellow element, sulfur, in its brimstone and flowers-of-sulfur forms. The teacher produced an elaborate and expensive piece of glassware, a Kipp generator, to demonstrate the process of $FeS + 2HCl \longrightarrow FeCl2 + H2S$, and Patrick and Garven paid rapt attention to how it was done. Even though neither boy entertained any aspirations or interest in the chemical field, they, like all real boys, knew that $H2S$ is, in reality, rotten egg gas.

The principle Patrick and Garven learned was to drip diluted hydrochloric acid over a sulfide such as ferrous sulfide. The generator apparatus was a triple globed affair with an upper elongated and tapering flask descending down through the middle of another, bi-globular flask. The tapered end of the upper and separate flask was open at the bottom, and ingress and egress were controlled by a stopcock.

The chemical process occurred in the middle chamber which contained the ferrous sulfide. When the stopcock of the upper flask was opened, acid was noted to run down the central stem then up into the middle globe containing the FeS where the reaction took place. Upon closing the stopcock, pressure developed within the middle globe, and in this way, the acid was pushed back up the long stem causing chemical activity to stop; so the reaction could be limited and controlled. The successful demonstration by the teacher delighted the boys with a vigorous outpouring of hydrogen sulfide—putrid smelling, rotten egg gas. It was as near perfect as anything the boys could have imagined for their purposes.

Patrick was so taken with what he had gleaned from the lesson that he induced Garven to engage in some extracurricular laboratory review as well.

Garven was as enthusiastic a student as his lab partner in this educational enterprise, and, together, the boys staged a night raid to enhance their participation in laboratory chemistry. By the light of a three-battery penlight, Patrick showed Garven his discovery about the connector hole between the two classrooms. Together, they recapitulated the day's experiment, adding a refinement. They bubbled the H2S into cool water in a beaker, assiduously sealed all openings with paraffin, and the boys securely inserted the latex tubing leading from a side port of the generator to the doorknob hole. They rearranged the glassware so the rotten egg gas generator would not be seen accidentally by the casually curious, and returned to their dorm rooms.

The following day Garven and Patrick impatiently waited in the physiology class while the teacher droned about the digestive system and how acid ate up food in the stomach, and how bile helped to dissolve the rest. Fascinating. When the teacher busied himself with an experimental setup opposite the chemical pantry, Garven slipped out of his physiology class, through the empty chemistry teaching lab, and into the closet room and lit a Bunsen burner under the flask of water with its dissolved rotten egg gas. Then, he just as surreptitiously made it back to his seat unseen. With less than ten minutes of class time left, the first faint odor of putrefaction began to waft into the room next door. There were a few sniffs, then a few more. Soon the stench of rotten eggs permeated insistently into every crevice of the nearby classroom. The rotten egg smell was unmistakable and unendurable. The alert physiology teacher reacted properly and evacuated the giggling and rowdy boys from the classroom. Security was called to search for the gas leak or for the hole in the sewer system.

A little of that smell went a long way; and shortly, the entire second floor of the classroom building was evacuated. By ten, the rotten egg gas generator had been ferreted out, and the Gestapo began its methodical search for the culprit or culprits. No one knew. No one was telling. No amount of threats could cause a break in the student ranks. No one would own up to the guilt even after the alarmed chemistry teacher explained in a solemn assembly about the terrible poisonous nature of the gas.

"The school was lucky to have averted a medical disaster," he said. "It definitely was not funny," he stressed.

The students, evidently not listening closely, thought it was funny, a fact that perturbed the chemistry teacher.

"When air containing a very small amount of H2S is inhaled, headache and nausea result. It is unsafe to breathe, for an extended period, even one part to two hundred of the gas. Larger concentrations cause paralysis of the nerve centers of the lungs and heart. People have been known to suffer sudden severe falls."

The chemistry teacher was very serious and intense in his delivery of the description of the dire consequences of sniffing rotten egg gas. For some reason related to the perverse nature of boys, the entire student body, nonetheless, found the episode excruciatingly funny. They told and retold the story, embellishing the anguish of the faculty with successive tellings. They drew caricatures, left chalked slogans on various and sundry blackboards, and every time a prank was pulled, a note would be found signed, "THE GASSER". The Gasser went into Burton-Cagle legend not only for the sheer hilarity it had created but for the resolute refusal of anyone to break and confess or identify the Gasser or Gassers. It was a triumph of prep school *Omerta*, a code greatly respected by the boys.

Garven and Patrick, though at one time strenuously interviewed, as were all of the chemistry students, never wavered. No one ever seriously suspected them, and they stayed mum.

CHAPTER
Ten

David Applegate got gentlemanly Bs but was capable of doing much better. He had a wide variety of interests including physics and engineering, old cars, and architecture as well as the universal pursuits of girl watching (and hoping), and sports. He was the originator of the great prank of the spring semester, the only misadventure that would be prominently memorialized in a photograph and displayed in the foyer of the main administration building for the wonderment of succeeding generations of students and parents.

David suggested his idea and enlisted the help of both of his roommates, and Garven drew in Patrick and his two roomies to cope with the sheer magnitude of the project. Hamilton Templeprince had been the third headmaster of Burton-Cagle and had passed on to his Maker while still in the office. Out of respect for the venerable old administrator, or by neglect of the buildings in question, the old man's Model T Ford had vegetated and collected cobwebs in an outlying building for thirty plus years.

David reveled in the collection of old vehicles in the unused building and hit on the idea for his project because of his particular admiration for the Model T. The underlying concept was innocent enough—the school should honor one of its early headmasters by displaying his vehicle; for the Catholic at heart, a kind of venerable relic. David inveigled P. Pot and Garven, which was not too difficult, into working with him, in their copious free time, to build a jury-rigged derrick to haul the car to the top of the steeple of the campus church.

It was a world easier to conceive of the idea than to come up with a workable plan that would not get them all caught or killed. It was quite another aspect to execute the plan. That is why Garven brought Patrick and his roommates into the plot. For nearly a month the six boys worked to polish the car, get its wheels moving again, to build a pre-fabricated disarticulatable tower that could be hidden on the grounds then erected with reasonable facility and alacrity in the dark, and to procure some huge industrial pulleys and two-inch anchor rope in the post wartime shortage era. They built a ramp way so the old car could roll to its final resting—hanging—place. They practiced and drilled and, in every way, worked with a discipline that would have pleased their teachers immensely except for its nefarious design and purpose. After the event, and a discussion of the effort that must have gone into it, the faculty lamented that such pains were so seldom known to be applied to class work.

After consulting the almanac, David, the titular head of the project, selected a Saturday night in early May when it was supposed to be moonless. A number of the teachers were going to be away from the school, attending the national convention of preparatory school faculties for the last four days of the week. They were expected back Sunday night. Only the skeleton security staff, the luckless faculty officer of the day, Grantlin Hereford, and a couple of janitors were going to be at the school for the weekend. Everyone agreed on the day for the reasons David enumerated, and when Saturday night came, the conspirators pitched in with a will.

The tower went up first. It took longer than they had rehearsed because this was the first time they had done a major portion of the assembly in true darkness. True to the almanac's prediction, there was no moon at ten o'clock when the boys started. The parts of the sides of the tower were pulled up by the brute strength of the boys hauling on ropes attached on the top, at the middle, and —for safety's sake—on the bottom of the open walls. They laboriously attached the separate wall segments together, and basked for a moment in their success. The makeshift tower stayed upright. It was midnight.

Garven and Patrick climbed the ladder-like supports to the top of the structure, affixed the pulleys to the hooks on the crossbeams, and passed the heavy rope through. David attached the end of the rope to the body of the Model T and passed it through the lower pulley that was attached to the tower support about five feet from the ground.

Using main strength, awkwardness, and a smaller set of ropes and pulleys, the hardy lads towed up the flooring ramp and left it suspended where it would be swung into place after the car was strung up above that point. Exhaustion was beginning to be a worry; all of the boys were soaked with perspiration. It was quarter to two.

The boys were all back on the ground and began to pull the body of the car up and off the ground, thanks to the miracle of the physics principle of the pulley, and to the long ago car strippers who had removed the engine, transmission, and all of the heavy metal that could be removed. Slowly, slowly, the dangling Model T ascended. With superhuman strength and endurance, the grumbling and sweating boys hauled the heavy hulk hand over hand to the top of the prefab scaffolding tower. David attached the taut rope to a bottom cross girder, and they rested long enough to gather strength for the final phase. It was three forty-five and without their having paid attention to the phenomenon, the moon had risen to bathe them in a curiously bright and gray-white light. It was like being spotlighted.

When the boys realized how vulnerable they were to exposure there in the natural spotlight, they had their first moment of pause, of self-doubt.

P. Pot said in a mildly quavering voice, "I have this feeling that we're being watched. I think they are just letting us work hard enough to get ourselves into deep crap, then they are going to catch us all like rats with no place to go."

"Stop worrying, Pot. Nobody's here. There's nobody to see us; I told you all about that," hissed David.

"Yeah, and you said there wasn't going to be any moon, neither. Look at this; its like being in Union Station," P. Pot grumped.

"So, whatta you want to do, quit?" asked Patrick practically.

The risks had occurred to him, but not very strongly.

"I don't think it would be so very unreasonable to have a vote about it, your majesty," P. Pot said in a challenge to David and Pat.

He was a pudgy soft-looking boy, but there was nothing weak-minded about him.

"This is undoubtedly the strangest place and time that democracy was ever formally practiced," said David. "But why not? This whole deal is going to go down in history as being on top of the weird list. Let's vote."

"Will the meeting please come to order, gentlemen?" intoned Garven in his most magisterial voice, marred by a nuisance slip to a higher octave that was occurring of late.

"Have we a quorum?" inquired Mr. Patrick Sullivan Kilcannon in full mock solemnity.

"Get on with it!" shrieked Harold Bird as loud as he could whisper.

Harold was the mildest of Patrick's roommates, and the one most often the butt of his extroverted roommate's practical jokes.

"Do you know what time it is?"

"Well, all right then. If there is no more discussion from the floor, will someone put the question?" asked Garven in his formal chairman's voice.

"Oh, for crying out loud!" carped Harold.

"Order!" snapped David, impatient at the out-of-order interruption.

Harold clapped his right palm to his forehead.

"I shall do my best to phrase the question in proper form for a vote, if you will bear with me," announced David.

"Oh, brother," sighed Harold.

The other five boys, now wrapped up in the theater of the vote, glared at the discourteous young fellow.

"Probably a freshman," said Patrick in his best sotto voce.

An undercurrent of snickering began.

David rose to his full height and said with dignity, "There will be no snickering. Gentlemen, need I remind you of the gravity of the situation at hand?"

The old hulk of a car chose that moment to make a noisy twist in the air above them as if to punctuate their attention on gravity. The boys were all laughing now, harder than if they had good sense.

David regained his composure and said, "The question is, shall we of the tower brotherhood continue in our quest for glory and immortality, or shall we leave this car dangling here and our job half-finished, and gain naught but the derision of our fellows?"

His voice was positively Shakespearean.

"Would you mind repeating that?" laughed Patrick.

"Oh, brother," moaned Harold.

"No whining," said Garven.

"I think we all have it. All in favor of glory, say 'aye', those in favor of ignominy and who want to quit and limp away, say 'no'," said David.

"Aye, aye, aye, aye, aye, aye," came the chorus.

"By Jove, the ayes have it!" David exclaimed, jubilant if not prudent.

"The time at the tone is four o'clock," grumbled Harold to no one in particular.

For all their bravado, the six boys were aware of the increasing light and of the greater likelihood of being caught in the act. They worked with a vengeance. The ramp went into place without a hitch. The car jolted a little too hard when they let it down into place on the inclined plane, but no harm was done. The massive rope was wound around the Hogan Memorial Chapel steeple twice in a memorable feat of daring-do by Patrick who was the only volunteer to leap across from the makeshift tower to the small walkway around the steeple's zenith. He stretched out full length and lay hanging over the ledge to tie the rope to itself to make fast the car to the building.

"And here's where my career with the Boy Scouts pays off," he said and fashioned an intricate knot ball of alternating grannies and square knots.

126

The car was nudged down off the ramp and allowed to swing against the side of the steeple. The vintage vehicle swung nicely away from the tower as planned; the vehicle settled its full weight on the steeple spine as worked out; and the steeple cracked with a sickening crunch and leaned frighteningly over towards the car in a maneuver that definitely was not in the plans. The guilty six collectively held their breaths as the nails flew out and the boards creaked and slowly gave way. The boys watched in horrified fascination as the steeple top bent and prepared to break off. No one dared breathe lest the wind thus created prove to be the last bit of pressure tolerated by the fractured spire.

Although the steeple creaked and groaned, it did not break off completely; the Model T remained in place dangling precariously from the spire with its green-stick fracture. The boys breathed. When they were satisfied that the steeple and the rope would hold, all six scrambled to reverse the assembly process, and removed the last vestiges of their scaffolding at six-thirty as the mesa began to fill with morning's first sunlight. They need not have worried nor hurried. It was a blissfully quiet Sunday. No one ventured out of a building where he or she could have seen the night's work before the gentleman's hour of ten, and the faculty advisor of the day did not chance to look up from his morning constitutional until around noon. It was he who first detected the anomaly. At first glance, he was only aware of something amiss, something out of place in the familiar picture he beheld. It was hard to place the alteration in a view that had not changed substantially in nearly thirty years. When it all connected, he was speechless. His day was ruined. Now he would have to do something. Exactly what was unclear, but something.

Mr. Hereford decided to wait. To think it all out. He had breakfast, a leisurely affair, prepared carefully with proper attention to each segment—the toast tanned, not darkened, the eggs exactly three minutes at a full boil, the coffee fortified with extra cream and three lumps of sugar. He needed the fortification. His procrastination did not yield any satisfying answers to his problem. He finally elected to play the public detective and called the prefects to round up the entire student body still on campus. Most of the students were off to town or had been picked up by their parents for one of the few free weekends of the school year. As it happens, Garven, David, P. Pot, Patrick, Harold, and their other roommate, Skipper, were among the absent.

"I don't suppose any of you gentlemen knows who hanged the car from the steeple?" Mr. Hereford asked to begin his interrogation of the students assembled in the Leslie Theater Auditorium.

One of the assembled students muttered to his companion, "It's 'hung' not 'hanged'."

His companion just shook his head.

There were no more than twenty-five students; they had all seen the outrage; and they were all hysterical. Mr. Hereford was not having a very good day.

"This is a serious matter."

Laughter.

"School property has been damaged."

Laughter.

"The house of worship has been defiled."

Irreverent, stronger laughter.

"I will not have it," he yelled above the growing din.

Peels of uncontrolled, tears-down-the-face laughter.

"I will be in my quarters all day. Someone here knows who did this, and I expect him to uphold the honor of the school and his fellow students and to come forward. Any communication will be held in strictest confidence."

"You can count on me", "Right", and "I'll be right over, Mr. Hereford" were just some of the whispered promises from the amused student body.

Mr. Hereford was shocked and dismayed when the day closed without a single volunteer coming forward. The students had fallen well below his expectations that day, he told his wife. She, too, fell somewhat short of his definition of propriety when she had to exit the room to avoid breaking down in front of her stodgy husband.

The headmaster and the rest of the faculty and the remaining students returned the following day to learn of the terrible travesty. There was a general weeping, wailing, and gnashing of teeth, a spate of promises and threats, a solemn assembly—all to no avail. No one ever knew for sure who had done the deed although there were rumors aplenty. Garven, David, Patrick, and company were prominently mentioned on the basis of reputation alone; but there was no proof; there were no eyewitnesses; and no one was telling.

The incident was dropped after a local construction company, marveling at the ingenuity displayed, let the hapless car down and righted and repaired the steeple for only two thousand dollars, give or take a little. Nothing more was said about the incident unless one counts the six identical discrete handwritten letters received by Peter Wilsonhulme of Emmett, Arizona; Andrew Applegate of Pacific Palisades, California; Darwood Graham of Houston, Texas; Kevin Kilcannon of Manhattan, New York; MacIntosh (Skip) Branden of San Francisco, California; and Harold Bird I of Vancouver, British Columbia. The letter stated simply:

April 6, 1946

Dear (First Name of Father),

We at Burton-Cagle School have had the misfortune to have a schoolboy prank go awry, resulting in costly damage to our beloved Hogan Memorial Chapel steeple. The cost of repairs was in excess of $4000.00, a sum we can ill-afford in these straitened times of ours.

Our investigation has failed to identify the culprits for a certainty, but perhaps with a more diligent effort, one including the local constabulary, we can be more successful. We would prefer to keep our efforts in house, of course.

We are making a general appeal for contributions to rebuild the damaged portion of our Lord's house. If you can see your way clear to help, your tax deductible contribution would be most welcome.
As always, cordially,

C.P. DM.
Carter P. Des Moines,
Headmaster

There was an overflowing of generosity from the fathers singled out for attention. A discrete inquiry or two by the curious fathers revealed that there were only six letters sent, and the implications need not have been more explicit. This was the way gentlemen did things. The school received six separate $4000 contributions for the new steeple. The refurbishment blended nicely with the handsome new Seth Daniels Memorial school library. It had been a good year for the building fund.

CHAPTER
Eleven

Garven proved himself to be no less an innovator than a follower. He was responsible for the last Burton-Cagle prank, worthy of recordable recognition for the 1945-46 academic year. Garven enjoyed poking around in Army-Navy surplus stores in his time off from school. The stores were a veritable treasure house of inventory in the early aftermath of World War II. The particular treasure that caught Garven's attention was an air force weather balloon, still in the box. For no special purpose other than that he felt he just had to have one, and it was cheap, Garven bought the heavy duty balloon. He also bought two used parachutes, similarly useful items.

Using his idle mind as the proverbial devil's workshop during one weekend of spring fever, Garven hit upon a truly ingenious use for the balloon. He did need some help with the unwieldy article and for proper performance of his proposed project. Garven solicited the connivance of Bradley Dreyer, a wanna-be-cool freshman, who was annoyingly enthusiastic for the prank.

Together Garven and Bradley slipped into the sleeping quarters provided for the faculty advisor of the day during an afternoon when the advisor for that particular Saturday, Doyle Penrod, MEd., was attending to his duty as the baseball coach. The two boys meticulously unfolded the cumbersome and huge weather balloon and spread it out as far as it would stretch around the cramped room. Garven opened the single window and hauled the hose connector tube to the window and let it hang outside. Then the boys inserted the high pressure garden hose used for sprinkling the wide expanse of the back campus lawn into the tube opening. The nozzle-tube connection was then wired and taped securely enough to be watertight and able to withstand considerable force.

Bradley turned the hose on full blast, and Garven stood in the room and adjusted the folds of the balloon as the water inexorably filled the balloon. When the level of water was about two feet deep in the balloon inside the room, Garven considered that he had done all he could. For one thing, the water-filled balloon was becoming horrendously heavy. Garven exited through the room's only door with difficulty, and he and Bradley used every ounce of their combined weights and strengths to get the door closed and locked. After five hours of filling, the water was seven feet high in the room, three feet from the high old fashioned ceiling. The water pressure seemed inadequate to fill it further; so Garven and Bradley turned off the faucet and left the nozzle in place as a utilitarian cork.

Garven waited until the general stir over the prank had generated a sufficient crowd before he came as an innocent bystander to see what the excitement was all about. The crowd of easily entertained boys tittered and joked, calling out to anyone who was so uninformed as to have failed to know already about this latest outrage. Teenage boys in general, and preppies especially, enjoy outrages. This one was a rousing success, and a carnival atmosphere prevailed. Even Mr. Penrod betrayed a grudging approval, at least he laughed and mingled with the madding assembly of lads venting their pent-up stores of boyishness.

Gratefully, Mr. Penrod thought. *There had been no damage done.* He decided that the sport had gone on long enough and undid the hose from the balloon's entrance tube with some effort. He warned the crowd of boys beforehand, and they were all gratified to see a geyser of pent-up water force gush out of the window. Several of the boys stripped to their jockey shorts and played in the spray as a shallow lake formed in the grass. When the water level descended below the level of the window opening, the flow ceased outside and the balloon exit tube settled into the room. There was a small flood, about two feet deep, but minimal damage. The soaking wrecked the ancient worn rug and the venerable old school desk. Replacement cost exactly $412.28, a modest sum for a memorable deed.

Dr. Des Moines' letter, in his own handwriting, was apparently sent at random to ten fathers, not including Dr. Wilsonhulme or Tuckman Dreyer, as it turned out. It read:

May 18, 1946

Dear (First Name of Father),

A prank committed by several of the Burton-Cagle boys has had the unfortunate result of property damage to our institution. As you can well imagine, we are not in a position to sustain significant losses in these straitened times and must appeal to our generous parents committee for tax deductible contributions to cover the loss. My estimate of the value of the fine old antiques that were destroyed was more than a thousand dollars. They are irreplaceable, and although it is possible that we can find less expensive substitutes; still, the loss is substantial.

Our investigation to find the culprit(s) has revealed suggestive evidence implicating several of the students. I regret to inform you that your boy has been mentioned. You can rest assured that I have personally seen to it that the police were not involved. I look forward to hearing from you.
As always, cordially,

C.P. DM.
Carter P. Des Moines,
Headmaster

The Burton-Cagle Parents' Endowment Fund received ten separate contributions of $1000 each before the last day of school in 1946. There was never a formal accusation made against any boy in the unfortunate incident. Garven Wilsonhulme was not even questioned.

CHAPTER
Twelve

Dr. Elmo Jaccialetti, fourth generation Italian, was the favorite teacher of the junior students at Burton-Cagle even though his subject was chemistry. He spiced his lectures and labs with what he called "gee-whiz" chemistry. He poured red liquids into clear ones to produce green liquids. He made things foam and crackle and get hot. He showed the boys how to make the greatest slime in the world.

"Now, young gentlemen," he began. "This is serious and practical chemistry."

The boys all listened intently. Whenever Dr. Jaccialetti started a lab with that statement, there was going to be something good.

He mixed a fifty-fifty solution of 3-5% Polyvinyl alcohol with sodium borate (Borax) and a little green food coloring and whipped it very quickly with a kitchen whisk. The resulting product was enough to make the most impervious girl cringe. The reaction's yield was an ooze the consistency of fresh snot. Every student committed the lesson to the most carefully preserved section of his lab notebook.

Dr. Jaccialetti made a volcano by taking a cardboard cone he had made and filling it half-full of $NaHCO_3$ and then pouring copious amounts of 5% acetic acid (baking soda and vinegar). In another lab he enthralled the third year students with liquid nitrogen. He froze a full bloom rose which was rather pretty. Then he broke the petals off as if they were made of glass. The boys could readily see the practical value of that chemical process.

The talk among the juniors was how to come up with a chemical stunt to rival Pat and Garven's "H2Scapade" from their freshman year. The pranks ranged from spreading an inch thick rim of well-aged Limburger cheese around a student's locker door to making flashers of red phosphorus linked with a dynamite fuse lit to go off in a series during a chapel devotional, fairly prosaic stuff. Patrick Kilcannon spent sleepless nights trying to come up with a topper for the rotten egg gas caper that wouldn't burn the old school down or land them in jail.

Garven had some sense. He liked Patrick Kilcannon, but Pat knew no limits and had no fear. Garven shied away from two or three of Pat's general exploits when he reckoned in advance that someone was likely to get hurt. Patrick had an unfunny bone sometimes. One of the those times, Eric Slater broke his leg and was out of play for the entire soccer season. On another occasion, nearing spring break, Thomaso Guittierez-Pondosa, the son of a wealthy exporter from Venezuela, had been induced to make a rudimentary Molotov cocktail that was to be set off by a cherry bomb to provide fireworks for a beach party. The handsome young Venezuelan scion of a prominent family had dropped the dangerous Mason jar prematurely out of nervousness and had sustained moderately serious burns on his arm and torso.

Although Patrick was never implicated in the sad affair, owing to a rigid adherence to the schoolboy *Omerta,* Patrick's popularity rapidly declined. He had difficulty inveigling even freshmen in his schemes. Garven remained a steadfast friend, one of very few, until the end.

The end came when the subject in chemistry was the compounds of nitrogen. Patrick had listened with no more than desultory and occasional attention until the chemistry teacher touched cautiously on the nitrates and derivatives of nitric acid and their use as explosives. He discussed black gunpowder, an extremely finely ground mixture of potassium nitrate, charcoal, and sulfur. Patrick's serious attention was kindled by the laboratory experiment that demonstrated the manufacture of dynamite.

"Do not, I repeat, do not ever attempt to do any of this on your own," the teacher, Dr. Jaccialetti, demanded.

He was deadly serious. The man was fun and had a captivating sense of humor when it came to chemistry, but when he was serious about the dangers of an experiment, he was completely no-nonsense. Garven made a solemn personal vow to comply. The thought of messing with the explosive stuff was enough to make his skin prickle. The red phosphorus was enough. That had given him an unpleasant reminder of the night back in Cipher before he left for Burton-Cagle, when Edward Sespootch had lit the dynamite stick with a short fuse, and he and his friends had barely escaped being blown to bits. Patrick, on the other hand, found the discussion and even the warning invigorating and seemed to take the latter as a catalyst and a challenge.

"The most unfortunate thing about dynamite is how easy it is to make. First, you have to make one of our nitrogen products we have been studying, nitroglycerin. This compound is prepared by nitrating ordinary grocery shelf glycerin by mixing it with nitric acid."

In the lab, the teacher prevented the dilution of the nitric acid by the water formed in the reaction by adding concentrated sulfuric acid along with the nitric acid. He kept the nitroglycerin constrained in its liquid form and added it to wood pulp.

"Voila!" he exclaimed with careful scholarly enthusiasm. "Dynamite."

He cut off a tiny fragment of the crude dynamite and exploded it with a minuscule amount of fulminate of mercury from the locked laboratory safe as detonator. The explosion took place in the heavy lead box out of sight of the students, but they were impressed with the ominous sound.

"Okay, Garven," wheedled Patrick. "We have to make some dynamite or even TNT (The product, trinitrotoluene, of nitric acid reacting with toluene to form an explosive fusible crystalline solid). We can blow up the old root cellar above Des Moines's house. It would be the most spectacular stunt to ever take place at Burton-Cagle. We'll make history!"

"Not we, paleface," said Garven making reference to the old joke about the Lone Ranger who, when faced with Indians attacking from all sides, asked Tonto, "What do we do now, Tonto?" and Tonto made the only sensible reply, "Who's we, paleface?"

"Come on, don't turn chicken on me!" exclaimed Patrick hardly able to believe he was hearing his old co-conspirator sounding like a wimp.

"I would not touch any of that stuff with a frozen rope," Garven insisted firmly. "That stuff is really dangerous; it's no kid's prank to mess with it. I am not going to have anything to do with it, and that's final. Don't even talk to me about it."

Patrick made a derisive sound like an overgrown chicken clucking, and flopped his bent arms in a pantomime of a chicken; but Garven held firm. Evidently, no one else would have anything to do with any plot to make deadly nitrogen compounds either, to the credit of their store of common sense, and the subject was dropped forever, so far as Garven knew.

He and the school were shocked into a pall of gloom and mourning after the student body returned from spring break to learn that one of the most popular third year students, Patrick Stewart Kilcannon, had been blown up at his home. He had been exercising his curiosity by making rockets out of lead pipes filled with black powder. He had used a mining blasting cap secured from an industrial dump site as a detonator. The old blasting cap was lethally unstable, and the rocket, which was more accurately a bomb, exploded in the boy's hands as he closely scrutinized the attachment of the cap to the lead rocket tube. There was talk of canceling graduation that year, but, finally, the school and the boys compromised on a plan for all of the seniors to wear black arm bands and for the attendees of the graduation ceremonies to observe a moment of silence in Patrick's honor during commencement exercises.

******

Through the junior and senior years at Burton-Cagle, Garven Wilsonhulme became so facile with Latin that he could translate:

Macrobius, S., VI, 2, 16: *"Multa dies variusque labor mutabilis seve / rettulit in melius, multos alterna revisens/ lusit it in solido rusus fortuna locavit."* (Aen., XI, 425-7). Ennius in VIII.
"Multa dies in bello conficit unus…let rursus multae fortunae forte recumbunt; haudquaquam quemquam semper fortuna secuta est."

[Macrobius, quoting Virgil: "Many a day and change of work in ever-varying life have brought back countless men to better state; and fortune, her eye now here now there, has had the laugh and set men anew on foundation form."
-Ennius in the eighth book.
"Many things does one day bring about in war… and many fortunes through chance sink low again. In no wise has fortune followed any man all his days."]

And fluent enough in written German that he could decipher simple descriptions, although he could not say that he could handle anything complex or sophisticated; and his spoken German was that of a child, a grammatical child, but a child nonetheless. He could not talk on the phone or cope with the radio or a recording of anything but simple conversation. He could handle this level of translation:

Jetzt sind wir auf dem Campus. Dieses College ist eins derbesten im Lande. Mehr als virtausend Studenten and Studentinnen gehen hier zur Schule. Sid sin siebzehn bis einundzwanzig oder zweiundzwanzig Jahr alt. In unsere Campus befindet sich die englische Abteilung. Die englische Qbteilung is die grosste, den alle Studenten mussen in ihrem ersten Jar Englisch belegen.

[Now we are on the campus. This college is the best in the country. More than four thousand men and women students go to school here. They are seventeen to twenty-one years old. You find here the English department. The English department is the largest because all of the students in their first year must take English.]

He could translate from German to English and vice versa at about that level fairly consistently, and presumed that that represented an enviable accomplishment. It did not trouble him that all of scientific German and most conversation with educated Germans would be more complex and exacting, and that he would be found wanting.

Math was not his field, his avocation, his diversion, or his aptitude. He could manipulate fractions, decimal points, percentages, inverses, and do some story problems although he could not bring himself not to hate them.

Firewood is cut into logs and built in piles called cords. A cord is 8 ft. long 4 ft. wide and 4 ft. high. To estimate the number of cords of wood, find the number of cubic feet and divide by 128. How many cords of wood are in a pile 12 ft. long, 12 ft. high, and 8 ft. wide?

-

Lumber is measured by board feet. A board foot of lumber is 1 ft. long, 1 ft. wide, and 1 in. or less in thickness. To find the number of board feet, when lumber is more than 1 in. in thickness, multiply the length in feet by the breadth in feet, and this product by the number of inches in thickness. How many board feet in a sidewalk 100 yards long, 6 ft. wide, and 11/2 in. thick?

-

One path lacks 2 rods of being 5 times as long as another. If both paths together equal 124 rods, how long is each?

-

A locomotive weighing 888 tons is going up an 8% grade at 8 miles per hour burning $8 worth of coal each hour. At the 8th hour, how much will it cost to blow the whistle?

Algebra was his weakest subject. If ever there was anything more useless and a source of plain annoyance, Garven had yet to find it. It bothered him no end that he was going to have to do more algebra when he got to college. It would probably be even harder than he had been subjected to at Burton-Cagle, he groused.

Garven learned to tolerate poetry, to find the deep inner meaning, even though he never believed for a minute that the poets actually wrote such hidden pearls. He personally accepted the poems at face value and pretended on paper to understand his English teacher's enthusiasms. His senior English paper had been, "The Wisdom from the Shakespearean Sonnets". He liked and commented with some conviction on *Sonnet 73*:

> "That time of year thou mayst in me behold
> When yellow leaves, or none, or few, do hang
> Upon those boughs which shake against the cold,
> Bare ruined choirs, where late the sweet birds sang.
> In me thou see'st the twilight of such day
> As after sunset fadeth in the west,
> Which by and by black night doth take away,
> Death's second self that seals up all in rest.
> In me thou see'st the glowing of such fire,
> That on the ashes of his youth doth lie,
> As the death-bed, whereon it must expire
> Consumed with that which it was nourished by.
> This thou perceiv'st, which makes thy love more strong
> To love that well, which thou must leave ere long.

Garven said, "In summary and in brief, medieval Shakespeare painted word pictures, images of sight and feelings, that teach profound lessons about life, acceptance, and love. He took the mundane and cyclic observations about fall, sunset, and twilight and let the quiet pleasure we can take from them be a comfort against the inevitable expiration of the day's fire and the coming of night and even death. Like Thoreau, who counseled that we should 'suck out the marrow of life', Shakespeare admonished the pursuit of love—to make it strong. Since no one can stave off the awful day, we can only make the most of the time we have, and we can do that by loving 'that well, which thou must leave ere long'."

Unlike most young men about to leave high school and to tackle the next challenge, Garven took mental stock of himself and of his aptitudes, accomplishments, and preparedness. Like most such young men, he found himself more than adequate, even quite impressive. He could read and write Latin and German. He had completed the math courses acceptably at one of the nation's most prestigious preparatory schools. He was able to converse grammatically and sensibly with the intelligentsia, recite the table of elements from memory, balance chemical equations, describe accurately the interrelationships of the several bodies of the United States government, spell, use the correct fork when three were presented, discuss the Bible as literature, and had a passing knowledgeable familiarity with Kant, Hume, Augustine, John Dewey, Don Quixote, Woodrow Wilson, FDR, the great religions, and with the planet's geography.

Garven C. Wilsonhulme, standing at the threshold of college and the rest of his life, and after careful deliberation pronounced himself fit and ready—a fine specimen of young manhood with an excellent future, indeed. In the arrogance of his youth with its selective memory and its susceptibility to suggestion from liberal instructors and other people with no experience with doing work with their hands, he could ignore the salient fact that he, unlike many of his less privileged contemporaries, lacked any marketable skills. He was all potential, nothing experiential, unless you could count his expertise at breaking horses on the reservation and executing pranks. Garven could not plow a straight row, dismantle and repair a carburetor, cook a dinner, lay a smooth cement sidewalk, bale hay, erect a scaffold, type sixty words a minute, estimate board feet in a standing pine tree, splice a wire, unplug a stuck toilet, swiftly and accurately manipulate the numbers on a spreadsheet, or do his own taxes; and he did not have respect for those who could. In that way, he was typical of his classmates and the rarefied social stratum wherein they dwelt. He felt that he had come of age and was a paradigm of his class, a long way from Cipher, Arizona, population 141.

******

"The boys of this venerable school have received the finest education available in the United States, in the world, I dare say," the commencement speaker was saying. "The class of 1948 is now part of the history of the school; they came as boys, and they leave as men, men who are well-prepared for the challenges of the future. If their record is any indicator, and I think it is, these young men will wear the mantle of leadership proudly and with distinction in the predictably foreseeable future."

Garven was standing bored and impatient to be on his way. He stood next to Evan Zabriski, where he always did when there was an official line. The two boys had the last two names in the alphabet in their class, and by virtue of the many queues in which they had stood, had come to be good conversational friends. Both of the young men were over warm in their black graduation gowns and wanted little more than for the endless speeches to be done and to have the certificate of graduation in hand. They had worked hard enough for it.

Dr. Des Moines gave his yearly speech:

"Let me share with you the accomplishments of the class of 1948; the best in Burton-Cagle's history, I might add. There are forty-seven young men graduating out of a starting class of fifty. Of these forty-seven, one hundred percent are going to college. They accumulated a grade point average of 3.81, a full point better than last year, and two hundredths of a point better than the best GPA ever achieved here."

He paused for the seniors to cheer.

He went on, "You might be interested in the colleges these fine scholars will attend in the fall. We have four men starting at Harvard, a full six at Yale, four at Stanford."

Garven tended to lose interest after Stanford was mentioned. He was going to Stanford. The only other guy he knew about that was going to Stanford was David Applegate.

Lyle Durche and even Edward Sespootch had come to the graduation with his mother and his new dad, Dr. Wilsonhulme. Dad had insisted and paid the transportation and keep for the two friends from Cipher and was ebullient with enthusiasm as he squired the awestruck Cipher boys around the impressive campus. It was the first time either of them had been outside the Arizona border; it was the first time Edward had been in a suit. He was uncomfortable, but it was worth it. He was bursting with unselfish pride for his old buddy, Garven. Garven had been kind of stuck up in his fancy school blazer, his English straw hat, and the striped school tie. Edward guessed that he was just showing off; he could tell that Garven was real glad to see an old friend from home. He needed to be able to brag to someone and the old friends were willing listeners.

"Seven of our boys were qualifiers in the finals of the national merit scholarships, two will have full rides. The senior and junior varsity soccer teams took the championships this year; the baseball team came in a squeaky close second in the Western Prep Leagues world series; and our tennis team just about took a clean sweep in the Prep League and in the state finals. We are proud of these young men."

Rachel was proud. She could not keep from crying every time she thought of the transition her son had made. He came to this awesome school a scared hick, she had to admit; but he was leaving on an equal plane with the *cremè de la cremè*.

"Our seniors have completed their courses in Greek, Latin, higher math, college level English, advanced writing, government, and, as you know, it is a requirement that every graduate be proficient in a modern foreign language. They have each written a graduate thesis. I have read many of them; they are fine original work."

"Not likely," thought Garven. His thesis had been the admission of the territory of Arizona as a state—The *Ditat Deus* state. It had been easy; he had gotten a raft of information from the state library when he was home for the summer before the '47-'48 school year. He copied most of it. Who was ever going to check in Arizona? He was pretty sure that most of the rest of the thesis papers were of similar scholarship quality.

"Now comes the moment we have been waiting for," said the headmaster. "This is what the boys have anticipated as much as the actual receiving of their diplomas. I will read the names of the recipients of the special awards; and as I do, I would like the young man to step up to the podium to receive the award and your applause."

Garven's academic record had been okay, more than okay, but not good enough to compete with the top ten from whom the valedictorian and salutatorian were selected. He did not have any illusions about getting an award. The names were read, and the proud young men graciously accepted the adulation of the pleased parents, faculty, and undergraduates. Garven received the Senior Sports Award, to his embarrassed pleasure. It was great, and he was totally surprised. He saw the pride on Edward and Lyle's faces.

"At last, we come to the highest award the school can bestow. Some years, we do not deem any graduate worthy to have the award. In fact, the Burton-Cagle Gold Medal has been given out only twenty-seven times in the school's forty-three-year history."

He glossed over the fact that the medal had only been introduced thirty-five years ago, eight years after the school's founding.

"The award is a combination of academic, sports, and service excellence. It is not ordinarily or necessarily given to the valedictorian, to the Prep League sports champion, or to the boy who logs the most hours in the schools service project of helping the poor of our community. Instead, it is reserved for the unusual individual that excels in all of these areas; it takes into consideration

141

the extent of growth the student has made at Burton-Cagle. In short, the Burton-Cagle Gold Medal is our attempt to measure the refinement of the best representative of our tradition. We always expect great things from our gold medalist."

Dr. Des Moines allowed an expectant silence to reign.

There was a shuffling, a minor agitation. The prestigious award would be an important door opener for its recipient. There was considerable ambition attached to the headmaster's words. Forty-seven sets of parents leaned forward expectantly.

"Garven Carmichael Wilsonhulme! Will you step forward!" Headmaster Des Moines announced. *"Ad astra per aspera! Ad augusta per angusta!"* [Through hardships to the stars! Through difficulties to honors!]

There was a momentary hush. Some were surprised, even shocked, at the unexpected medalist; some were dismayed and could not express their disbelief; and a solid four members of the audience were so thrilled they could not utter a sound at first. Edward Sespootch broke the quiet with a blood-chilling war whoop, the likes of which had never been heard in the staid halls of the dignified old preparatory school. Edward's unrestrained expression of joy and unselfish pride in his friend's accomplishment was so infectious that the reserve of the exclusive audience gave way to laughter and shouted praise. It was the best single moment in the life of Garven Wilsonhulme of Cipher, Arizona. His friends among the Apaches and the coyotes of his home town basked in his glow.

CHAPTER
Thirteen

In late August 1949, Garven drove alone from Cipher to Palo Alto and Stanford, California and onto the Stanford University campus in his nearly new 1948 Chevy coupe, the graduation present from his dad. He slipped into the handsome cashmere camel hair sport coat his mother had scrimped for a year to give him, and walked into the administration building to get directions. There were hundreds of bright and confident looking students accompanied by their proud and successful looking parents. Garven felt very much alone and lacking in self-confidence as he joined the throng asking the same set of questions of the painfully bored secretary.

He was given an agenda for freshman orientation week, a copy of the university student rules and regulations, a campus map, and an envelope with his name on it that contained a letter from the counselor to whom he had been assigned, and his dorm room assignment and a key. So far things were not so different from Burton-Cagle, just bigger; and he had survived there, even the period of home-sickness; and he guessed he would do all right here. Although Garven was apprehensive and nervous about entering the prestigious and academically demanding institution of learning, and was a little awed by the sheer size of the place; at least, he was not homesick. That had been a very painful period in his life as a fourteen-year-old, and he thought he could see suggestions of his remembered feelings in the faces of some of his classmates, the entering freshmen.

Garven lugged his suitcase up the stairs to the third floor of his dormitory which was named Madera House, a part of the Wilbur Hall freshman residence. He was glad that he had only the one bag with all his belongings because of the considerable distance he had had to carry it from the parking lot and to his room that was on the far end of the top floor hall. Each dorm had three floors and only one gender of occupants. The rooms were occupied by two students to a room, and Alan Crowder, his new roommate, was already there when Garven walked in with his big suitcase.

"Hey, man!" the pudgy and hail-fellow-well-met occupant of the room effused. "I'd guess you're Garven Wilsonhulme since your name was on the door below mine, and you're the last guy to arrive."

"Good guess," Garven puffed, winded from the carry and the climb. He managed a smile even though the guy seemed like a dork.

"I'm Alan Crowder, pleased to meet you." Alan said extending his hand.

It was soft and fat and clammy just as Garven had expected.

"Garven Carm... uh, Wilsonhulme," he said shaking the other fellow's hand.

He realized that he was more nervous than he thought and that he must feel a little inferior to the other guys to have almost reverted to his original name.

"Can I help you carry your stuff up here. Its a long ways, isn't it?"

"It's a long ways. But, no, thanks; this is everything."

Alan gave him a brief quizzical look and involuntarily tossed a fleeting glance at his own four suitcases and pile of books, papers, pens, typewriter, notebooks, and toiletries. His and Garven's eyes met as he did so, and Alan started to laugh.

"My mother packed my stuff," he said by way of explanation.

After he moved his things onto the desk and into the closet on his side of the room, he and Alan went up and down the hall to meet the other boys who were walking up and down the halls to meet the other boys. They chatted in each of the dorm rooms, usually with the parents who were reluctant to depart and to leave their sons alone for the first time in their lives. Garven saw a greater abundance of possessions than he had ever seen collected in one place before. The boys at Burton-Cagle had been rich, but space did not permit them to display their abundance at the prep school. At Stanford, the parents and the boys were determined to make room. Tempers flared as one roommate encroached on the space of another.

Freshman orientation week agenda required a meeting with the student's advisor in the morning and formal class registration in the afternoon. Garven's advisor meeting was late in the morning since "Wilsonhulme" fell in the nether end of the alphabet. The process was made as easy as possible because the upper classmen would not be arriving for another week for their registration. Classes started Tuesday next.

Garven put on his best slacks, shirt, sport jacket, and tie and went to the medical school offices to meet with his assigned counselor. Heinreich von Tauben, M.D., PhD was listed as Garven and six other freshmen's counselor because there had been such an overload of premeds signing up in 1949. Dr. von Tauben was disgruntled at the prospect of interrupting his research on the physics of heart action for such mundanities and was determined to allow no more than fifteen minutes per student. He would get through the whole process in the one morning and be done with it for the year if he had anything to say in the matter. Dr. von Tauben was not about to be anyone's surrogate father; these were adults. Once he had laid out the proper schedule for their studies at the university, they were on their own.

Garven was the last premed counselee of the morning and, by then, Dr. von Tauben's nerves were frayed and his usually short attention span for such university duties had been exceeded.

"Come in, young man; take a seat," he ordered, his Teutonic background and Prussian accent showing through its threadbare cover.

Garven sat.

"I take it that you are interested in a career in medicine, young man. Not so?"

"Yes, Sir," Garven answered nervously. "I wish to be a doctor."

Dr. von Tauben abruptly interrupted Garven.

"Don't give me 'wishes'. If 'wishes were fishes, we'd have a good fry. If horse turds were biscuits, we'd eat 'till we die' I think is the old American saw. You have to do the work. That is why I am here—to guide you. Please listen carefully."

Garven was expecting to get information to get off to a good start, particularly in mapping out the curriculum for a premedical education, about which he had only the sketchiest idea. He has also determined to make a good impression. Who knew? This man could make a difference of whether or not he was accepted to a good medical school and seemed to know the straight and correct way to his goal. Garven was attentive.

"Now down to business. I have spent fifteen years of preparation for my present work and will not bore you by making this a discussion. I will give you the benefit of my experience in an efficient manner and leave you to realize the wisdom of the program I have outlined for you as time passes. Here is your schedule for the next four years, all carefully worked out."

Garven had not expected the premedical course to be quite that cut and dried, and studied the course schedule before him quickly and with an occasional frown.

"Young man, you will see that there are several areas where choices and substitutes can be made," Dr. von Tauben said with as pleasant a face as he could muster, knowing how the young Americans cherished the concept of choice and the young man before him would appreciate his thoughtfulness.

The areas of substitution were all in the unimportant area of the humanities.

"But, there are to be no substitutes for the science courses nor for the study of German, the language of science."

"Thank you, Sir," Garven mumbled, overwhelmed at the magnitude of the task before him.

Since the young man seemed disinclined to converse, and the doctor was feeling the pressure to get back to his duties, von Tauben asked brusquely, "Have you any further questions, any way I can be of service as your counselor?"

"I can't think of anything right now. It's all pretty new to me, Sir. I guess I just take your word for it and register this afternoon."

"That's a fine attitude, young fellow. Although I am of the opinion that we already have far too many physicians in practice in the United States, perhaps you will be able to apply yourself and find your place in a good research institution or, failing that, persevere to become a specialist in one of the areas of need. The country doesn't need another GP in our lifetimes, I'd venture to say. Well, if that's all, let me wish you a successful stay at the university. If you have any further questions or need for assistance, don't fail to call on the advisor for premed, Dr. Carter, in zoology. We at the medical school value his efforts and his recommendations highly."

Dr. von Tauben shifted his attention to the important materials on his desk and purposefully picked up the pen he had been absentmindedly twiddling with from time to time to signal that the counseling session was over.

Garven exited without so much as receiving a second glance from the busy academician and found a bench on the quad that was occupied by only one other freshman, a dowdy girl who, gratefully, did not indicate any need to engage in conversation. He unfolded the schedule sheet prepared for him on legal size paper and neatly typed by the counselor's secretary. The first quarter of work consisted of twenty credit hours made all the easier by the inclusion of a physical education course worth three hours, Garven's choice as to the exact activity to be determined by him. Twenty hours did not seem like so much, and the young man wondered briefly at the small script, nearly illegible, handwritten note in the margin, "This will build your character."

Most of the classes outlined were pretty straightforward, Garven reasoned; Freshman this and Introductory that. He had English Composition, German, Chemistry, Physics, Botany, History of Western Civilizations, and the free choice PE class. That sounded like a lot of class time every day until Garven studied the University Course Handbook to find out that the classes met only three times during a week, or even only twice as in the case of Botany and "Hist. West. Civ.", as the Handbook abbreviated it. His registration packet had a practice sheet in the form of a calendar to permit him to arrange his classes in a plausible and doable fashion. After the first go-around, Garven switched to using a pencil because the times the classes were offered kept conflicting with other classes. It was a frustrating experience. Garven could not see why they did not simply use the format that Burton-Cagle had. It seemed an unnecessarily complicated process.

He had not finished by lunchtime and discovered that he was very hungry. He had a pass for the lunch line for the first week but would have to buy his card for the full quarter by Wednesday. That was the deadline for all certifications: library, student body association, athletic and cultural activities, and for registration to be on any of the freshman teams. The administrative tasks before him seemed daunting, to say nothing about the actual classes. He elected to forget about them all for the time being, and to take his place in the lunch line with the other ninety occupants of Madera House.

The lunch line was predictably slow, which Garven had anticipated based on his experience at Burton-Cagle. The servers were obviously college students whose enthusiasm was, on a scale of one to ten, about a minus three. But the food itself was a revelation. He and his fellow prep school students had joked about their institution having put saltpeter in the mashed potatoes to calm the raging hormones of the boys, but saltpeter would have improved the flavor of the fare at Madera House. There was white bread, macaroni and processed cheese, mashed reconstituted potatoes, canned string beans, and an amorphous patty that the unsmiling server called "mystery meat". There was the same fruit-flavored punch made from industrial powder that institutions all over the world buy from the same outlet and which carefully avoided any contamination with real fruit juice. There was also the option of drinking the reconstituted dry milk powder that no one selected. Garven guessed this balanced meal had balanced out the protein.

He crowded into a table for six with three guys from the second floor and four from the first. There was not much talk until the boys had stuffed themselves. They were all still a little unsatisfied; but, while it was okay to go back for seconds of everything but the meat (using the term loosely), no one thought it was worth waiting in the still long line again for more of the carbohydrates. The questions were predictable:

"How'd you like the slop du jour?"

"Where're you from?"

"Whatch're major?"

"Whatch're dad do?"

"What high school'ju go to?"

"Oh, yeah? Did you know...Steve Patterson, the all-state quarterback?... Emily Langston, the one with the scrumdolious set of knockers when she was a ninth grader?... Marko Antonovich, who kicked the crap out of the Milwaukee High fullback, what was his name?... Remember where we used to meet after the East High games and go get smashed... Reggies' Diner—no ID, no hassle, just high prices for anyone who didn't look twenty-one?"

"Goin' out for football? Track? Lacrosse? Golf? Nothing? Really, nothing?"

The answers had only a little more variety but the same general predictability:

"Milwaukee. Hey, me too... Phoenix, Arizona... LA... San Diego... Winston-Salem. That's in North Carolina. Oh, yeah? Sounds like England."

"Premed...Pre-law... Pre-dent... Premed... Zoology ...Can you make a living in Zoology?... Engineering.... What kind? Civil... Electrical... Chemical... Premed."

"Doctor... Lawyer... Dentist... Surgeon... Biology professor... Civil engineer... Electrical engineer... Chemical engineer... Doctor."

"Milwaukee West High... Milwaukee East High... Burton-Cagle School in Pacific Palisades, California... Glendale High in The Valley... San Diego Union High... Wake Forest Prep School; it's by the Blue Ridge Mountains."

"Oh, yeah, I remember him.... Oh, yeah do I remember her. You should have seen her sister.... I heard it was Antonovich who got his clock cleaned.... Reggies' got closed down, I heard.... We had a grocery store on Garner and the expressway that didn't check as long as you went after ten when Sid Mason or Manny Pachecho were on. Didn't cost extra."

"I'm gonna try.... I was alternate all-state half my senior year.... Maybe, but I'm probably too little. I saw the varsity; they're monsters.... Nah, I gotta study, premed, you know....What's lacrosse?... Really?... My dad said I only got in here because he was a veep of the alumni. I spent enough time in high school on football. He says it's time to get on with the real world; I guess he's right. Everybody's gotta make a living..... Not even golf?"

Registration was a nightmare, even without the upper classmen. The entire process took place in a single room, the gym floor at the Athletics Center. There were rows of collapsible tables identified by placards attached to slat-wood uprights as being the registration desk for one class or another. Garven plunged into the center of the thronging milieu. After waiting in a stupid line for what seemed like half and hour, he was told he was five minutes early; they weren't quite ready for the Ws. The 100 series of physics were all filled. He could take the 150 series for honors students; they would waive the special requirements.

The grad student manning the botany desk looked at him quite seriously, "You sure you want to take botany? It's a 200 series. I don't know why they don't make frosh biology a prerequisite," he said.

"My premed counselor told me I had to take it, and this quarter, no fail," Garven said holding back his exasperation.

He still had four more lines to stand in and a trip to the coaches' office to sign up for some team. He had not even decided on which one yet.

"No skin off my back," the grad student said and shrugged his shoulders as he recorded one more student for the make-or-break class for zoo majors.

"You'll be-e soo-rry."

The chemistry series was only taught at ten on MWF, which conflicted with the physics series; so, Garven had to go back through the physics line again. The physics course then conflicted with the time for his botany lab; so, he had to go back through the botany line again.

The grad student smiled smugly, "Back for more punishment? Maybe I can interest you in Problems in Tropical Botany?"

"Thanks just the same," Garven said bitingly. He was going nuts.

Four hours had elapsed, and the tables were starting to be dismantled before he got all of his classes verified. He still had to see the premed counselor and to get to some coach. He was a mess.

Dr. Carter was a taciturn, crisp, no-nonsense authoritarian. His face was frozen in a perpetual downturn.

"One more doctor to be?" he asked with a taint of sarcasm.

"Yes, Sir," Garven answered, determined to put himself in the best light he could.

His dad had warned him about Dr. Carter—the man had more influence on whether or not a guy got into med school than any other single person at Stanford.

"Let's see your schedule. Half of you take a basket-weaving major and skip all the hard sciences until you're seniors and then wonder why the med schools don't just grab you up, what with your high GPAs and all."

Garven figured he wouldn't be faulted for having a basket-weaving major.

"Pretty stiff schedule…Mr. Wilsonhulme. You sure about this?"

"Well, yeah. I mean, Dr. von Tauben said I should take these. What do I know, Sir?" Garven asked, his voice tired.

"Von Tauben again. You're the sixth premed in here today with this schedule. That old German still has you all signing up for the pre-Hitler schedule. If you survive, you'll be the best educated scientist the university can produce."

"I hope so."

"You can drop out of any class without getting an incomplete before two weeks into the quarter. If you find you can't hack this schedule, get back to me. I'm in the Zoology Building. Good luck."

Dr. Carter was already looking at the next young man's papers and was motioning him forward. Garven staggered out of the huge room and found his way to the signups for athletic teams.

"Too small," he heard at the football desk.

"No experience, no tryout," he heard at the swimming and lacrosse desks.

"Come and see us if you can run the 220 in under 34, the 100 in 13, or can clear 5-2 with a western roll in the high jump. Otherwise forget it," he heard at the track and field office.

Garven forgot it.

"Hey, great! C'mon in. We can use a wiry guy like you. Whadda you go, 130?" came the first positive response, this time from the wrestlers.

He should have got the hint when he looked around for the coach and found only wrestlers.

"More like 136," Garven replied. He was warming to these enthusiasts.

"You can starve down. We really need someone in the 130-pound class. Right now you won't have any competition. Whadda you say?"

"I don't have any experience."

"We'll teach you."

"Who's the coach?"

"He couldn't be here today," Garven looked at the guy's face to see if his nonanswer had been intentional or just an oversight.

"Is Stanford any good? I mean, you do okay in the PAC?"

"Okay. We're kind of a new team."

"How new?"

The two wrestlers at the sign-up table looked at each other sheepishly.

"Hey, c'mon. Give it a try. It's a great sport. You can be on the varsity team even when you are a freshman. All the girls can't wait to groove with the varsity players. It's the big time."

"How new?" Garven persisted.

"Around two years," the wrestler flinched as he admitted it.

"I'll think about it," Garven said, but in reality, the alternatives were not all that available or desirable.

He wasn't going to get on one of the glamour teams, and no one but the nerds played intramurals. Why not give it a try?

"Look, so it's not Iowa or Minnesota. You can get in on the ground floor here—chance to be a big fish in a little pond, maybe."

Garven shuffled his feet and knitted his brow in concentration. The two wrestlers could detect the nibble at their bait and kept quiet to avoid interrupting the positive looking turn of facial expression.

"How often do you workout?" Garven asked.

"Every afternoon before supper. And you gotta run every morning to get into shape. That's crucial."

"What if I miss some practices?"

"You'll be like everybody else. Look, we're a small bunch. We look out for each other. It's a good way to get an 'in' to the fun stuff at Stanford. You'll like it. You look like you can handle yourself."

"Oh, what the heck! I'll do it," Garven said finally.

For better or for worse, Garven Wilsonhulme had just made the Stanford Varsity Wrestling Team.

There was no supper at Madera House that first night because of the Jolly-up at Florence Moore, the main girls' dorm. The traditional Jolly-up was the welcoming party for all incoming freshmen and had been held the last Monday night in August for twenty-five years. Garven was starved, and if nothing else good came of the introductory party, he could expect to get some decent food, maybe even some protein that was called something besides "mystery meat". He figured he had better not miss any opportunity for a little protein. He washed the frustration and anxiety of the day off in a cool shower.

The nervous freshmen milled about; the men surreptitiously eyeing the women and vice versa. That took Garven all of ten minutes. Most of the females ranged from plain to skaggy. Even Cipher, Arizona had more good looking girls, he decided. Five, to be exact. It was obviously true, what they said about beauty and brains not going together. He went to a food-laden table surrounded by a bunch of freshmen and some upperclassmen, all of whom appeared to be jocks and began to forage with them. The evening was not going to be a total loss.

"You were the right half for Hollywood High. Varsity, right? That's gotta mean something. I can't see how Troy Denton got a scholarship, and they wouldn't give you a tumble. You oughta go see Coach Woods personally. Maybe you can work something out. Even a walk-on is a reasonable shot here. We need some good meat, let me tell you," the most gregarious upperclassman was saying to the muscular blond freshman.

"I'm gonna be on that team. I got a lotta hustle. I'll make it. I'm not gonna take it personal that I didn't get a scholarship," the heavyset freshman replied earnestly.

Garven was so small in comparison to the jocks around the table that, at first, he had trouble being noticed. The conversation drifted in and out of football, and Garven was able to contribute at intervals because he had learned very early at Burton-Cagle that an almost encyclopedic knowledge of football and baseball were essential for making your way into the ranks of the campus and other movers and shakers. His knowledge did not come from any particular enthusiasm; he studied the sports in a calculated way. It stood him in good stead now.

After a while, when the subject of football was beginning to wane in the group's interest, another of the upperclassmen football players took notice of the wiry, sandy haired kid with all the latest facts.

"You a jock?" he asked

"Yeah," Garven answered. "I'm a wrestler," he said flatly.

"That so?" The older jock was more interested. "I heard our wrestling team wasn't so hot."

"That used to be the case. We're going to change that all around this year. Got some new meat. Watch what happens."

"You varsity?"

"Yeah."

"You sure? I'd have taken you for a freshman."

"I am. You can be on the varsity squad as a freshman in the individual sports."

"Like tennis?"

"Um hum."

"How'd you get to be on the varsity? You must be pretty good, huh? The team hasn't even had tryouts yet, I'd bet."

"Got a scholarship," Garven answered and wondered why he had felt the need to tell a white lie. Anyway, this guy wouldn't know the difference.

"Jeez, really? That's something!"

Garven was feeling a surge. The opportunity to embellish was inescapable.

"I told them I wouldn't come otherwise. It's not like it's Iowa or Minnesota, you know," he went on.

He was beginning to have something of the feeling of being a fish in the pond, at least. It would take a little more to feel like a big fish.

"Hey, Denny," the jock said to his crony. "This guy's on the varsity, and he's only a starting freshman!"

Dirk asked Garven, "What varsity?"

"Wrestling."

"Oh, yeah, that's great. Wrestling is a good sport, gives the little guys a chance, you know? It's not the size of the dog in the fight," Dirk said. "It's the size of the fight in the dog."

Garven thought the guy could have gone all night without making that observation about his size.

The remark was not ill-intended, and Garven was drawn into the group even after the subject changed several times. He was feeling good, getting full, and thought he was going to make it here. He, then and there, decided to be the best wrestler in Stanford's history.

A cooking pot gong was sounded to get everyone's attention. It took two more gongs and a bellow from the master of ceremonies before the crowd quieted down enough to listen to the program.

"I've got a few announcements for you, freshmen," the master of ceremonies, a senior, yelled once the noise began to subside. "First, the frats have to leave you alone for two weeks. No contact until the fifteenth of September, that's two weeks before pledge night. You should report any violations to the Greek council. Second, the frosh party will be at Half Moon Bay this year…again, and you will board buses Wednesday night by dormitory floors, no exceptions. Third, the administration decided the party can't be a weenie roast this year, too suggestive, I guess."

The girls tittered, and the jocks laughed uproariously. Garven joined them even though he did not think it was all that funny.

"Fourth, or third or wherever I was, the bonfire on Friday night for the Big Game on Saturday will be the sole responsibility of the Class of 1953. See me about where to get the wood. I have to tell you that the usual jerks from Menlo Junior College and the Neanderthals from Palo Alto will do their very best to light the bonfire on Thursday like they always try to do. You wouldn't want it to be said that you were the only class in the history of Big Game Bonfires to fail to protect your stack of kindling. The honor of your class is at stake."

"Fifth… now that has a nice ring."

Everyone laughed.

"Fifth, there is to be no, and I mean *no* violence around that bonfire. That comes straight from the president. He doesn't intend to see a repeat of last year's debauchery… And I quote."

Everyone laughed heartily. "Last year's debauchery" was infamous. It had been the biggest and best debauchery in the history of Big Game Bonfire parties.

"So, no repeat of the fighting and drinking and slipping off into the shadows like last year, understand?" And in a prominent stage whisper, "And like the year before, and the year before, and the year before that."

The crowd was laughing and warming up to each other now.

"We do not want to have an improper tradition at Leland Stanford, Jr. University. And again, I quote," the master of ceremonies said in all mock-seriousness.

The class of 1953 was developing real enthusiasm for an improper tradition now.

"Six… You know, it's been so long. I've come to think of that as nothing more than the number between five and seven."

There was a noticeable quiet and a puzzled look on the frosh faces. The seniors, there as chaperones, had heard the spiel before and began to laugh. A few of the more raunchy freshmen boys caught the reference and laughed with them. So did several others who had no idea why they were laughing.

"Enough of this kind of talk about sex. I am directed to call your attention to rule twelve in the handout about rules and regulations you received. If you would be so kind as to follow along with me."

He made an elaborate effort at straightening his paper and adjusted his glasses to read the aforementioned rule.

"There will be no inappropriate PDAs."

He paused for effect.

A serious girl, who looked like a plain but certainly a nice girl, raised her hand and asked politely, "What is a PDA?"

"Public Display of Affection."

There were hoots.

"I will disregard the rowdies in the gathering," the master of ceremonies said looking offended. "Let us continue. These are serious matters, ladies and gentlemen."

"Rule Thirteen in the official rules and regulations for student behavior at Leland Stanford, Jr. University…doesn't it make you proud to be going to a junior university?"

The crowd laughed enthusiastically. He had gotten them by surprise with that quip.

"Rule Thirteen, like its predecessor, concerns fraternization between the genders. The sexes, if you will. This regulation strictly limits the visitation rights of those of the masculine gender in the habitations, specifically, the dormitory rooms, of those of the feminine gender. The matrons of Dormant Hall… "

He allowed time for the appreciative chuckles to ripple forth at his accidentally on purpose mispronunciation of the correct Dorman Hall which was the old name for Florence Moore Hall as it was now called after the rich benefactress.

"The forces for good in our community, these guardians of virtue, will not permit any male to be in any female's room at any time. That's certainly clear and simple, isn't boys and girls? You will be subject to the mercies of the faculty and student disciplinary council for any infraction. In short, you will be expelled forthwith. A word to the wise.

"I have been privy to the councils of the University that breathe only rarefied air, and I can announce with pleasure that a lounge will be provided at Dormant and at Feebles, forgive me, I mean, Peebles (the irreverent sobriquet for Crothers Hall, so called because of Jessica Peebles, who had lived there the first year after its dedication, and who supposedly had preached free-love. It was more wishful thinking than anything), where men may be seated in the same room as women on a social basis during daylight hours—until six on weekdays and until ten on Fridays and Saturdays. There will be a chaperone, one of the forces for good in our community, present at all times, you will be pleased to know."

The freshman class gave a collective groan then laughed at the image.

"Let me caution again about those PDAs," he concluded his recitation of the announcements and the regulations.

He took a sip of his drink. It looked suspiciously like beer, but since no alcoholic beverage consumption was permitted on Stanford campus, Garven presumed it must be ginger ale.

"Now, for some statistics about our beloved alma mater. First, about the ladies."

He adjusted his glasses and pretended to read from a paper on his podium.

"Ah, yes. We have more women enrolled this year than in any year in the past. That is Really Fine. Absolutely R.F.!"

At that, for some inexplicable reason, the seniors began to laugh uproariously. The freshmen looked bewildered.

"I don't get it," Garven said to the senior jock standing next to him.

It was evident that the rest of the younger members of the audience didn't get it either because they were all making the same comment to their nearest upperclassman.

"Really Fine is long for R.F., which really means…uh, how can I say it in polite society?"

His jock friend clapped both hands over the ears of the nearest freshman girl and said, "This isn't polite society anymore, go ahead and say it."

"I'm sensitive," the first jock giggled and blushed, to his chagrin. "It means 'rodent fornication' or some variation."

Garven thought the guy was hurting for material. He looked around to see if anyone else was looking bored with the inanities. Seeing no one, he put on a having-fun face like the faces that he met. The murmur fluttered through the crowd, and, shortly, everyone was chuckling at the Stanford tradition to which they had just been introduced. Even the very proper girls smiled indulgently to show that they were good sports.

"More statistics," the master of ceremonies continued when the audience would let him. "If all of the girls in the freshman class, the class of 1953, were laid end to end… " he paused and looked about with a serious demeanor… "I wouldn't be surprised."

He was gratified by the general whoops of laughter from the crowd that had warmed up completely now. He was having a good time.

"It is my duty to tell you how the Stanford Honor Code works. I know you are all thinking that the students have the system, and the teachers have the honor. Not so. Seriously, it's simple: Exams are conducted on the honor system. You sit in chairs three seats apart and in alternate rows. I remember my freshman trig class. I asked one of my friends who was about as much of a mathematician as I was how far he had been from the correct answer on our midterm. He said, 'Two seats'. I said, 'Well, I proved that X is equal to zero.' My friend said, 'All that work for nothing.'"

The laughs were beginning to diminish, and Garven found himself getting bored and yawning. He got up as unobtrusively as he could and quietly made for the door. In the hallway by the door he met a tall, lean young man, probably a freshman, who was putting on a windbreaker and headed for the exit himself. Garven held the door open for him.

The other young man said, "Hi, I'm Frosty McTavish, 'Forest' to those who don't know me or to professors."

"Garven Wilsonhulme. Pleased to meet you, Frosty."

As they were closing the door, they caught the master of ceremonies' last feeble joke, "Dean Winslow has stated firmly that he is going to stop smoking at Stanford, if it is the last thing he does. I think that is great of him, don't you? Next thing, though, he'll be trying to get the students to stop, too."

Frosty rolled his eyes, and Garven laughed at Frosty.

The two boys stepped out into the cool fall evening.

"I've had enough for one day. Guy was kinda funny, but he was trying too hard at the last," Frosty said.

Garven nodded in agreement.

"You're in Madera, aren't you, Garven?"

"Third floor. You, too?"

"First."

"Are you going to the welcoming party at Half Moon Bay and the bonfire stuff?" asked Garven.

"I really hadn't planned to, if you want to know the truth," Frosty answered. "I am something less than a social animal at best, and the rah-rah stuff isn't my forte."

"Me neither. I'm glad to find someone else who isn't such a phony. The rah-rah is bad enough, but it irks my butt that everyone acts like they're way into the Joe-cool college stuff."

The two boys talked and became friends, the best that the two generally untalkative young men were capable of on short notice. They had in common their dedication to a medical education. It was doubtful if either freshman really knew what a doctor did with any degree of sophistication, but they were unshakable in their conviction that they were going to be doctors no matter what. Before they went to their separate rooms, they had agreed to go to the kid stuff together. At least, they would have someone to talk to. Garven was feeling like he wished school would start already; must be something wrong with him.

******

Garven and Frosty were bored at the beach party at Half Moon Bay that night. Neither of them was facile in dealing with girls, and it was deflating to see the girls pair off with more sociable freshmen, not that any of them were so gorgeous. The only girls with boobs, Garven could see, were the fat ones. The sense of lost self-esteem and accomplishment was increased by Garven's nerdy roommate, Alan Crowder, joining them. Garven felt like the proverbial wallflower, or whatever the male equivalent was. He hated being grouped with the nerds, and it looked like he was allowing himself to be categorized in the ranks of the socially inept. He vowed to do something about that.

Day three of orientation week proceeded with the same contrived and irksome overenthusiasm as the preceding days. There was a tour, with senior students as guides of small groups, of the university's facilities that occupied most of the morning. In the early afternoon, the class divided into co-ed teams to play touch football with the usual reminders to the boys to mind where they touched. Nonetheless, there were some complaints of touching above and beyond the call of necessity of football. Garven looked pretty good out there, and Frosty demonstrated real athletic ability as long as he had the security of having friends like Garven close by. Otherwise he was a definite hang-back guy. Neither of them shined or came to the attention of the handful of reasonably attractive girls in the class during the games, nor in the mandatory jolly-ups that evening. If anything, Alan Crowder, Garven's roommate and first class nerd, did better in the small group party atmosphere provided by having one floor of freshmen boys get together with a girls' floor, than any of Garven's small circle of acquaintances. It was revolting.

CHAPTER
Fourteen

Building the stack of kindling wood on Friday night for the Big-Game bonfire was a different and more successful story. The Big Game was the yearly football rivalry between Stanford and U.C. Berkeley across the bay. The freshman class was responsible to build a huge stack of boards to create a bonfire for the pep rally on the night before the game. Every year, the Berkeley students teamed up with the junior college and high school students from Palo Alto and Menlo Park to set off the fire prematurely to spoil the pep rally.

The Stanford freshmen, by tradition, were obligated to fight for the honor of the school and to keep the interlopers away. Sometimes the good-natured frolic took on a more ominous tone and became more a riot of over-privileged children. The Stanford administration kept a jaundiced eye on the whole tradition since the more aggressive men returning from the armed forces after the end of World War II had gotten rough; a few injuries had resulted—none serious but certainly enough to raise eyebrows. The so-called honor of Stanford remained intact after years of concerted effort by the school's united foes to foil their rally. The faculty council strongly doubted that a real riot, or even an isolated serious injury to a student, especially a Stanford student, was acceptable in defense of that disputable definition of honor.

It never occurred to the students for a moment to doubt the price of Stanford's honor. A cracked head on a Menlo Park Junior College student was not too terrible a price to pay. Garven became fully involved in building the precarious stack of boards with all the attendant daring-do required to get the higher parts of the stack completed. The stack swayed and groaned until even the most intrepid of the freshmen adventurers could not be inveigled into taking up the figurative last straw. Garven, being small and strong, held the distinction of having placed the topmost board. With the momentary notice he achieved by doing so, he forgot his opinion that the bonfire was more college-kid phoniness.

Even Frosty and Alan absorbed themselves with the rest of their classmates in the silliness of the rite of fall and despite their pacific natures, and willingly took up their cudgels and accepted a place in the all night guard vigil to protect the sacred wood pile. Garven, although small, had a certain presence, a toughness, that inspired the ranks; he gravitated quickly into a leadership position, making schedules, finding boards that made good weapons, and sending girls off to procure as many baseball bats as they could find.

It was shortly after midnight, and the sky was a deep starless black, when the first probes were made by the enemy. Alan Crowder made the first sighting and contact. He was walking his assigned guard beat, carrying a two-by-four in an aggressive stance, when he walked smack into a young intruder feeling his way in the dark towards the stack. He was carrying a small can of gasoline and a box of matches that constituted *prima facie* evidence of complicity in the nefarious enemy plot. Alan, who was not exceptionally sharp about such matters, figured out who he was dealing with the instant the can and box of matches clattered noisily to the rocky ground. Uncharacteristically, he swung the board around and felt it decelerate with hard contact against the skull of the interloper. The blow was hard enough to numb Alan's hands; so, he dropped his board. The Menlo Park kid, just fourteen, let out a sickly groan then a keening howl. Alan was startled back into his usual pacific nature and turned tail. He ran into Garven.

"What happened?" Garven asked excitedly.

"I hit somebody!"

"Somebody Menlo?"

"I think so. I hope so. Do you think I'll get into trouble?"

"He wouldn't know you from Adam. It's as black as a mine shaft out here. Maybe you scared the whole bunch of them off."

No such luck. The Menlo and Palo Alto toughs and wannabes backed off for a while to think out their plan. It was not going to be easy, obviously. They debated whether to surround the Stanford freshmen with a thin circle of attackers and to pick off the guards one at a time or to select a weak point and crash through in a commando attack, light the bonfire kindling, and dash away into the night. A Palo Alto High senior argued against the encirclement plan because it spread them too thin and even the smaller guys would be one-on-one. A Menlo Park Junior College sophomore argued against the flying wedge concentrated attack plan because it put all their eggs in one basket—they would have only one shot at the bonfire. He pointed out to his cohorts that they would have to pause during the attack long enough to light a torch or at least a box of matches. The guy lighting that fire would be the target of every bruiser the defenders could muster. They voted, and Palo Alto won. The attackers would form a single wedge phalanx and crash through in a blaze of glory.

Devon Upshire from Florida was in his element as one of the Stanford freshmen defenders. He was an ardent student of all things military, and had insisted that they chip in and buy a roll of bailing wire. He persuaded Garven and four other serious freshmen boys to work with him to set up a tangle of wire to which were attached old cans and other metal debris all around the bonfire, leaving only a small bare space that only the Stanford students knew about. When word of Alan's coup against the attacker had gotten around, the freshmen ring leaders herded the rest of their classmates into the inner circle with the wire between them and the Menlo Park and Palo Alto invaders. The wire was far enough away that it was nearly invisible in the inky night darkness. Garven found that he could see better if he kept looking away from the bonfire site in a thirty-degree arc and concentrated all his attention there.

He did not have to concentrate for long. At precisely 2:00 A.M., a blood-curdling set of screams and battle howls erupted on the southeast corner of the freshmen's laager.

"Geronimo!" "Banzai!" and assorted similes of Rebel Yells pierced the night.

The invading hordes—about twenty-five of them—began crashing towards the focal point of their attack zone at an all out run. The lead boys could not stop their headlong progress and found their legs hopelessly entangled in the bailing wire defense perimeter. They began to fall and to bunch up, trying to hold on to each other to keep upright. The center and rearguard, unaware of any problem and unable to see, ran up the backs of the frontrunners, bringing down the lot of them. The mighty commando force became a helpless cursing knot of flailing arms and legs.

The Stanford freshmen demonstrated a varied reaction. Those in the direct path of the onslaught deserted their posts immediately along with some twenty percent of the class. Most of this bunch slipped quickly into the blackness out of harm's way. Another thirty percent, not knowing what to do or what more attack could be in the offing, froze uselessly in place and would not budge despite the pleadings of their more aggressive mates.

Garven, Frosty, and Devon Upshire paid no heed to caution; gave no thought to the possibility that this brouhaha could be a diversion and that more attackers could be coming from another direction, ignored the possibility that they could be hurt or that they might cause serious damage to a nice boy participating in what was, after all, only a group boyish prank, and ran pell-mell into the center of the melee along with about half of the Stanford Class of 1953.

Like his heroes of the Charge of the Light Brigade, Devon Upshire raised aloft his saber, a Little League ball bat, and cried mock heroically, "Into the breach, men! Follow me!"

Given the fact that Devon was clumped into the center of the pack, his inspiring cry was neither logical nor logistical; but it was no less satisfying to him.

Fists flailed, kicks struck home, boards and ball bats resounded off heads. Garven got punched hard on his ear, all the more painful because it was a glancing blow. Alan Crowder brought up the rear; and when he saw that real fists were striking real faces, he kept his place. Devon and Frosty stood back to back with Garven and the three boys lashed out with great satisfaction connecting with Menlo Park noses and Palo Alto stomachs until their arms were growing weary and their knuckles were scraped and hurting. No incendiary ever reached the protected bonfire kindling. The record was intact.

As abruptly as the fracas had begun, it stopped. As if one person, the fighters heard the unmistakable sounds of an even greater common enemy. Police sirens and horns rent the air behind the knot of battlers. Cop cars and paddy wagons roared up to the edge of the defense perimeter, a couple of them becoming ensnared in the bailing wire. Car and spotlights and two dozen flares lit up the scene with a dazzling brilliance. Most of the combatants froze in place, fixed as surely as if they were butterflies whose wings were pinned to a display board. It never occurred to them to defy authority. Visions of disaster for their barely commenced college careers appeared vividly in front of their freshman eyes. The townies had more explicit visions of the inside of the Palo Alto jail; for some it would not be the first time.

Garven Wilsonhulme, not large for his age anyway, made himself small, and slipped to the periphery of the gaggle of sheepish looking former brawlers. He picked his way gingerly over the tangles of wire, then dashed off into the surrounding darkness outside the lights. Ten steps later, he was securely enmeshed in the unyielding embrace of one of Palo Alto's finest, a stocky brute of a man. Garven was going no place. The boy tamely followed the cop back into the light and towards the waiting paddy wagon. The cop's grip was like a steel vise, and he had the advantage of keeping Garven's arm twisted painfully behind the diminutive freshman's back. Garven gave no resistance.

There was a confused crowd of boys and even a few of the more progressive Stanford girls being pushed and shoved into the two waiting paddy wagons. There were far more young perpetrators than could fit into the available bench seats or could be crammed into the space, even standing. There were nowhere near enough cops to deal with the rowdy crowd. The minions of the law were entirely dependent on their intimidating presence, and upon the predilection of the well-bred and educated Stanford neophytes to be obedient citizens. Garven was not naturally so inclined; in that regard he had more kinship with the ruffians from without than the Stanford students within. Garven did not regard himself as having a particular obligation to the Establishment, tending instead to view it as a collective set of institutions to be used when beneficial, and to be avoided or circumvented when necessary.

This was definitely one of the times when circumvention was in order, to Garven's way of thinking. The difficulty was the force being applied to his arm. When a Menlo Park Junior College football player type needed a crack upside his head with a nightstick, Garven's cop found himself the only available one to handle the responsibility.

"Listen, you snot-nose," he snarled at Garven in his most intimidating growl. "I gotta quieten down that punk. Stay right smack here, or I'll find you and give you some of the same. You unnerstan' me?"

"Oh, yes, Sir," Garven meekly replied, his face fervently demonstrating his heartfelt wish to comply to the letter with the nice policeman's orders.

The cop felt reassured and released his grip on Garven's sore arm, then he wedged his way through the unruly crowd and remonstrated with the football player with his night stick. It took several remonstrations before the young fellow understood the full gist of the burly cop's argument. Garven got out of there the second the cop let go of his arm. He simply stepped into the middle of the two lines filing confusedly into the backs of the paddy wagons and then into the blackness between the two police vehicles. No one paid the slightest attention to him in the midst of all that frenetic activity. Garven slunk silently into the gloom of the night and was swallowed up in darkness. He adjusted his eyes and trotted as noiselessly as possible the two miles back to his dorm room.

The newspapers had a field day with the story the next morning. The constabulary released the freshmen to the custody and responsibility of the Stanford officials pending the institution of formal charges. Those Menlo Park and Palo Alto participants without prior records were released to the recognizance of their parents, and the escapees took long deep sighs of relief. President Cheevers called an emergency faculty council meeting and assigned damage control to the members with the smoothest public relations histories. They were armed with bundles of free tickets for athletic events, symphonies, plays, and fashion shows. It would cost the university a small fortune but nothing like what would happen if the scions of some of the richest, best educated, and most influential families in the United States were actually to be slapped with the ignominy of criminal indictments.

The city and county prosecutors were screaming "Riot! Incitement to Riot! Assault and Battery! Mayhem!" and were already planning their next career advancements on the basis of their showing in the spectacular trials to come.

The university would need all the schmooze it could muster in the days and weeks ahead.

President Cheevers then held an extraordinary assembly for the freshman class on their fifth day at the university. He was furious and made every effort to let it be known to the malefactors.

"I am directing my comments to the minority of you who were directly involved in these sad events, those of you whose names adorn the police blotters of our adjoining city. Bear with me, those of you who did not besmirch the honor of Stanford by engaging in the scurrilous and low-life behavior."

Garven felt proud of himself for being found on the side of the angels in this affair. He looked about him with a genuine hurt that his fellow students could have been so foolish. Frosty read all the hypocrisy in Garven's glance and rolled his eyes in a gesture of recognition. Frosty's name, fingerprints, and his front and side-view photo were a part of the police blotter to which President Cheevers referred. Garven smiled back at his new friend beatifically.

"The university will expend every effort to help make this sad event nothing more than a prank that got out of hand rather than the felonious activity the relevant prosecutors are insisting upon. Nevertheless, every person, male or female, who was involved will be subject to the full brunt of the student-faculty honor council. This is as good a time as any to acquaint you with a couple of fine Stanford institutions. For that purpose, I have invited this year's president of the student body, Mr. Carlyle Gammett, to enlighten you on the Contribution Hours and the Corporation Yard," the president said and paused to give the senior student time to join him at the podium. "Mr. Gammett," the president said, by way of short introduction.

The aristocratic, slim, modishly dressed, twenty-year-old assumed the focus of attention as if born to it.

"Ladies and gentlemen of the class of 1953. This is not a very auspicious beginning from a class that had such promise. The remainder of the student body is ashamed of your performance."

He paused to allow the full effect of his statements to impact the errant underclassmen.

Frosty whispered to Garven and Devon, "Do you suppose anyone else in the student body knows about this screw-up besides him; and if they do, do they give a crap?"

The other two boys snickered.

"If you are convicted of an infraction against the rules of good order or against the honor code of Stanford, the disciplinary council can deal with you in any one of four ways. You can receive a reprimand. You can be assigned Contribution Hours that are community service activities in which you can work until your sentence is fulfilled. You can be assigned to work at hard labor in the Corporation Yard, affectionately known by several generations of students simply as the 'Corp Yard'. Corp hours are spent either laying track for the three hundred yard long Leland Stanford, Jr. Railroad or tearing up track, depending on the status of the line on the given day that you start your corp hours. Corp hours can only be worked off on weekends and all punishment hours are to be completed within the quarter when the infraction occurred or as directed by the council. The final option is to mix and mingle the punishments."

He stepped down from the podium without further comment. Questions were not in order from the disgraced class.

Saturday was Big Game day. There was as great a deal of hoopla and the super enthusiastic upper classmen arrived on campus to start their new year and to revel in the excitement of the 'fall gridiron classic' as it was so frequently designated by the cheerleaders (both male and female, Garven learned to his uneasy surprise) and the Popular People on Campus, and the Greeks. The regular people were not given to such gushing, especially since Stanford had not won a single football game in any of their memories, let alone a Big-Game with U.C. Berkeley. The regular types were back for a good time anyway; Big-Game was a great excuse to get a keg and get juiced up on the beach before coming to the stadium to boo the Stanford Indians and to see if they could screw up the cheers so earnestly conducted by the enthusiastic cheerleaders. Not that there was a need for another excuse for the college students to have a beer party.

Stanford was losing at the half to no one's great surprise. The flits and nerds in the band marched up and down playing marches and fight songs while the students in the stands hooted and made disparaging remarks. The NROTC (Naval Reserve Officer Training Corps) precision drill team marched flawlessly twirling their rifles and flag standards in precise union. There were no war vets in the organization despite a fairly large contingent of returnees from the armed forces back to school. The bored and irreverent students, led by some GDIs (Independents, as they identified themselves. The Greek letter frat brothers added the G.D. abbreviation as an expression of their lack of fondness for their social inferiors.) spontaneously broke into a song that was soon joined by all of the student fans. To the tune of the Disney Mickey Mouse Club Song:

M-I-C-K-E-Y-N-R-O-T-C, Mickey Nerots,
Mickey Nerots, forever, ever hold your
banner high. M-I-C-K-E-Y-N-R-O-T-C

It was a rousing part of a good time afternoon if something less than an affirmation of the university's involvement with the military or the football team. Stanford's Indians lost again, although there were few students left in the stands at the end of the game to take notice.

CHAPTER
Fifteen

The best part of the entire orientation week for Garven, as it turned out, was the Sunday afternoon exchange with a dorm group at Mills College. The ultra-exclusive small girls' college sponsored opportunities for its students to make contacts with the promising young men of carefully selected like-minded colleges and universities. U.C. Berkeley undergrads, generally assumed to be plebeians, were seldom invited. Garven was accorded an automatic first class status by virtue of his being a Stanford student, and he did not need to do anything special to be accepted. He felt no reason to be nervous or to have to perform or to be a phony, and it was the first time all week, other than during the fight, that he had felt completely at ease.

He met Sandra Hill, a lissome creature for Odessa, Texas who treated Garven with a warm friendliness that won his heart. She was "the daughter of a very rich but eccentric, wild and woolly, Texas oil millionaire," she told Garven.

Garven felt he could let down and tell the friendly girl about his real background. She was the only person outside Arizona whom he had told that he really came from a place called Cipher, Arizona, that was about as big as its name would suggest. He told her about breaking broncos with his Apache friend, Edward Sespootch.

Sandra scrutinized his face, and when she assured herself that he was not putting her on, said, "Mah daaddy would just love y'all, Gaahven!"

Garven passed a little time with some of the other girls but found a way to get back to Sandra as often as he could during the afternoon without being too obvious about it. He tried and failed to sit near her during the fine dinner catered by the main dining room staff. He realized that he was being silly, but he had pangs of jealousy when the Texas beauty paid attention to her dinner partner or to one of the other of his dorm mates.

He was successful enough to get her to agree to have him call her, and "Puhhaps the two of us caan geht togethah one tam."

He was too excited and flustered by the handsome and sophisticated girl to remember to get the phone number of her dorm. But knew that he could easily find her next week and arrange a date. His mother had always said he might as well fall in love with a rich girl as a poor one, and this looked like his chance. In his enthusiasm, he believed her when she said that he would be able to win over her millionaire daddy. Things were looking very bright for the young gentleman from Cipher, Arizona as the first day of the first quarter of his college career started at Stanford University the following morning.

The first day of every class began with a full lecture and assignment, no orientation, no settling in. It was a mild shock to Garven with his preparatory school education, but came as an intimidating revelation to many of his fellow students that this was not high school, and this was not a party school. He was enrolled in a first year German class having had four years of high school German with students who had never seen nor heard the Teutonic language before. Likewise, he learned that the botany class in which he had enrolled at his faculty advisors insistence was the domain of zoology majors and most of his classmates were at least sophomores with half a dozen hard core classes of university biology behind them as preparation. There were some areas where Garven was really going to have to hump, he could see that. Anytime he was in a class necessary for premed, he found the premeds to be the worst D.A.R.s in the university as competitors. It was going to be a challenge from day one.

On the far wall of the English class was the following sign:

"HINTS ON PRONUNCIATION FOR FOREIGNERS"

I take it you already know
Of tough and bough and cough and dough?
Others may stumble but not you,
On hiccough, thorough, laugh, and through.
Well done! And now you wish, perhaps,
To learn of less familiar traps?

Beware of heard, a dreadful word
That looks like beard and sounds like bird.
And dead: it's said like bed, not bead.
For goodness sake don't call it deed!
Watch out for meat and great and threat
(They rhyme with suite and straight and debt.)
A moth is not a moth in mother,
Nor both in bother, broth in brother.
And here is not a match for there,
Nor dear and fear for bear and pear.
And then there's dose and rose and lose—
Just look it up - and goose and choose,
And cork and work and card and ward,
And Font and front and word and sword.
And do and go and thwart and cart—
A dreadful language? Man alive!
I'd mastered it when I was five.

His assignment in English Composition was the write an essay on "My Best or My Worst Experience" due the next class, two days hence. He had found English a breeze at Burton-Cagle; so, he did not sweat that. He would be able to get easy As in English and German, given his strong background. That would leave him time to concentrate his efforts on the rest of his classes, especially the hard sciences. He had a natural ability in the sciences, he prided himself; so, he figured he would be able to set aside time to make a showing on the wrestling team without interfering with his scholastics.

Late that afternoon, Garven walked into the gym and looked around for the wrestlers and their mat. It was not in sight. He went into the weight room and asked the first athlete he saw, a powerfully built Negro, where the wrestling class, the team, worked out.

"Don't know," the body builder replied in between grunts and strains.

It took Garven two more approaches to the people in and around the athletic center before a secretary finally gave him directions to the basement. He trotted down the stairs and followed the noises of men straining and exerting to the dungeon-like cement room with the old gray mat filling the entire floor.

"Hey, sorry I'm late," Garven said to the first man he encountered, a sweaty, panting wrestler.

"No sweat, man. Who're you?"

"Garven Wilsonhulme."

"Pete Barnhienel, glad to meet you. You going to work out with us?"

"Guess so," Garven said thinking this was the most casual class and team he had ever seen.

"Good, great. How much do you weigh, Garven?"

"About 136."

"Ooh," he winced, "that's Hector Trujillo's weight. He was the Pacific Coast Conference champ last year. If you really want to know, he's by far the best guy on the team. You will want to lose six pounds. We don't have anyone at 130."

That was the second time he had heard that suggestion.

Garven thought, *I'm already too skinny. I don't have six pounds to give away anywhere, I don't think, but I'll give it a shot.*

"You have to bring your own workout gym shoes, otherwise we have all the sweats, tights, and pads; anything like that, you need. You have to wash the stuff yourself, unlike their Lordships, the football players. That's why it stinks so much around here."

It truly did stink there in that unventilated room.

"Okay, weigh in, get your stuff on and come on out on the mat. We'll do our calisthenics together. You need to meet the rest of the team."

"This is Garven Wilsonhulme; he's a freshman, just starting," the gregarious wrestler called out to his teammates.

He, like all of them, had the minimum of scalp hair and moved with a habitually wary cautiousness. The two wrestlers whom Garven had met on registration day nodded a greeting.

"Don Strathem."

"Derek van Leventhal, glad to see you out."

"Hi," Garven returned.

"Warm up a while, then let's get you matched up with somebody. Maybe you can pick up a few pointers," suggested Derek.

"I need more than a few," Garven said with no false modesty.

He watched the other wrestlers and copied what they did.

He was tired from skipping rope, and doing push-ups, sit-ups, squats, and leg lifts before Derek again centered his attention on Garven.

"Garven, this is Steve Mandella. He's the second latest guy on the team—he's the worst wrestler, though. Hector is the latest; he's not even here yet; you'll notice. How about you two working out together for a while?" Derek asked.

"Sure," the two said in near unison.

"Glad to have you on the team, Garven; we need some new meat."

"Glad to be here."

"You want to start with some take-downs, or what?" Steve asked.

Garven did not know enough about the sport of wrestling to be confident with "what" or what might be included; so, he said with false confidence, "Take-downs are fine."

Steve showed Garven arm drags, trips, one leg, and two leg takedowns. As soon as Garven thought he could protect himself against one attack, Steve switched to another. It was a good, tiring, educational, and demoralizing work out. Garven was sure he would never be half as good as Steve, and Derek had said that Steve was the "worst wrestler on the squad". This was going to be tough.

After another of Madera Hall's filling carbohydrate cafeteria dinners, Garven settled his two pillows at the head of his bed and set out his books for the night of studying. He was one chapter into the history of Greek art and theater, and starting to become interested, when his roommate Alan started to talk.

"Garven," he said. "Who'd you get for Western Civ?"

"Danielson," Garven answered tersely and reread the paragraph he had been on when Alan interrupted him.

"I got Sievers."

"Um hum."

"You going to read all that stuff they assigned, or are you going to use the outline?"

"Um hum."

"Well, which?"

"Which what?" Garven asked, only partially diverting his attention from the required reading.

"The text and library stuff, or did you buy a Coopers *Western Civ* outline at the bookstore?"

"I don't even know about the outline. I guess I'll just do the reading. It's kind of interesting anyway."

"My cousin went here, and he said you couldn't make it through the year, at least not through Western Civ, without using the outline."

"Huum, zat so?" Garven said, aware that there was a little pearl of wisdom being offered. "I'll have to get one—one of those outlines— tomorrow. There must be two hundred pages of reading; I am on the waiting list in the library for one of Danielson's books even then."

Garven started back to his studying.

"I'm going to try out for the play," Alan said changing the subject.

"Um hum," said Garven back in his book.

"We're going to do *Our Town*, and I'm going to be in it. My cousin said the law school admissions committee likes the applicants to have a well-rounded undergrad career; you know, have some extracurricular activities. He said, I mean, my cousin, Tucker, said they like things like debate, extemporaneous speaking, oratory, and thespian. That's drama," Alan continued talking progressively more rapidly as he warmed to his subject and more loudly as he unconsciously tried to overcome his roommate's lack of interest in the one-sided, nearly stream-of-consciousness conversation.

It was as if he thought Garven was hard of hearing.

"That's good," Garven mumbled and reread the same paragraph. It was beginning to sound familiar since he had started back at that point in the Western Civ textbook three times now.

"I liked my English Comp prof. He's right from England. Used to teach at Oxford. Really knows his literature. I guess he knows about writing. I hope so. My cousin, you remember, I told you about Tucker; he's a lawyer now; passed the California bar last year…What was I saying? Oh, yeah, Tucker said English Comp. is critical; and I mean critical with a capital C for law school. You have got to be able to write well. They have you write an essay on the law school application, did you know that?"

"Um um," Garven mumbled getting a trifle annoyed at losing his place once again.

He could not concentrate. Alan's prattle came across as mind numbing prating. He could not really get what his roommate was saying, and he was losing ground in his reading. As his frustration mounted, so did his annoyance. He turned away from Alan and tried to read one more time.

"Did you have to write some dippy thing about "what I did last summer?" you know, something like that?"

Alan continued totally unaware that he had no audience and never considering the possibility that his conversation was not altogether appreciated.

"Um hum," Garven muttered gritting his teeth.

This was impossible. He would try one more time to read about Oedipus then he would either have to give it up or tell his roomie to stuff a sock in it.

Alan took a short rest. It had to be tiring, talking all the time. He opened a bag of potato chips which resulted in a particularly nerve jangling crinkle-crackle of the bag each time he put his pudgy hand into the opening. He was halfway through the bag when Garven's patience came to an end.

"Hey, Alan. I'm trying to study, you know, hit the books. I have assignments. How about some peace. You can make all that stupid noise later!" he said with clear enunciation of each syllable for emphasis.

"Jeez. This is the first day of school. Nobody, *nobody* studies on the first day of school. You'll burn out, man. Lighten up," Alan said peevishly.

"I don't want to lighten up, Alan. I want to study. You do it your way, and I'll do it my way. I'm in premed, and that's tough, okay?"

"Well, la de da. Big premedder. Big deal!" Alan snapped mockingly.

He turned on his radio to a bang-bang rock and roll station slowly tuning through the static to find the most offensive musical drivel possible.

Garven started to seethe.

"Shut that thing off, dork! It's time to get some studying done. Give me a break!"

"Dork!" Alan retorted with offended pride, "name calling is the last refuge of weak minds," and turned the volume on the bang-bang up.

The music had a throbbing bass, maddeningly repetitive lyrics, and the singers positively yelled some inanities about lost eternal love. Alan loved it. He saw the anger mounting in Garven's face, and loved the music all the more.

"Turn it off!" hissed Garven abandoning all efforts at studying or civility now.

He had not asked for trouble, but his petulant and selfish blob of a roommate was making an effort to have a confrontation. So be it. He would get his contest. Garven was going to study, if he had to cold cock Alan. He was way past reasoning.

Garven started to get up out of his position on the bed. Alan was used to threats. He liked to annoy people; he had to admit; and he knew nothing would happen because this was Stanford; and fighting was considered seriously déclassé at the exclusive institution. He actually looked forward to provoking that look of impotent fury that he had tormented out of his high school classmates at the best of times. He did not associate with the low-life types that settled their problems with their fists; so, he knew he was physically safe. Garven would settle down and forget this little tiff in no time just like the rest of them had done. He turned up the radio with a dispassionate look on his face.

Garven advanced towards his roommate who glared back at the angry boy with a taunting grin.

Alan knew nothing would happen.

"We're going to shut off that rotten radio now," Garven snarled.

Alan waggled his shoulders in a theatrical display of fear, still keeping that maddening grin. He was enjoying Garven's mounting anger and especially the accompanying bluster. The skinny guy from Arizona looked funny, all red in the face.

When Alan made no move to shut off the radio, Garven took three steps towards it, tore the plug out of the wall; then twisted off the volume and the tuning knobs. He presented them to Alan—two knobs in four pieces. Alan did not look nearly as amused.

"You broke it! You ruined my radio, you jerk! That'll cost you twenty-five bucks!" Alan screeched.

Garven felt like he was losing control and made a conscious effort to dampen the vehemence of his responses. He stepped right up to Alan's round fat face and looked malignantly at the narrow eyes. Instead of hauling off and pasting him squarely on his bulbous beak as he really wanted to, Garven jabbed Alan directly on the end of his nose with his stiffly pointing forefinger. Alan's head snapped back as if he had been hit with a pile driver. He had never been hit before. It hurt terribly. He started to cry.

"Shut up, you twinkie!" Garven snarled down at the now cowering boy.

Alan knew he was not dealing with a gentleman. Of all the guys that he could have gotten as a roommate, he had to get this Neanderthal. He knew better than to do anything more, however. He shut up.

Garven made a sharp about-face, scooped up his books, papers, and pencils into an untidy bundle, stuffed the bundle in a disorderly wad into his briefcase, and left for the library vowing never to study in his room as long as that creep was his roommate. His adrenaline had pumped him up so much that he stayed until the study kiosks at the library closed. He was able to get through all of his Western Civ reading and wrote the first draft on his English Comp essay. It was so good that he doubted that he would have to make any significant changes. It turned out to be a good night's work. Garven smiled to himself when he acknowledged the contribution his anger had made—he would have to do it again, he thought.

He did not admit to himself that he had stayed late to avoid facing his roommate again that night. His easily sparked temper had once again come close to getting himself trouble. When he calmed down, he knew he had to keep his self-control. This had been such a simple, stupid little thing to get mad about. What would he do if something really important interfered with him? Kill somebody? He made a resolution to count to ten or to a thousand the next time he started to get mad.

Alan was asleep when Garven let himself back into his room well after midnight and was still asleep, or looked like he was, when Garven left for breakfast the next morning. He had his chemistry lecture in the morning and the lab in the afternoon. He also had physics and botany that morning.

Chemistry was the classical student nightmare. The first day, the very first day of class, the professor gave a quiz. A surprise pop quiz—the lowest weapon in the professorial armamentarium. It was a huge two hour long multiple guess test; six pages, two columns each, long.

Dr. Rodowsky wrote his name and the title of the course, Chem 101, on the black board then announced, "This examination is for placement purposes only. It will not affect your grade in the course in any way. In order to give you the most individualized help possible, we divide the class into quiz sections, A through Z, based on your performance on the test. We assign graduate students to each of the quiz sections with the foreknowledge of where you stand in the class and with a pretty good idea of your background and needs in the study of chemistry. Do your best, but don't worry overmuch. It doesn't count on your grade for the course. Remember, the honor code is in effect. Sit in alternate rows and seats. Switch now, but don't open your test books until I tell you to do so."

Garven thought he was going to have diarrhea right there in his seat. He found himself hyperventilating and struggled to get hold of himself.

"I have a better background in chemistry than the schmucks from public schools," he told himself. "You're okay; take it easy," he repeated to himself over and over.

"Open your test booklets to the first page. Do not go on. Fill in your name and the date in the blanks indicated."

Garven wrote hurriedly. His name looked like it had been scrawled by a third grader just learning cursive. He had to get control of himself. He peaked at the question and answer sheets. On the last sheet, he saw the number of the last question, "250." He thought he was going to faint.

"All right, begin," the professor announced as if it were the start of a foot race. "You have exactly two hours. When I say stop, I want every pencil to drop. It is a violation of the honor code to continue past time. Is that clear?"

No one spoke up. The papers rattled; the pencils scratched on the answer sheets and doodled and figured in the margins; there were noises of distress, moans of indecision and gasps of disbelief at an unfamiliar question here and there throughout the huge lecture hall. The cumulative effect was a low throaty whine reverberating throughout the classroom. Garven found the questions none too difficult once he got into the test. He calmed down. The questions were high school level and had a strong emphasis on the periodical table that Garven had sweated so many hours over at his prep school. He was confident of his answers on ninety percent of the questions, and was sure he would get a significant percentage of the ones he was less confident about by the old law of averages for guessing on multiple-guess type tests.

He was on the last column of questions when the professor disturbed the class's concentration with, "Five more minutes, ladies and gentlemen. Better begin finishing up and check over your work in the few remaining minutes. I'll warn you again when there is one minute left."

Garven hurried through the last four questions, determined answers acceptable to himself, then made a realization that almost caused him to cry out in shocked desperation. His answer to the last question was three spaces short of the spaces on the numbered answer sheet. He had been so careful, but it was a rushed, timed test; and somehow he had screwed up and must have left out three questions somewhere along the way. He had no idea where he had made his mistake, but he realized that he would be marked off for every question after the spot where he had made his fatal mistake. He could only hope that it was not very far up the line.

Garven could feel the seconds tick away like a Chinese water torture dripping on his psyche as he raced up the questions in reverse order trying to discover the site of the error.

"One minute remaining," the professor announced.

Garven's heart sunk into a drum beating tachycardia. He could not find his mistake. He calculated that there was no more than twenty seconds left, maybe less, when he found where he had gone wrong. He had gotten hung up on a question for several minutes at about the halfway point in the exam and had made a mental note to come back to the difficult question rather than wasting precious time at that point. He absent-mindedly had turned the page neglecting two remaining questions on that sheet, and continued with the remaining questions. His big mistake had been to place the next answer in next blank without leaving the three spaces blank. Every answer after that was wrong. He was frantic.

Garven furiously began erasing his answers and trying to fill in the correct answer from three spaces away. It was almost impossible to keep his correction system straight, especially because the stupid eraser did little more than create a smudged black mess. He scraped viciously at the filthy carbon deposit on the eraser to get it to do a better job. He lost track of his place. Twice, he tore through the test paper. He was pouring sweat, and his heart was going like a race horse.

"Time," the professor stated.

Papers rattled, pencils dropped all over the lecture hall. Students cried out in muffled frustration and failure. Garven's pencil and eraser flew down a few more spaces. He did not dare to look up.

"Put down your pencils and pass your test booklets forward on your row."

Garven got in two more changes before the girl in the desk in front of him turned around to find out the cause of the delay in receiving the booklets on her row. She saw Garven write a hasty last letter in the answer column and gave him a nasty disapproving look. Garven returned her gaze with a snarl of his lip and passed the books ahead. He was sick, physically sick.

The rest of the day was soured for him. He could not get his mind off his fiasco. He castigated himself, called himself all sorts of demeaning vile names. He could not concentrate on the physics lecture. The only thing he remembered about the lecture on Ohm's Law (Volts = Amps × Resistance) was the mnemonic for remembering it: Virgins = Are Rare, and having to take the chemistry lab that afternoon just rubbed salt in the wound.

"Get your lab supplies and meet your lab partner for the year. That's the person to your right, starting with the row of Bunsen burners and sinks nearest the door," said Mr. Terwilliger, the chief lab instructor, a grad student due to get his doctorate that coming spring.

Garven said, "Hi," to Gwendolyn Daugherty, the student on his right.

She was mousy and wore glasses. She looked smart.

Garven thought, *She couldn't be that homely and dumb too.*

She could probably help him through lab; it looked like he would need all the help he could get. Garven was still depressed.

"The results of the test today will not be posted as such," Mr. Terwilliger said. "You will find your name under the quiz section to which you have been assigned posted on the cork board by the supply room next lab period…that's on Thursday. I will instruct quiz section A, Mrs. Henderson will have section D, I think it is. Yes, D. And Mr. Trent will have section K. They will be with me here on some Tuesdays, and you will meet the rest of the quiz section instructors in due course. Any questions?"

Garven was full of questions, but did not dare open his mouth. He had a bilious enough taste in his throat without making some kind of public fool of himself and adding to his misery. No one else raised a hand.

"All right. Today we are going to take the lab period to familiarize you with the equipment itself. My biggest concern personally is that you don't blow us all up; so, let's start with the fundamentals of the Bunsen burner and the methane hook-up for it."

Garven made an uneasy peace with Alan but knew that the creep was still bent out of shape with him. He took off for the library to get a good night's study in and to polish his composition on "My Worst Experience" for Comp class tomorrow. He was still revved up about the test when he finally got home at midnight. He had forgotten wrestling practice altogether.

Garven dropped his composition on the stack on Dr. Nicholson's desk and noticed with a quiet sense of accomplishment how neat and professional his paper looked compared to some of the others. He had fitted the composition into a card stock paper folder, a nice touch he had picked up at Burton-Cagle. Dr. Nicholson gave out the assignments including one to write a critical essay on one of the short stories they were to read this week. The essay was due the following week.

German was a surprise. So much so, that he wondered briefly whether he had signed up for an advanced class by mistake. The unfriendly Teutonic matron who taught the class, reminiscent of lovely Frau Mueller at Burton-Cagle, was a stern and no nonsense believer in drill. Up and down the vocabulary list, conjugate the action verbs in present, past, and present perfect. A crisp *"nein!"* for the slightest error left the student embarrassed and to his own devices to discover the correct usage. It was an uncomfortable position to find one's self in the good Frau Professor's special circle of attention because of repetitive mistakes. Pronunciation was not considered particularly important.

"Reading and understanding the language of science is," Frau Dr. Lutz repeated at intervals.

The homework consisted of over two hundred new words for each class period. The student was expected not only to know the words in the context of a sentence, but to have the correct conjugation in mind when called upon. Garven did know something about German, but he felt thoroughly intimidated. He could only imagine what the freshmen felt who were encountering the confusing language for the first time. Even the German class he had counted on as being easy was going to be a hill for a climber.

Physics, even the dumbbell physics designed for premed students, was more a math class than anything else. Mathematics had always been Garven's weakest suit; that is one of the main reasons he selected premed. Everyone he talked to told him he did not need math, definitely not calculus, for premed, not even for physics. Wrong.

"It is true," Professor and Nobel Prize Laureate, Ingemar Rolffsson, had said, "We will not rely on calculus here, but you will nonetheless have to be facile with the elements of college level algebra and trigonometry, and volumetric geometry."

The first lectures sounded like calculus to Garven, despite the professor's assurances. He figured he understood about ten percent of the lecture. He had been warned to take very detailed notes and to forget the textbook since the tests came right out of Rolffsson's expositions. He was in the process of writing textbooks for undergraduate physics majors and also for non majors, like premedders. Garven wished the professor would hurry and finish the books so he could memorize the material and not have to worry about whether his notes were accurate. It was not a question of learning physics. Nobody learned physics.

"Physics is a discipline to get through, a hurdle." Garven's dad explained premed in general, and especially physics, as being "the equivalent of going through pledge week to get into a fraternity. What you do is worthless, but you have to prove you can do it anyway; so, the frat brothers, or professors, as the case may be, will let you into their club."

Garven was a good memorizer and was pretty sure he could suck in and regurgitate out enough material to get a good grade. He had to.

During the break between classes on Thursday, he gave Sandra Hill at Mills College a call.

"She is out," the desk matron tersely informed Garven.

She did not know when the young lady would return, but she would leave a message.

The moment he had been dreading all week came Thursday afternoon in the chemistry lab. Frosty, who was also a premed major and always seemed to have the inside skinny on classes and grades, told him that the most important thing about chemistry, the only important thing about chemistry from the point of view of a premedicine student, was to get into one of the top two or at worst, three, quiz classes. All of the 'A's were given out to the students in those classes. For one thing, Terwilliger made up the weekly quizzes, and the A through C quiz instructors made up the two mid-term exams. It was a serious mark of pride for the top three instructors that their quiz sections garnered the high grades, and they were not above stacking the deck in favor of the students in their charge by going over the quiz material in advance.

Garven knew he had to get into a good quiz class, and he also knew he was not going to get there because of his three-dimensional screw-up on the lousy placement exam. He could just wait to see how terrible it would be.

CHAPTER
Sixteen

The quiz sections were listed along the west wall with twenty-six sheets of neatly typed names, ten per quiz section, except for sections A, B, and C which had five each. In a mood of grim foreboding and depression, Garven started looking for his name from the Z end.

"Thank the stars and deities," he sighed when he failed to find his name in the very last section.

He could guess what the denizens of that section would be like— callused knuckled jocks who were one generation out of the trees, education majors and poly-sci nerds—birds of a feather.

"Section P. Oh, no, Section P," Garven read, moving his lips.

His heart dropped to the bottom of his chest. He looked around to make sure no one knew him and pretended that he was looking in the higher sections. He was very close to crying and had to make a conscious effort not to let the tears spring out. His lab partner, Agnes Gooch, or whatever her name was, looked at him with motherly concern.

"You feeling okay, Garven? You don't look very well. Do you know where the dispensary is?"

"I'm okay. Something I ate, I think."

It was lame, but it was all he could think of for the moment.

"I'm in B. I saw you looking at A; are you in Terwilliger's section?"

"I'm not sure," he lied, looking intently at an acid hole in his lab coat. "I didn't get a chance to check all of the sections out yet. I'm going to do it after lab."

"You are a cool guy," Gwendolyn said. "I could never wait to see the results of a test. I'm just too too nervous."

That was just what Garven needed right then. Someone to chat him up. The last thing in the world he wanted to do was to talk to anyone, and the oldest member of the three sisty uglers would not have been his choice in the best of times.

Gwendolyn asked again if he felt okay, and when he assured her that he was fine, she timidly asked, "Are you going to the Dormen Hall Sadie Hawkins Day party on Saturday?"

"I haven't even heard about it," Garven said starting to squirm in his seat.

"You know who Sadie Hawkins is, don't you, silly?"

Did she think he had just flown in from some monastery in Outer Mongolia where their funnies didn't have "Lil Abner"?

"Yes," he said pleasantly.

"Well, this is a party in honor of the Dogpatch custom of the girls asking the boys to a hoe-down once a year, you know."

A hoe-down? he thought acerbically.

She looked like an easterner if he had ever seen one. What would she know about a 'hoe-down'.

"I read Lil Abner, too," was all he said.

Gwendolyn was looking at him with that funny kind of look.

Oh, oh, he thought. *I don't think I like this.*

She summoned up courage from way down inside and very softly asked, "Garven, would you, I mean would you come... uh, be my, I mean, my, my date for the Sadie Hawkins party?"

She drew in a deep breath, almost a sigh.

"I would really like to go with you."

In the two seconds before he answered, Garven ran the vision of the entire evening of the Sadie Hawkins Day Party and Dance over the screen in the back of his eyes. Diminutive and short Garven prancing around with Gunnhilda, the Troll. She did seem like a very nice girl, *For a fat girl, you don't sweat much,* kept running through his mind as he strove for a decent way to turn her down.

"I'm sorry, Gu... uh, Gwendolyn, my aunt, that's it, my aunt," he could have laughed right out loud at himself. "She's coming in from, uh, San Francisco to see me. She can only be here on that one day, Saturday wasn't it?"

Gwendolyn nodded crestfallen, knowing that this was going to turn out like every other social effort she had made in her entire life.

"Much as I'd love to go with you... it sounds like lots of fun."

He was laying it on too thick. It would better to just say it and be done with it. Garven felt like two cents.

"I understand, Garven. You don't need to explain," she said looking away from him with her large brown doe eyes that pooled memories of a lifetime of small hurts.

"Okay, I'm sorry about that day; maybe we can do it another time," Garven said and regretted his impulse immediately.

"You don't have to say that if you don't mean it. I know I'm not popular or good-looking or anything, but I'm a decent human being. I don't scare puppies or kids, and I'd like for us to get to be friends as well as lab partners," Gwendolyn said with real dignity. "I hadn't thought that would be such a painful thing."

Garven was impressed with her integrity and thought that it reflected badly on his own. She was so plain though; a guy had a reputation to protect, didn't he?

They were both saved by their lab instructor's voice describing the experiment of the day, something about the difference between physical reactions and chemical reactions. The lab pairs each took two beakers of water. Garven suddenly developed a particularly intense interest in the work at hand. Gwendolyn said nothing more about dating.

Garven remembered to go to wrestling workout that day. He needed the physical release badly. His ego could use some upbuilding, but it was unlikely that he was going to find any such uplift on the wrestling mat, if his luck ran as usual for the day. Pete Barnhienel, Steve Mandella, Don Strathem, Derek van Leventhal and a wiry muscular Hispanic whom Garven presumed was the vaunted Hector Trujillo were all doing their mat work when Garven walked into the smelly lair. A moose of a man, hairy and paunchy, was skipping rope pouring sweat. He was big but appeared soft, almost feminine but in an ugly sort of way. Garven had a flash of the typical Stanford girl that the Jolly-up master of ceremonies had alluded to. He had to turn aside to keep from showing a wry smile as the moose galumped awkwardly tangling his feet in the jump rope.

"Garven," the wrestlers on the mat said in what sounded like a sort of ill rehearsed unison.

Garven nodded in return. He dressed in his sweats and came out on the mat.

"This is Jack Larimer, Garven. Jack, this is Garven; he's the newest member of our exclusive little club," said Don Strathem.

Jack extended his large but soft and pudgy hand for Garven to shake.

The Hispanic looking man walked up to the little group.

"I'm Hector. Hector Trujillo, Garven. Glad to know you," he said.

"Hi, Hector. I'm Garven Wilsonhulme."

"You want to do some mat work with me, Garven. I understand you and I are pretty close to the same weight," Hector asked.

Despite his strong mestizo features, the Hispanic man spoke with flawless and unaccented English.

"Sounds good to me. Let me warm up for a few minutes first. Soon's I get up a sweat I'll holler."

Hector put his right thumb up in the air in agreement and returned to a series of very rapid two armed and one armed pushups, sit-ups performed with both legs and torso elevating at once, and a bouncing duck walk that made Garven wince just to watch. He was nowhere near as springy as Hector, he had to admit. He was not sure, but he figured that he was not as strong as the Latino either.

When Garven had worked up a lather and the reverses of the day were beginning to fade from the forefront of his consciousness, he signaled to Hector. He could not help but notice that the other wrestlers slacked off in their calisthenics and their wrestling practice with each other and were covertly glancing in the direction of the two 136 pounders. Garven knew it was to get a chance to watch Hector perform, or maybe to see if he, the new-comer, had anything to offer.

Hector asked, "You want top or bottom to start? If it's all the same to you, I need to work on reverses and counter reverses."

"I need to work on everything; so, reverses are as good as anything," Garven said almost apologetically.

He was nonetheless determined to make a showing, to look decent.

He had paused for a second; then, he said, "I'll take the top. Okay?"

"Okay." Hector placed his body in the kneeling position in the middle of the area of the mat the two men had staked out for themselves. He looked like a panther ready to spring. Garven remembered another one of Dr. Wilsonhulme's quotes; "He who rides a tiger may find it difficult to dismount." This was beginning to look like one of those situations.

Garven had watched the other wrestlers in the floor position; so, he had a vague idea of how to hold the Latino panther beneath him.

"Got to put your left hand above the elbow, here," Hector directed Garven. "Your thumb has to be on the back of my arm, not all the way around it. That's right."

Garven adjusted himself sensing the coiled muscles under his touch ready to spring.

"Hey, Derek! Come and slap the mat for us, okay?"

Derek bent down in front of the two wrestlers like a referee, raised his right hand, palm down; and when he was sure both men were ready, slammed his hand on the mat with a resounding snap.

The movement was so fast, so perfectly executed, that Garven was still mentally getting ready when Hector sat out, that is, turned his body away from Garven's; so, they were facing opposite directions. Garven remained suspended in his kneeling position, but Hector was now sitting. He threw his brown right arm over Garven's triceps and deftly inserted his hand between Garven's thighs. Garven's arm extended almost involuntarily to reduce the strain as Hector's weight suspended on it. Hector levered himself over Garven's arm and back around Garven's hip continuing the fluid movement until the two wrestlers had completely reversed positions.

Garven did not know what to do next; so, he struggled to free himself from the iron grip and steel band arms of last year's PAC champ. He was beginning to see why he was the champ. No matter what he did, Hector was always one step ahead of him. His weight was always located in just the right position to feel very uncomfortable to Garven. Soon Garven's legs were ensnared in a figure-four leg hold by Hector, and he felt the strong insinuating fingers worming their way up under his right arm and his lateral thorax. The more he squirmed, the farther that arm sneaked through his defenses. It was like the proverbial camel's nose under the tent flap at first, and by now the camel was in up to his shoulders.

Hector worked his arm up over the back of Garven's neck in a progressively troublesome half-Nelson and began to pry Garven over onto his back. Garven was desperate not to get pinned. He braced himself, spread his legs, squeezed his arm as hard as he could against Hector's pry-bar of an arm. He felt himself gradually turning over to be pinned. Garven decided to make a final effort, hoping to catch Hector unawares. He suddenly rolled over onto his back to dislodge himself from his surprised opponent or even, he thought, to judo roll Hector on over and off him. Wrong!

Garven's maneuver was the classical mistake of a rank novice. He succeeded only in rolling neatly in under the champion After Garven's deft move, the opposing wrestler's chest ended up crushing down on his own. He was pinioned in place by the arm crooked around and behind his neck. He could move his legs all he wanted, but his back stayed fixed to the mat. He was pinned. Less than a minute had elapsed since Derek had slapped the mat. If he were not so tired, Garven would have been humiliated.

"Hey, amigo, you did good!" Hector said in both good grace and good humor.

There was not a hint of condescension in his voice.

"Let's try it again. This time you take the bottom. We can go through my way of doing a sit-out slowly. Maybe, if it's okay with you, I can teach you a little something, okay?"

Garven lacked humility when he started the day's mat workout with Hector Trujillo and became angry each time the agile Latino wrestler bested him then dissembled the most recent maneuver and taught Garven the wrestling finesse that had been involved. Gradually over the next two hours, Garven gave in grudgingly to the recognition that he was dealing with an exceptional athlete, a champion. Then he gradually accepted the generosity of the senior student who was trying to impart his experience and acumen in the sport to the lowly freshman. Finally, Garven submitted himself to Hector as a master teacher and began to learn. Hector recognized in the proud defensive gringo a kindred spirit of sorts, a born wrestler, and persisted.

"I have to get back to the books, Garven," Hector said at six o'clock to Garven's intense relief.

The younger boy was truly exhausted but had been too proud to admit it.

"You look like you could use a little rest yourself, amigo."

"Yeah, I'm a little winded," Garven panted.

"If I may, a little advice?"

"Why not? I have everything to learn. Anyway, Hector, thanks for taking the time with me. I know I was acting like a spoiled kid," he shrugged his shoulders in resignation.

Hector nodded and smiled gently.

"I also know I'm not much of a wrestler. Yet. But I can be. I am going to work at it. I am going to beat you one day!"

Hector laughed. He was delighted in the change in the freshman's attitude.

"I'll welcome the day. But, amigo, I am not going to throw any match just to make you feel good. Remember that. Anyway, what I wanted to suggest… you don't do as well as you could, even now, because you are not in good enough shape. You've got to run, a good five miles every day. Every day."

"I know. But I don't have time. Premed takes up all my time. I don't have a social life; I hardly get to take a break to crap."

"So, crap quick," Hector laughed. "But you're a wrestler, and some day you'll be a great one. Right now, you could beat a third of the guys you will meet in matches if you were in decent shape. I'll guarantee they won't be yet, either.

"So I'll get up an hour earlier. Maybe I'll just stop going to bed. Pretty soon when I meet myself coming, I'll just be going."

"Good idea. *Hasta mañana*," Hector said as the two headed for the showers.

Garven thought his own Spanish accent was better than Hector's. He was determined to beat Hector if it was the last thing he ever did.

After a recurrent boring carbohydrate supper and a few unpleasant words with Alan Crowder, Garven headed for the library. He was not sure his legs would carry him. He was beat. He stopped at the pay phone in the library entrance foyer.

"Hello," he said when the desk matron at Mills College dorm where Sandra Hill roomed finally fetched the Texas girl to the phone.

He had had to put coins in twice before connecting with Sandra, and he hardly had enough dimes to permit a conversation. Certainly there was no time for the preliminary chit-chat he had rehearsed.

"This is Garven."

"Who?"

"Garven Wilsonhulme. You know, from Stanford. We met at the exchange party up at your dorm a week ago."

"Oh yes. Youah from Phoenix, rat?"

Her tone became friendlier.

"Right."

The operator's voice interrupted.

"Your three minutes are up. Deposit another dime for three more minutes, please."

Garven put in the dime, his second to the last.

"Anyhow, are you doing anything this Friday?"

"Oh, deah, yes, yes Ah am. Ah have another engagement."

The word sounded so formal.

"I'd really like for us to get together. We hit it off so well at the party. You're a swell girl," that sounded so sappy, but he meant it. "I mean, uh," he felt a little foolish; why was he stammering. "What about Saturday? We could catch a movie or something."

There was a brief pause. "Sorry, Ah… Ah'm booked up then too. Ah'm really sorry. Maybe another time, Gahdnah, okay?"

Garven would have been more impressed with her sincerity had she at least remembered his name. Maybe he was just being paranoid. One more try.

"What about next Friday or Saturday?" he asked as nonchalantly as he could.

"Oh, yes, why don't y'all call me then, Gahdnah? Yes, that would be great."

"Uh, are you going to be free then or what?"

"I can't be sure. It's too early to tell. Give me a call, ya heah?"

The Texas accent was more pronounced it seemed to Garven.

"Your time is up," came the annoying interruption from the long-distance operator, "deposit one more dime for an additional three minutes, please."

Garven fumbled in his pocket for the coin.

"Gahdnah, Gahdnah. Ah, y'all still theah?"

He could not lay his fingers on the elusive last dime.

"Gahdnah, have y'all hung up?" her voice was becoming insistent.

There it was. He inserted the coin and hurriedly said, "Look, Sandra, I'm running out of dimes. I just want to know if you are interested in going out with me or not. I don't want to waste your time, you know."

Sandra was feeling the press of time. Her roommate was standing at the top of the stairs pointedly gesturing at her wrist watch to indicate some deadline or other, and Maybelline Harper was impatiently waiting her turn for the phone.

"Of couhse, Gahdnah, of couhse I want to see y'all. Now call me next week, ya heah? Ah have to rush now. See ya."

She paused a decent interval then quietly put down the receiver.

That was enough for one day. Garven forgot about studying altogether and pushed his weary bones back to his dorm room. He said nothing about the horrible loud music Alan was playing defiantly. Garven slept quickly and peacefully despite Alan's pointed refusal to lower the volume when Garven gave the blaring radio a look of unmistakable annoyance. Garven dreamed briefly of making clever rebuffs to an imploring Sandra Hill, oil heiress from Odessa, Texas.

******

On Friday, The *Palo Alto Daily Herald* carried a third page, two paragraph follow-up article on the near riot of two weeks before. The small article described the police investigation that had concluded that it was nothing more than college spirit that had gotten out of hand a bit. The only charges that were still pending were on three Menlo Park juveniles who had records of previous violence. The *Stanford Chronicle* (The Chrony) included no mention of the fights at the bon fire before the Big Game, but on page four did mention that a group of twenty-five fathers of Stanford freshman were making a generous contribution to the campaign to the refurbishing of the Leland Stanford Jr. Memorial Church (Mem Chu).

On Friday, Garven screwed up his courage and made an appointment to see Dr. Rodowsky, Chairman of the Department of Chemistry. It was naive of him, he found out. When he arrived at the department office, the formidable secretary looked over her pince nez glasses and informed him that the chairman was not in today.

"But I had an appointment," Garven protested mildly.

"Are you a student, young man?" the imperious secretary asked in a condescending tone.

"Yes, ma'am," Garven replied.

"An undergraduate?" she asked.

They were descending the evolutionary tree. She was bored with a ritual that had been re-enacted thousands of times during her guardianship of the professor's busy door.

"Yes, ma'am," Garven answered again, pretty sure where this was leading.

"The chairman does not see graduate students without an appointment being made by their lead professor in advance. He does not see undergraduates at all. I am sure you are aware of just how busy the Nobel prize laureate is, young man," the secretary said in what appeared to Garven to be a deliberate effort to be both offensive and annoying.

Maybe she called him "young man" out of affection, but he could not give her that much benefit of the doubt. He had no choice but to remain polite and to eat his ration of what she was dishing out.

"But I need to see him. It's important."

He was pleading, he realized, but it was necessary. He detested the woman for reducing him to groveling.

"Mr. Terwilliger sees the undergraduates, Mr...what was your name again?"

"Wilsonhulme, Garven Wilsonhulme," Garven said dejectedly.

"Shall I call the graduate student secretary for you, son? Perhaps she can make an appointment with Mr. Terwilliger. I am sure he can handle any undergraduate problem," the professor's secretary said with slightly pursed lips as if dealing with an unpleasant taste.

Garven noticed that she accentuated the diminutive, 'son'.

"I suppose so, yes, please."

The call was made; and to Garven's relief, he was able to get an appointment with Mr. Terwilliger at four-thirty that same afternoon. He thanked the secretary for her kindness. She was too busy with her desk full of non undergraduate matters to look up. Garven considered himself dismissed. He was about to thank her again, this time for the opportunity of wasting his entire morning, but he thought better of it and just left for his English class.

The day was running true to form. In the English Composition class, he got back his first composition of his first week at the university. He was counting on the grade here to off-set his reverses in chemistry and botany. He saw the big red C-minus standing out on his paper as nastily as the "A" on Hester's dress front. It was a shock. He felt like crying at first, then was certain it was some mistake. That was it. He could get this blight changed easily. His certainty wavered, and he faced reality when he began to come out of his own black cloud and began to see the students around him registering the shock at their marks.

"What'd you get?" asked the pimply faced boy across the aisle.

Garven was not that thrilled to advertise his mediocrity.

"Okay," he said, the untruth showing up clearly on his face.

"I got a C-minus," the boy persisted, looking at Garven for his answer.

Cripes, Garven thought. *Leave me alone*

But what he said reluctantly was, "Me, too. I got a C, too."

"I think they give real low grades to start with so you don't get too cocky. You know, so you will work harder."

That made Garven feel a little better. Not much better. Not enough to damp down that feeling of a rising flood water licking at his neck. He had to do better, or he could kiss off any hopes he had of getting into medical school. Medical school? He would be lucky to graduate in poly sci at this rate. He made an appointment to see the English prof that same afternoon. Wrestling was getting the short end of the stick again. That could not be helped.

He was supremely prepared for Western Civ, and it showed. It made his morning, what was left of it, to be able to discuss for a full ten minutes of class time with the professor on the comparison of Greek culture and law with the Code of Hammurabi. Forty percent of the class grade came from class participation, and he was off to an excellent start. At least something was working out that day.

Four-thirty came all too rapidly. He went to Mr. Terwilliger's closet sized office on the eighth floor of the chem building and expected to be left to sit around and twiddle his thumbs for another hour; so, he would be late for his appointment with the English prof at five. Mr. Terwilliger was punctual, however. At four-thirty-one he opened his door and apologized for being late.

"Come in, Mr. Wilsonhulme, have a seat. If you can find one," the slender, pale, overworked scholar said.

He cleared a pile of ungraded blue book test pamphlets from a dilapidated old swivel stool for Garven.

"What can I do for you?"

"I came to talk about my placement exam. I screwed... I mean, I made a mistake on the numbering on the score sheet. I got a terrible score; so, I'm in quiz section Z or something like that."

"Well, I don't know what I could do to help, Mr. Wilsonhulme."

At least he had the name right. Garven could take slight solace in that small factor even if the words were not at all encouraging.

"Please, Sir. If you would just take a look at my test, you would see what I mean."

He was pleading again. He felt like he was going to spend his college career on his knees.

"What I mean is, I'm not nearly as dumb as that test shows. I can be one of the best students in the chemistry department, but with this, I'll never get a chance."

"You will have the same chance on the tests and therefore to get a good grade as anyone else, don't you presume?" said Terwilliger knowing that was not quite so.

In all fairness to the young man's plight, he had to admit that the sign in Orwell's book, *Animal Farm* as amended by the animals, "All the animals are equal, (some are more equal than others)" did apply in the introductory chem course. He did not have to admit it aloud, however.

"You look so earnest. I'll tell you what I'll do; I'll look at your test book; and if what you say is true, I'll move you into a higher quiz class."

"Great!" exclaimed Garven, the joy and relief flooding his features.

He waited for Mr. Terwilliger expectantly. He did not seem to be ready to leave the overworked grad student to attend to the commitment another time.

Terwilliger saw his own earnestness of a distant eight years ago and yielded to the power of the young man's persuasive look. He rummaged in the alphabetically arranged boxes of blue books until he found Garven's. He took a ruler and followed through the answer booklet until he came to the smudged area. His ruler then moved at an oblique angle to the end. He mentally counted and then calculated. Garven could all but hear the mental gears clicking.

"Including the smeared section and the three empty blanks at the end of the answer column, you missed a total of seven questions on the test if I accept your explanation, Mr. Wilsonhulme. Frankly, I have to admit that would have put you in quiz section A. I'll give you the benefit of the doubt and compromise. You know, I don't usually make this sort of allowance. If you make it known, I will be inundated with guys and their requests."

"I know, but this is kind of a special case," encouraged Garven seeing that things were beginning to go his way.

He was afraid to say too much and break the spell.

"So, what I'll do is get you one of the best quiz instructors in the whole group, and we'll see how you do with him. Let's see, which section is Greg Allen teaching?"

He ran his finger down the course instructor list. "Yes, 'I', quiz section 'I'.

"I'll move you in there."

He made an erasure on the far end of the student list and penciled in Garven's name in what Garven presumed was an empty slot in the quiz section "I" list. Garven continued to have a crestfallen expression.

"Don't look so down; that's a heck of a lot better that 'P', don't you think?" asked the grad student a trifle unsettled by the lack of a display of gratitude.

"I guess so. What do I have to do to get into your class? Into quiz section 'A'?" Garven asked by way of an answer.

He was certainly tenacious, thought Terwilliger, like a certain kid he remembered from eight years ago. It was obvious that this kid was not going to go away. Subtlety was obviously lost on him. Terwilliger was amused, and he was also behind on correcting his section of the second year quizzes.

"Look, I have a lot of stuff to get done. I'll make you a specific deal. If you ace the first three section quizzes, and Mr. Allen agrees that you are 'A' section material; I will move you up to my section. How's that?"

"Hey, terrific. You won't be sorry. I will get the highest scores you ever saw! Thanks, Mr. Terwilliger. Thanks a lot!"

Garven was beaming, the misery erased from his face.

"Get out of here now, and let me get back to work then," Mr. Terwilliger said good-naturedly.

Garven was glad there was at least one human being on the faculty. Maybe he had a chance to come out of the crap pail he had been in after all. He was feeling upbeat when he ran to Dr. Nicholson's office arriving out of breath but on time.

CHAPTER
Seventeen

"Take a seat," the English professor's secretary directed.

Garven was overheated from his run from the Chemistry building. He sat on a straight backed steel chair with four or five other upset looking young students. He presumed they had all come for the same reason: the first composition results. He also presumed that Dr. Nicholson had heard every excuse and protest possible that day and in all of the days he had been dealing with students. Garven was sure he was not going to get anywhere with the same old boring pleadings; so, he decided to take a different tack when his turn came.

The secretary called out his name, and Garven passed through the entrance to Dr. Nicholson's inner office making room for the glum-faced student who was leaving.

"Good afternoon, Dr. Nicholson," he greeted the professor. "Thank you for taking the time to see me."

That was refreshing, thought Nicholson. *Most of these spoiled brats think I only exist to move them through freshman English as painlessly as possible.*

"I came about the results of the first English composition," Dr. Nicholson," Garven said after the fatigued professor bade him sit with a gesture. "Just like everyone else."

At least he was right on target, thought Nicholson.

"What can I do for you, Mr...Mr...uh,"

"Wilsonhulme," volunteered Garven helpfully.

"Yes, Wilsonhulme," he said almost musingly and waited for an answer.

"I'd like to ask a question, and maybe that's all I need to know," Garven said.

The professor did not seem inclined to say anything; so, Garven continued, "Is it true that Stanford, well, that you, give lousy grades at the start of the year so we won't get lazy and will feel that we still have to work hard for a grade? And that we can expect grades to improve later. I will tell you the truth. I am in premed, and I can't afford a C. Not even one."

"Your concept could not be more wrong, Mr. Wilsonhulme."

Garven was afraid of that.

"Then what can I do to get a good grade, then?"

That was indeed refreshing. No begging or pleading, no presentation of how well the student had done in the past and this must be some mistake. It was a straight-forward question that deserved an answer in kind.

"I guessed the reason you made an appointment to see me this afternoon; so, I took the opportunity to review your composition. Are you ready to hear, in all frankness, why you got a 'C-minus'?"

"Yes, Sir. And I'd like to know how to write better to get a better grade."

"The 'C-minus' was generous. I know you used to get 'A's for this kind of work in high school, but this is not high school. You are now a student at one of the best universities in the world. It is expected that you will leave here able to express yourself clearly, succinctly, and accurately. I am not teaching a creative writing class; it is neither desired nor useful for you to be clever or elaborate or to use so-called big words to impress me. I want you to be able to tell me and anyone else who needs to get something out of what you write, exactly what you want to express. Tell me what you have to say, not what you think will be fancy enough to get a good grade. I am personally sick and tired of grades and would do away with them entirely if I could."

He took a breath.

"I thought that's what I did," said Garven.

It was a real question, not an argument.

"You didn't. Let me impress that on you. This paper," he indicated Garven's nicely typed work, "is a good example of what not to do in declarative expositions."

Garven was beginning to wish he had left well enough alone.

"Am I really supposed to believe that the worst thing that ever happened to you was losing some soccer game at a prep school nobody cares about?"

That stung a little. Garven's sensitivities rose to defend Burton-Cagle, but that seemed unproductive for his cause; so, he let it ride.

"In a minute, I am going to ask you what really was the worst thing that ever happened to you. First, though, let me comment on the content of this paper. I see that it is very neat, well presented; and for that I thank you, believe me; but I am most dissatisfied with the essay itself. It is stiff, stilted, doesn't seem real. You know what it really sounds like? It sounds like a freshman English composition, maybe even a high school product. The vast majority of them are unreadable. They drive me crazy."

Jeez, thought Garven. *I really set him off. He's going to remember me for all the wrong reasons. I need to learn to keep my trap shut.*

"The piece is full of words right out of the thesaurus; words of dubious usage. The whole thing is jerky and hard to follow. I think, at least I hope, you can do better. First of all, how about a subject? Tell me, I mean for real, what is the worst thing that ever happened to you?"

Garven squirmed in his seat, uncomfortable with the penetrating intelligent gaze and uncomfortable with the prospect of sharing his privacy. He had not interpreted the assignment as having been serious, not that serious at least. He did not want to discuss the real worst experience of his life. He wanted to forget it. He put up a smoke-screen.

"Did you give any As, Dr. Nicholson?"

"One, to a woman student who told of the best experience of her life and did so with a fresh sense of humor and with a real zest. It was well written to boot. Now, please tell me what the worst experience of your life was."

"That's pretty personal. I feel kind of funny talking about it. It's private."

His face showed pain.

"It is not my purpose of invade your privacy, Garven," Prof. Nicholson said, glancing quickly at his student list for the first name, "but that is the only way you can get at the heart of this exercise in writing. I think for your purposes, this composition has to come from the gut."

Garven looked at his professor's face and saw nothing threatening there. He needed the grade; and if this was what he had to do to get an 'A', so be it.

He sucked in a breath and blurted, "When my father, my real dad, left me and my mom."

"My mom and I", Nicholson corrected in a very gentle voice.

"Right."

"Then go write about that. I am the only one who is ever going to read it if that is what you want. I mean, besides yourself. Tell you what. If you will re-write, or I should say, write again, this essay; I will consider changing your grade. And stop worrying so much about the grade. We have a new composition almost every week and three tests. You have plenty of time to get the grades. Instead of concentrating on the grades per se, why not try to learn something. Try to learn to write. That a deal?"

"Yes, Sir. I'll give it my best shot."

"And a small hint. Try to avoid clichés like 'my best shot'."

"I will have a new paper to you by Monday."

"That's the spirit."

Garven made it to the last hour of wrestling practice. He had a lot of pent-up energy and the workout did him good. He spent most of his time being Hector Trujillo's dummy, it seemed like; but he did seem to be learning something about the fine points of wrestling. He found himself liking the sport progressively more despite knowing nothing about it two weeks previously.

Alan Crowder's mess had worked its way over onto Garven's side of the room; clothes, papers, books, slide rules, plastic right angles, a compass, and the *coup de grace*, a pair of dirty under shorts. Garven threw the extras back onto Alan's side, making sure to align it up precisely along the invisible line of demarcation between the two sides of the dorm room. He moved the shorts with the slide rule so he did not have to touch them. It was a shudder just having to do that much.

Garven met Frosty in the cafeteria, and the two friends made the usual comments about the starchy character of the food and both scanned the emptying tables for scraps of abandoned protein. It was disgraceful, they agreed, for affluent Americans to be scavenging.

"Garven, my roomie is a three-dimensional dork," Frosty said as they ate their second dessert, scrounged from the tables next to theirs.

"What does the three-dimensional mean in this instance?" asked Garven out of minor curiosity.

"That's a dork anyway you look at one."

"I know what you mean. I will be lucky if I don't kill mine. You met Alan Crowder, right?"

Frosty nodded in remembrance.

"I mean, he is easily the biggest jerk I have ever met."

"It is going to be a very long year, my friend, having to be civil to Martin Bolechein every day. It strains my being even thinking about the long passage of the future stretching out before us."

"Somebody might drop out, and roomie dear can move into that place."

"If the guy with the single room is willing," said Frosty. "It would have to be someone who had never met Martin, is all I have to say."

"Alan Crowder is the messiest jerk in the school. He has some kind of special amplifier on his radio so it blasts you right out of the room. Anything I say just makes it worse. I have to live in the library."

"Boy, you could be talking about Martin Bolechein of Detroit. Martin and Alan sound like the perfect pair, the perfect marriage."

Garven put his hand over his head to simulate a light bulb, "Ding," he said. "I have an obvious idea. Brilliant, but obvious."

"And great minds do work in the same way, I deduce," Frosty said with a conspiratorial little laugh.

"So, how do we make it happen?" queried Garven. "And how fast can we make it happen?"

"And if we don't make it happen, can we plead insanity at our murder trials?"

"I'm in favor of a direct approach. Maybe not homicide, exactly; but I say we just tromp in and tell them they have been switched. We can tell them they will love the change, which is undoubtedly the truth."

Garven was all for heading for the two rooms right now. It had been a day of confrontations.

"No, my man, we have to be subtle and outflank them. If Alan thinks anything like Martin, they would both stay in the rooms they way they are assigned just to thwart us," cautioned Frosty.

"I have an idea that might appeal to the slobs once they get a chance to think about it."

"Ooh, good. Sounds corrupt and devious. You are beginning to sound like my kind of guy," said Frosty, ready to listen.

"You know how we play hearts up on the floor every Friday to determine who goes to the laundry for this week's sheets and towels?" Garven asked, looking around to make sure there were no eavesdroppers, as if anybody would care. "And you know how that dumb Michael Poletti gets cheated and has to go get the sheets every time?"

Frosty nodded, not sure quite what Garven was getting at.

"I don't think either Alan or Martin has a clue what is going on. So, we could set up a game this weekend that gave a really valuable prize, like, say, your roommate's bodacious view, or a free trip to San Francisco to the Hungry, I to listen to jazz with a date at the losers' expense. Hank and Peter would help us if we told them what a worthy cause it was. The way this has to work, is that I have to win that choicest of prizes, your roommate's bed."

"Since I can't think of a worse idea, let's set up the game for Saturday after our illustrious football team gets beat by UCLA," agreed Frosty.

"Done," said Garven, and the two conspirators shook on it.

CHAPTER
Eighteen

Garven squirreled himself away in the library all Saturday morning and from the end of the game with UCLA until the crucial game of hearts that night. He wrote and rewrote his English composition harrowing up emotions and conflicts that had lain dormant in his own heart of hearts since that day eight years ago when his father had written, "Good-bye, Rachel. Good-bye, Aloysius. I was just not meant to be a husband and father. You'll be better off without me."

The man had walked out the door and into the noonday glare of the Phoenix sun. Garven remembered shielding his eyes against the sun; and when he was able to look directly into the street, his father had driven away. It came as a bolt from the heavens upon Garven; but he supposed his mother had seen it coming, had fought about it with his father or something. Garven waited by the screen door for his father to return. After two hours, Rachel had gently placed her hand on his shoulder and directed him into the living room where the two of them sat and stared quietly at each other until supper time. Garven was two days shy of his tenth birthday when his dad deserted Rachel and Garven leaving them with a car that did not work and a surprise pile of debts. They had already been served with an eviction notice from their apartment earlier in the week. The day his father abandoned them, Garven lost his religion and decided that he would never again depend on anyone else except himself. He would become a coyote.

At first, it had been hard to understand; then, with the passage of days and finally, months, it was hard to accept. All Garven could digest of it was that he had been rejected. His own father had left him. Garven was left with the uneasy sense that he had done something terrible to drive his own father away. It took the boy the better part of a year to come to an emotional comprehension that he would never see the man again. It took more than a year for Garven to stop blaming his mother, then to ease up on himself, then finally to condemn his father. He ended up with an unquenchable ember of hatred for the dad who had deserted him and had left him and his mother destitute. He had never trusted another human being again for the rest of his young life.

He found it difficult not to swear at the man on paper and had to hold back his tears as he typed the composition that described the pain and fury and hatred. He had no trouble filling in the required three pages. He found the vocabulary and made no attempt to organize the words and phrases in any deliberate way. He simply told his English professor the way it was; what he had never before told anyone. He was very tired when he finished the last sentence at eight that evening.

He had eaten two hot dogs at the game that Stanford lost to UCLA by twenty-four points. Otherwise, he forgot to eat through the whole day. By time for the game of hearts, he was famished and had to drive over to a Dairy Queen in Palo Alto for a cheese burger, a bag of greasy fries, and a chocolate malt before he could think clearly enough to cheat his and Frosty's room-mates with the required finesse.

The two nerds were so gullible that they jumped at the chance to participate in the high stakes game of hearts. Martin never did figure out the fact that he would lose no matter what happened since his bed and his room were the prize. The other hall mates casually paired up; so that, it was as natural as could be that Martin and Alan became a team. Martin and Alan were as blind as Michael Poleti during the weekly games to determine who had to pick up the laundry; and for some reason completely obscure to Garven and Frosty, failed to see even the most flagrant passing of cards between their opponents, the withdrawing and replacing of bad cards into the deck sitting on the table in Frosty and Martin's room.

"Who farted?" Hank Quinton asked.

As the general tumult of denial and accusation proceeded, he passed two more hearts to Peter Bedford behind his chair, an awkward move, made all the more difficult because of the limitations of self-control imposed by hard-to-control laughter. Peter now had practically every heart in the deck.

He folded and reveled in his victory. Martin and Alan were oblivious as usual. Frosty had to explain to the two dupes that they had played the last hand, and they had lost. Martin had to give up his room to the pair that had accumulated the highest point total for the evening.

It took a few minutes to register before Martin asked plaintively, "But where's my room going to be?"

He seemed so sad that Hank and Peter were practically rolling on the floor with suppressed mirth. Martin cast a very quizzical look at the pair as if they had taken leave of their senses.

There followed a quick tally of the points. Peter looked a little disappointed when he saw that he was not the winner despite the veritable coup on the last hand. He was apparently having some difficulty remembering the overall plan in the excitement of the contest.

"Martin, since I will be moving in with Frosty, and therefore my bed will be vacant, you will be roommates with Alan," Garven explained kindly and patiently.

Martin was a math major and these complex social interactions were beyond him most of the time.

Alan smiled at Martin.

Martin said, "Oh, okay. Seems okay with me. Okay with you Alan?"

It was more than okay with Alan who was glad to be rid of the nasty tempered Garven. He could handle Martin. He looked on the math major as new meat.

Frosty asked, "Which team won the most games tonight? They get the trip to Frisco to North Beach."

To his surprise and delight the tally showed that he and Garven were the winners of the highest number of games as well as points.

"Why am I not overly surprised?" groused Peter.

He was not exactly sure how, but it did seem like he and Hank had been snowed here just like poor old Martin and Alan. This had cost some money. Only ten bucks a head; but still, it was the principle of the thing.

Garven and Frosty, who had kept themselves fairly poker faced during the general merriment that came from Hank and Peter at Alan and Martin's loss, remained above the fray when Hank and Peter looked askance at them. Hank shook his head. He could not figure how he and Peter could have been cheated; they were part of the scam. So, he just let it drop.

Garven moved in with Frosty, and Martin moved in with Alan. It proved to be a very salutary arrangement for Garven and Frosty; and given their disagreeable personalities, the other new set of roommates was no worse off than before.

Garven held out until Thursday of the following week before he called Sandra Hill at Mills College again.

"Hello, it's Garven Wilsonhulme from Stanford again," he said as soon as he had waited through the chain of command to receive her salutation,

"How naace to heah from y'all again, Gahven. How ah y'all doin'?"

He was tempted to reply that we were all doing fine, thank you, but was pretty sure the implied confusion over which all was being referred to in the Southern speech mannerism would not be appreciated. He was pressed for time that day; so, he got to the heart of the matter.

"Sandra, I would like to take you out. Would you like to go on a date with me?"

"Ah would simply love to, Gahven. Ah truly would, Ah'm sure," she paused delicately.

"But…" Garven prompted, reasonably sure of the impending objection.

"Yes… but, Ah am simply ovahwhelmed rat now, don't y'all see?"

He did not see but held his peace.

"Puhaps y'all could call again when thangs auh not so terribly hectic."

"Tell me, Sandra, are you interested in going out with me or not? It would be easier on both of us if you would just tell me straight out that you don't intend to go with me ever than for us to play this telephone game every week."

Garven had grown tired of the polite niceties, and it showed in his tone. He had not meant to alienate the southern belle, but it was silly to maintain a pretense that they could not connect because of some scheduling difficulty if the fact was that she never intended to go on a date with him in the first place.

Sandra was not accustomed to such bluntness. She much preferred the face saving devices built into the refinements of communication between cultured southern ladies and gentlemen. She guessed she could hardly expect better from the nouveau riche in the untamed west. It was becoming a bore. She decided to reply in kind.

"Well, Gahven, if y'all find that y'all cannot maintain the civilities, then Ah must inform y'all that Ah will not be able to return your calls nor your attentions, regrettably."

Garven gulped a little.

"Thank you for your frankness, Sandra. I will not bother you again. I wish you every success," he said in a subdued voice.

Perhaps she had been too abrupt, but what was done was done and undoubtedly for the best. The young man seemed disturbingly similar to a raft of others who seemed to pay undue court as soon as they became aware of her status as the heiress of the oil fortune. It was her lot to bear, she sighed inwardly.

"Why thank y'all, Gahven. Ah do wish y'all the very same. Ah must rush now. Thank y'all for callin'. Good-bah now," she said and put down the receiver before Garven could say his good-bye.

He winced. His pride and ego were bruised; and the more he thought about it, the more angry he got. He looked around to see if anyone was nearby since he had left the door of his dorm room open during the call. Seeing no one, he launched into a long hissing recitation of every curse, profanity, blasphemy, obscenity, vulgarism, and scatological phrase in his catalogue. He felt much better afterward and forgot the Texas girl before he left his room for class.

He had one more day before he would be docked if he quit Botany. He had to decide that day. If he dropped out of the class, he would be out of the whole series—botany, invertebrate zoology, and vertebrate zoology. The down side to that choice was that he would be behind in his agenda for completing his premed series. He had learned that he could get into some medical schools with only three years of premed if his grades were good, and he could secure some good letters of recommendation. This choice could foul up that schedule. He was not overly found of academics, and cutting the preliminaries by a year was very enticing.

On the plus side, he had learned on his own that his premed advisor had been full of crap. Garven thought he knew more about premed requirements than the eminent Dr. von Tauben over there in his ivory tower. In the first place, it was not necessary to take the advanced zoology course; the standard premed curriculum was designed to include the lesser straight biology series. Premedders shined in that series and bombed in the advanced series historically. Garven hated to give up, but cold reason demanded that he get out while the getting was good. He was doing lousy so far and could see the handwriting on the wall. For one thing, he could not really understand plant anatomy, the xylem and phloem, stamens and styles, or the Linnael nomenclature system that he was required to know. It was like reading the geodetic survey. He could not keep his mind on the subject long enough to learn sufficient material to pass the tests. There had been two quizzes; he had done miserably on both of them.

Garven absentmindedly glanced at Hoover Tower as he passed it on the way to the Biology Building. He smiled at the flesh colored smooth shaft of the tower itself which was capped with a red tile cupola. No Stanford student before or since could look at that silly structure without thinking of the sacrilegious name everyone used for it, 'Hoover's Last Stand'.

The lecture today had been on more of the systematization of botany as an independent discipline. Professor Ingrid Nordstrom, Stanford's eminent palynologist, had suffocated the class with a complete breakdown of phytogeography, plant ecology, population genetics, cytotaxonomy, cytogenetics, phytchemistry, fine structure morphology, plant sociology, bacteriology, algology, bryology, pteridology, paleobotany, and with especial enthusiasm described considerably more than Garven could ever want to know about her niche, palynology, the study of modern and fossil pollen and spores. Fossil pollen and spores, if you can imagine! Garven felt like he had been chloroformed.

Lab that afternoon consisted in adding to his required herbarium by which he was supposed to learn taxonomy. As if he could see how the vapid subject of taxonomy would help him to be a doctor. He thought it was tiresome and pointless to attach the dried pieces of weeds and sticks to standardized paper sheets and could not keep his contrary opinion from showing on his face. The lab instructor assured the class of enthusiasts (except for one, as near as Garven could tell) just how valuable all of this was going to be in their careers as the various plants changed, evolved, or became extinct. Garven irreverently thought extinction would be a good thing.

Garven had to admit to himself that the only aspect of the laboratory that made the class bearable was likely to be his downfall. The lab instructor was a buxom Swedish graduate student majoring in microbiology. Her main positive attribute was a set of partridge sized and shaped breasts that she displayed innocently, frequently, and tantalizingly to him in her ill-fitting loose front blouses. She was unaware of clothing styles and apparently oblivious to the effect she had on men, preoccupied as she was with her scholarly pursuits.

Helga Torvalt leaned over Garven and the sophomore girl who had been assigned as his lab partner to give a critique about how the two of them were attaching the stupid parchment dry weeds to the tedious papers. It actually seemed to matter to his lab partner, and she was put out with Garven because of his slap-dash approach. Miss Torvalt was very helpful, especially because the more he fumbled and smashed the brittle plant specimens, the more she needed to lean over and direct his activities. Garven could only concentrate on one thing at a time, and he gave into the most pressing, that of peeping down Miss Torvalt's blouse front. On her part, unobservantly unaware of his true interest, she was getting annoyed at his ineptitude. His lab partner was neither blind nor anyone's dummy. She could see where his eyes were going, and she did not appreciate his randiness. Typical man. Finally Miss Torvalt wised up and caught Garven's yearning stare at her fronts, and with a look of distaste at the silly freshman student and a sisterly look of recognition between her and the lab partner, huffed away.

Garven recognized that he had not helped his cause any but resented his lab partner's need to make reference to the *faux pas* nonetheless.

She said archly, "Nice going, Garven. Get a good eyeful? Think it was worth it? We won't see her again all quarter. That ought to work just dandy for our lab grades don't you think?"

Garven could just roll his eyes back in his head and mash more dry weeds onto the stupid page spreading more glue than the two partners would need for the next ten sheets. She gave a theatrical sigh. Garven signed the withdrawal papers right after the class. He knew when he was beat.

He was only two weeks into the quarter; so, he took a chance and signed up for the regular series. The grad student he talked to told him it would be tough, but he thought Garven could catch up and get his biology series back in sync. Garven still had his twenty hours of credit going for the quarter and could still realize his goal of finishing premed in three years.

Dr. Nicholson made Garven go through two more drafts of his first paper before he would let the freshman turn it in. It was well past any kind of reasonable deadline, and Garven knew that the professor was doing him a favor. In addition, he was taking time to critique Garven's declarative and expositive writing on the subsequent compositions; so, Garven's work was rapidly improving. He was getting 'Bs' regularly, and could see for himself that his work had changed enough to merit the better grades. He was proudest of the 'A' Dr. Nicholson finally awarded for his first paper. That was the real thing.

"I enjoyed your work," the professor had written when he handed it back to Garven.

So, thought Garven *Maybe I'll make it here, yet.*

Nevertheless, his view of the future was not all that positive; in fact, not all that clear.

-The End-

Excerpt From Saga of a Neurosurgeon Book Two

Anything Goes

He found himself seated in the front seat drowsily listening to the soothing cultured voice of Dr. Edith Brawlbecker, Associate Professor of English. Sweltering alongside him in the next seat on the front row was Forest McTavish who was equally somnolent.

"Last period we divided into two sections--the first group choosing to analyze for us Conrad's, *Heart of Darkness*. The reports on that allegory are due at the end of the period today. No later," Dr. Brawlbecker announced.

Garven and Frosty had been so preoccupied with the gathering streaker scandal that they had both chosen to concentrate on the second of Dr. Brawlbecker's two choices, Herman Melville's, *Moby Dick* because it would not be due for another week. They had had a week to prepare their comments and had known that their in-class oral participation would be tallied as part of their overall grades. Nevertheless, neither had prepared adequately and banked on the improbability of being called on to wax eloquent at any length.

"Now we turn to Melville's work. For purposes of discussion, let me read to you an excerpt. I want you to evaluate the allegorical implications of this passage as a prolegomenon to our class discussion today," the professor said.

Garven spelled 'prolegomenon' phonetically as best he could on a small note sheet and included a question mark. He showed the note to Frosty who returned a negative shrug of his shoulders.

"For those of you with the *Official Stanford Reading Series*, I will be reading from page 385: I will skip about, so follow closely:

"Oh, my Captain! my Captain! noble soul! grand old heart, after all! why should any one give chase to that hated fish! Away with me! let us fly these deadly waters! let us home! ...What is it, what nameless, inscrutable, unearthly thing is it?; what cozzening, hidden lord and master, and cruel, remorseless emperor commands me; that against all natural lovings and longings, I so keep pushing, and crowding, and jamming myself on all the time; recklessly making me ready to do what in my won proper, natural heart, I durst not so much as dar? Is Ahab, Ahab? Is it I, God, or who, that lifts this arm?...

Ahab crossed the deck to gaze over on the other side; but started at two reflected, fixed eyes in the water there. Fedallah was motionlessly leaning over the same rail."

Dr. Brawlbecker paused to let the power of the passage have its effect. As she had done for seventeen years, she looked out over the vapid, disinterested faces, hoping against hope to see an upturned set of eyes burning with her same passion. She thought she caught a glimmer of interest from a small young man on the first row.

She made a quick check of her seating roll and said, "Mr. Wilsonhulme," and was glad to see the appropriate head bob in her direction in response. "Mr. Wilsonhulme, what can you tell me about this whale? What is the meaning of *Moby Dick?*"

Garven was moved to ask what there could possibly be about whales that would interest a professor of humanities. As he really saw it, there were whales, and there were whales. He liked the book, all right, but saw it only as a great story. Somehow English teachers all felt the need to ruin a perfectly good yarn by analyzing it to death, by seeking the deep inner meaning. It was just a story about hunting a big white whale, for cripes sake.

He was about to speak when Frosty leaned toward him and quickly whispered, "Hey Garven, why don't you tell old Dr. Ballbreaker that you think Moby Dick is some kind of venereal disease?"

That struck Garven as hysterical, and he had to choke to suppress an uncontrolled and disastrous laugh.

"Excuse me," he coughed out. "I know this is supposed to be a big allegory and to have a deep meaning, but couldn't it be like Upton Sinclair said--just one of the world's great stories, a tale of men and whales and the sea?"

She was offended, disappointed. Garven could see that. He knew better that to suggest that something in English class was just a good story and to hint that the search for its meaning might be futile, or worse, that it might spoil the story. He wanted to kick himself. He remembered the time at Burton-Cagle when Mr. Harcrest had gotten all enthusiastic about William Blake's poem, *Tyger, Tyger*. Harcrest quoted the first verse:

"Tyger, Tyger burning bright,
In the forests of the night,
What immortal hand or eye,
Dare frame thy fearful symmetry?"

"Billy," Harcrest had asked singling out Billy Dell Geodes, the most con-crete thinking person on the planet. He was an Okie.

"Billy," he had said, "Tell us what this poem is all about?"

"It's about tigers."

"What kind of tigers, Billy?" Mr. Harcrest had prodded.

He was after that hidden deep meaning, Garven had known that.

"What kind of tigers are there?" Billy had asked innocently.

"Well, there are tigers and there are allegorical tigers," Mr. Harcrest had pursued becoming a bit put out like all English teachers did when somebody could not get that deep inner meaning stuff.

"Jeez, and I thought there were just tigers and tigers."

AUTHOR CARL DOUGLASS, a former neurosurgeon turned fulltime author, writes with gripping realism because in all his books he has been there

and done that in some measure. He grew up in a small town where fighting was the rule, not the exception. He was determined to escape the sameness of geography, intellectual outlook, and career prospects of the majority of his contemporaries. In complete naiveté, he applied to only one well-known major university for his undergraduate work, and to everyone's surprise, he was accepted. He found himself out of his league scholastically and had to work like a Hannibal to find a way or make one to succeed in that rarefied atmosphere. His goal of success was to become a neurosurgeon, and he did it. His career in academia and the military as well as his work as a medical humanitarian provided the background to produce the riveting tales that have made their way into his remarkable books.

HONORS, AWARDS, AND MEMBERSHIPS
Phi Kappa Phi University Honor Society
Alpha Omega Alpha Medical Honor Society
BS (Medical Biology) degree—magna cum laude
MD—magna cum laude
CDR/MC/USN

American Medical Association
American Association of Neurosurgeons
Congress of Neurological Surgeons
Fellow of the American College of Surgeons
The Association of Military Surgeons of the United States
Life Member of the Medical Society of Vienna
Diplomate of the American Board of Neurological Surgery

Past President, Our Community Foundation, Wasatch County, Utah
Past Medical Liaison Officer, Deseret International Foundation
Past Chief of Surgery,
Antelope Valley Regional Medical Center, Lancaster, California
Past Member-at-Large, Central Medical Committee,
Utah Valley Regional Medical Center, Provo, Utah
Past Member, Utah State Foster Care Review Committee

www.ingramcontent.com/pod-product-compliance
Lightning Source LLC
Chambersburg PA
CBHW051654260626
47170CB00004B/1500